WALKING
ON
CHALK

By

Kiersty Boon

Published in 2008 by Legend Press

For the many people who have inspired me… my mother (with a special thanks for her patience in editing and proof-reading this book), my children and, perhaps most of all, the people of Worthing, Hove and Brighton, who provided much of the inspiration for the characters within these pages.

Also, Paul Squires for giving his permission for me to interpret his wonderful poetry, from his book The Puzzle Box, with my descriptions of Ern's street-art.

Thank you.

CHAPTER ONE

'Bloody hell!' Kate muttered, desperately trying to run in her squeaky new stilettos. 'Please don't let me be late!'

It was January and the sun was taking it's time to rise. A peachy hue was beginning to glow in the sky, which Kate hoped would soon brighten the sombre grey stone of the town centre. An icy breeze whispered through the street, making her wish that she had at least put a scarf on, but the TV weatherman had promised her that it was going to be 'unseasonably warm later', nice man that he was. The morning was slowly edging in and it was bright enough for the muted streetlights to be pinging off one by one as she ran. Her suit jacket flapped, sending a cold blast through her thin cotton shirt. She slowed down in order to swerve right into the main pedestrian street, as the shops were just beginning to spur into life, with closed signs turning to open and the bright spotlights lighting up the mannequins in all the stores she knew so well. She faltered as she whizzed past Monsoon and quickly scolded herself for even being momentarily distracted by the temptation of 'SALE' signs in the main display. It was the last Friday of the month and she new they would soon be stocking up with all the Spring Season's clothes that she would have to wait until summer to buy, when they would finally reduce them to a price she could afford. It was very rare for Kate to not be working a season behind when buying clothes but luckily, the English climate often rewarded her by throwing in the odd hurricane in summer or snow in late spring.

Kate carried on half running, half skipping along the pavement and soon felt a curl work loose from the French plait that she had pulled

1

and pinned her hair into earlier that morning. She stopped in front of a large freshly washed window and tucked the curl back behind her ear. She was about to set off again when she looked at her whole reflection in the gleaming glass. She stared into her own eyes and scanned down to her smart black suit, which skimmed her hips so perfectly, her calves contained within nude Pretty Pollys and finally those wonderful new black court shoes. She allowed herself a small smile. Kate looked at this stranger looking back at her; all starch and pleats with perfectly applied make-up. It was a stark contrast to the jeans and floppy sweaters she felt comfortable in but she knew that she looked amazing. 'You may look amazing but it will mean nothing if you miss the appointment, silly cow,' she whispered aloud. With a frustrated tut, she quickly kicked off her shoes and hitched her skirt up slightly to allow her legs more freedom to move as she ran. The slabs were icy cold but felt good on her already sore feet.

With her shoes dangling in one hand and her portfolio in the other, she kept her head down, scanning the pavement ahead so that she could avoid any dogs mess or pavement pizzas left by the revellers of the previous night.

She swerved to avoid a pony-tailed busker who had stooped down suddenly to pull out his clarinet from its carry case. Her foot trod on something, crushing it instantly. She inwardly groaned and closed her eyes, stopping immediately and hoping that it had not been a snail, knowing that snail juice dripping off her heels would not be a desirable accessory to her image.

Kate looked down and saw bright blue chalk crumbled on the concrete. She quickly lifted her foot to brush the blue powder away, unaware that she was swearing quite loudly, whilst her mind was jumbled with panic about this latest blip to her supposedly 'stress-free, herbal tea, deep breath and stride-with-a-smile' start to the morning that she had promised herself. Her brain was so befuddled that she didn't see the man approach her.

'Thanks for that,' the man said. 'That was my last cobalt blue.' He sounded irritated and patronising, as though he was scolding a small child.

'Sorry?' Kate replied politely but with no hint of an apology in the word, as she was still brushing the dust from her shoe.

'You just crushed my pastel. I was going to use that.'

2

She looked up and saw that the man was dressed in a thick coat with a shabby, dark hat. Kate couldn't see his face as he was kneeling down to pick up the powdery remains of his chalk but she could gauge from his voice that he was angry. She felt flashes of guilt at how genuinely pissed off he sounded. She quickly bit her lip and battled in her head as to whether to be remorseful, or use this man as the brunt of all her morning's frustration. Her mind was already cursing him and another stupid delay, but she bit her lip harder and let the words scream inside her head... 'It was only flippin' chalk for chrissakes and have you any idea how scared I am about this morning and would you like to try and squeeze your toes into these stupid shoes and take my place and I'll play with chalk all bloody day? Hey? Would you?'

Instead, she took a deep breath before opening her mouth and quietly muttering 'Sorry.' Kate could see he was swirling his fingers through the chalk dust, rubbing it into the pavement to create a bright puddle. She took a deep breath and spoke a little more clearly. 'I am really sorry.' The man made no response. She tried again, saying gently 'Perhaps you could use green instead?'

He looked up at her and she offered a weak smile but he did not reciprocate. 'No. I can't. It has to be blue,' he said. His words were stiff and clipped. Kate caught a hint of an Irish accent as he continued, 'This cobalt is the exact colour of her eyes. Don't you understand?'

Kate sarcastically congratulated herself on managing to find the only weirdo in Worthing wandering the street at 9 o'clock in the morning. She studied him closer and took in his clothes - his coat that had certainly seen better days, the dark grey felt hat with the brim all twisted and squashed. He could have easily been dismissed as a tramp but his skin was clear, he was clean shaven and there wasn't a hint of the weather beaten look that most of the local park winos were blighted by. He saw her studying him. He stood up, brushing his hands together to rid them of the dust and faced her. He studied her for a few moments before finally returning her smile.

Kate was instantly transfixed by his eyes, which sparkled as though they were dancing with some private joke. She looked down to his mouth... it was the shape of Cupid's bow. Kate suddenly realised that she was staring at him and shook her head to pull herself together.

'I'm really sorry. Perhaps I could reimburse you?' She began to frantically root around in her bag for some change, which made a few old bus tickets and a half eaten tube of Polo's tumble out onto the

3

pavement and start to roll away. She scrambled after them, collecting all but a single bus ticket, which was swept up and carried away by the breeze. The man made no move to help her. She returned to where he was standing and started to unzip her purse. He shook his head and held up his hand.

'No. No matter,' he said, looking quite offended, 'I can manage.' Kate returned her purse to her bag and quickly said, 'I'm sorry… I really have to run. I'm very late.' She turned away, hoping that she sounded apologetic enough and began to run again. 'I'm really sorry!' she shouted over her shoulder.

The man watched her running up the paved walkway. His smile broadened, as he saw her hop over some dog's mess and drop her left shoe, which led to her dropping her portfolio as she bent to pick it up. He heard faint strains of 'Bugger. Stupid bloody shoes,' as she bundled everything up again and carried on running.

He sat down on the pavement, crossed his outstretched legs and reached into his pockets, pulling out an array of coloured chalks. The busker started to play his clarinet and the street artist hummed along to the melody as he made the first broad sweeps of colour against the concrete. 'What a wonderful way to start the day,' he thought to himself. 'It would seem I have a new muse.'

CHAPTER TWO

A few hours later, Kate slammed the door of the office closed and walked down the wide marble steps to the street. 'Bastards,' she whispered under her breath. 'Utter, bloody bastards.'

She kicked off her shoes and picked them up, muttering 'Stupid shoes. I never liked you anyway'. The big toe on her right foot had poked through the fine nylon of her stockings and the freed, freshly painted, candy pink nail smiled up at her. Kate dismissed it with a tut and bit her lip to stop herself from crying. She put the portfolio between her legs and pulled her hair out of its Kirby grips with her free hand. Her dark curls tumbled down over her shoulders as she ran her fingers through them to set them free. 'I am NOT going to cry,' she thought to herself and bit her lip a little harder.

Kate began to walk back along the pedestrian way. The shops were now in full throw of the January sales. People were teeming into and out of every doorway, laden down with bags of all imaginable colours. Kate loved her town. Even though most of the faces were strangers to her, she felt like she belonged. The choice of where to start anew had been made easy when she'd seen the beach and the town, which was an easy commute to London should she ever need to resort to going back to the Big Smoke for a job. She still looked out of her bedroom window each morning and marvelled at the vastness of the sky unimpeded by tower blocks or smog.

Although the town had a huge population of pensioners, there was enough variety of people for it to become a magical place on days like today. There were never really any grand dramas to throw the community off balance or upset their contented way of life. As far as Kate could remember, the only time there had ever been any kind of scandal was when the telephone company tried to replace the traditional red phone boxes with shining aluminium booths, the previous year. It had been the talk of the local paper when the men and women, in true Dunkirk spirit, had campaigned vigorously to 'save' their heritage. Some had chained themselves around the old metal boxes, with everyone cheering them on and plying those grey-haired protestors with sweet tea and currant buns. Of course, they'd won the campaign, which had just meant they could all go back to complaining about how the telephone boxes always smelt of wee and had prostitute's cards plastered all over them. That little escapade summed up her town really; if it ain't broke, don't fix it and if it is broke, don't fix it either.

Kate could just hear the clarinettist in the distance playing 'Blue Moon'. The soft music momentarily distracted her from the seething quarrel in her head but the burning humiliation of the morning soon seeped back in. She told herself to let it go and forced herself to take some deep breaths.

'You can stick your job, you pompous arrogant gits,' she'd said to them. Kate sharply winced at the memory. She had tried - really tried - to hold her tongue and she was sure that she'd meant to say, 'Thank you very much, you lovely people. I appreciate your time' but it had just come out wrong. She found that happened to her quite a lot.

It didn't really matter what she'd said by the time she'd walked out the door, as when Kate stood up, her heel buckled causing her to lurch to one side and knock over a jug of water. She watched as the iced liquid quickly sped across the shiny tabletop, soaking their papers and dripping into their laps, to groans of 'bloody silly woman' from their side of the table. 'Shit, sorry,' she'd said, before running out with tears stinging her eyes.

Kate shuddered. 'Bloody silly woman, they called me,' she thought. 'BLOODY SILLY WOMAN! Why couldn't they have called me a bitch or something? ANYTHING would have been better than 'bloody silly woman.' She could see her favourite cheap'n'cheerful clothes shop to the right and decided to pop in to buy herself some flat shoes. People could pretend that shopping doesn't make you feel better but Kate knew that when hugs weren't readily available, a carrier bag containing some new and colourful thing felt almost as good and that life wasn't too bad.

A few minutes later, Kate stepped back out into the sunlight with her new red and white polka-dot flatties gleaming in the sunshine. She took a deep breath of the fresh sea air. Shopping had woven its magic and calmed her down. She had begun to leave behind the memory of the arrogant suited and booted that she'd just had to endure an hour's worth of dodgy air-conditioning with.

She took another deep breath as she drew closer to the main stores. All the wonderful aromas of the street floated into her like gentle whispers; freshly baked cakes from the patisserie, lilies from the flower stall and the wonderful rich coffee of the local café were an intoxicating mix.

Kate allowed the busker's music to set the rhythm of her walk, as she made her way to the coffee shop. People were milling around, enjoying the winter sunshine. Their light chatter was occasionally broken by the excited scream of a child or an explosion of laughter as someone enjoyed a joke with a friend.

She reached the small coffee shop and pushed open the heavy glass door. She was immediately blasted with the sound of beans grinding, cups chinking together, as well as the loud whirr of the milk frother. This was one of her regular haunts and Tony, the Barista, greeted her like an old friend. She winked at him and dropped all her bags onto the sofa next to the bar.

'Hey Tony. Could I have a cappuccino to go?' she asked wearily.

'You sound fed up. You want some extra chocolate on that? Put a smile back on your face?' Tony grinned.

'That would be perfect. Thank you, Tony.' Kate smiled before collapsing on the sofa next to her bags, feeling the air in the sofa whoosh out of the slight tear she knew was just at the back of the cushion she was sitting on.

Tony chuckled and set to with a loud clank as he banged the old coffee sludge into a tin, refilled and clipped it into the grinder whilst using the other hand to froth some milk in a small metal jug. Kate leant an elbow on the battered arm of the sofa and propped her new polka-dot shoes up on the coffee table. She looked around Tony's café. She loved its friendly atmosphere and its dark comforting colours. People-watching was one of her favourite pastimes and the huge windows that overlooked the street allowed you to become a hidden observer to the humdrum passing by. She had spent many hours inventing lives for folk as they walked on with their current mood hinted in their faces.

To one side of the café, there were shelves which covered the entire wall. They were stacked with hundreds of well-thumbed books - classics and poetry, fact and fiction, along with a small notice that asked for any old books to be donated, for which they would receive a free coffee. She loved looking through those books. Often there was a little dedication in the front, or some idle notes that a student had made, which made the whole experience of reading them a little more special… as though you were sharing a secret with the original owners. Sometimes she would exchange a few words with another regular as she passed their table but mostly she liked to sit on her own, enjoying her book or scratching quick sketches down in her pad, of the lives she imagined were passing by.

The other side of the café had some posters of cups of coffee, which had obviously been taken in some European backstreet with ambitious designs dusted with chocolate powder onto the frothy cappuccino topping. Kate didn't like them at all. They felt like gatecrashers to this wonderful comfortable get-together that Tony had created.

'Any pastries today, Kate?' Tony said.

'Not today thanks, Tony. I've got some serious thinking to do,' Kate replied, standing up slowly and dropping the exact money into his hand. 'I'll see you tomorrow.' Tony nodded a farewell and started whistling along to the radio.

She bundled all her bags up under one arm and tentatively held the scalding coffee with the other. Her taste buds were already screaming for their caffeine hit.

As she stepped back into the street, she stopped for a moment and closed her eyes, feeling the faint warmth of the sunlight on her face. The sounds in the street could have come from anywhere in Europe with the busker playing and the gentle drone of people's conversations as they walked by. That thought was shattered when Kate heard someone shout, 'Ere luv. Look where you're bleedin' well goin'.' Kate opened her eyes and stepped out of the way of a middle aged woman pushing a double buggy. She smiled apologetically at the woman but that was only returned with a tut and a shake of the head. She looked around to try and find a bench. The busker had started a new tune and was now playing 'Stranger on the Shore'. The song sent her memories of her dad and her brain flickered up a recollection of an old LP, with Acker Bilk on the front, smiling in a bowler hat. Kate looked around and saw that all the benches were taken by old men, unwilling to accompany their wives into any more department stores or old women, with their blue rinses, gossiping to each other. She made her way over to a low wall that surrounded a flower bed of purple and red pansies. Kate was careful not to crush them as she laid the bags down next to her. She sipped gently at her coffee, watching the young busker, who swayed in a smooth motion as he played, his foot tapping time as the notes carried him and his audience away.

A young mother came to the side of Kate and unclipped her young child from the buggy. The little girl climbed out and stamped her feet on the ground in time to the music, whilst her mother jabbed a text message into her phone. Kate smiled as she watched the child twirl around with a giggle before clapping her hands, so pleased with herself. As she caught Kate's eye, she stopped clapping and beamed a huge smile. Kate mouthed 'hello' to her and took another sip of her coffee forcing her eyes in another direction so that she didn't get hoodwinked into playing peek-a-boo or similar for the next three hours. She didn't know why it happened but children seemed to like Kate and although she loved playing with little people, she drew the line at entertaining other people's children in the street. Kate could hear the mother talking on the phone through gritted teeth. It was obvious she was having a row with whoever was on the other end of the line. Kate stood up and moved away so that she wouldn't overhear. She'd had enough angst of her own for one day, without taking on other people's too.

It was only then that she noticed the tramp she had spoken to that morning, sitting on the concrete over to the left. That side of the street was still in shadow. It looked dull and lifeless by comparison to the happy throng on her side. His back was hunched away from her but she could see that he occasionally stretched his spine and tilted his head to one side as though watching something on the ground. The clarinettist finished his piece to a gentle ripple of applause. He gave a slightly embarrassed bow and people started to move away, tossing coins into his case.

Kate wanted to go and see what the tramp was up to but was nervous after their exchange earlier that morning. She decided that her day couldn't get much worse, so she wandered over to his crouched figure.

'Hello again,' she said.

The man turned his face to look at her and smiled with his cupid's bow mouth. 'You must be cold sitting over here?' she asked, as she leant forward and looked over his shoulder.

Kate felt goose-bumps rise on her skin and all the sounds from the street faded into a slight hum, an ineffectual background noise, as though the only things that existed were her, this man and this magnificent sight in front of her. When she finally found her voice, she spoke quietly.

'That's stunning. For goodness sake…' She paused to catch her breath, 'that is simply stunning.'

CHAPTER THREE

Kate stared at the chalk drawing on the pavement. There, on the ground, encapsulated within a concrete slab no more than two feet by two feet, was the most exquisite picture, projecting a fantastical scene. It was a swirl of colour, intricate in some places, faint hints of tone in others. Bygone characters stared back at her from their powdery bed - Jezebels and Pimpernels, Pirates and Thieves - in a bar scene that oozed sophistication within its debauchery. Kate could almost smell the atmosphere and hear their laughter baying with the clatter of tankards, whilst the motley gathering celebrated life. In the foreground, stood a woman with her hair pinned behind her head, except for a single curl that fell over her face. A child tugged at this woman's thick, velvet skirt. Just behind her there was a table with three men seemingly having an argument, pointing fingers, all of them dressed in fancy garb. She could just make out that one of the men was a Priest and another was wearing a top hat, with a pencil moustache that gave him the appearance of one of those old fashioned magicians. They were being observed by a man who was wearing a battered felt hat and who looked very much like the artist who'd drawn them. Through a window at the very back of this scene, there was the outline of two Chinese men watching on.

It was a surreal and fascinating illusion. The intense colours exploded from their resting place and into Kate's mind transporting her into the moment that these characters were creating.

The man remained silent as Kate knelt down beside the tramp. Not really aware that she was speaking her thoughts aloud, she asked him,

11

'How could you do this in just a few hours? Why would you do it on the street? It's magnificent.' Kate's hand hovered over the picture. It felt as though her fingers would submerge into the painting and become part of the scene, if she were to dare to touch it.

She suddenly realised why the blue chalk had been so important to him. She knew that pastels weren't cheap. She jabbered another apology, 'Oh, I am so sorry I crushed your cobalt blue. Is it okay? I mean, was it okay? I mean... I'm sorry.... Again.'

She took a deep breath and looked at him. He replied very quietly, his voice calm, happy and as smooth as silk.

'Oh that's alright, lovely lady. It is the colour I normally use for her eyes.' He pointed to the curly haired woman in the foreground, 'but I can see now that the shade was a little too dark. Her eyes are just a touch lighter.' Kate felt herself blushing as he pointed to the woman in the picture and she realised that there was a distinct resemblance to herself. The artist continued, 'You crushing my blue has made everything just perfect.'

Kate looked back into his eyes. She felt completely confused by the rush of feelings she felt for him. She couldn't pin a single one of them down to mean anything, apart from perhaps a frantic, unsettling panic. She had to remind herself to take a deep breath again. Their eyes were still locked as she asked,

'Would you like a coffee? I mean, as way of an apology. It's the least I can do.'

He studied her face for a moment before asking, 'Where were you off to in such a hurry?'

'A job interview,' she replied. He nodded his head slowly and smiled as Kate said, 'I didn't get it though. I think I just managed to make an idiot of myself.' She groaned before asking again, 'So? Would you like a coffee?'

'Thank you,' he replied. 'That would be most kind.' Kate left her bags next to the artist's patch as she walked back over to Tony's.

As Tony was making Kate's coffees, she turned and stared through the window at the street artist. She felt totally overwhelmed by what he had created on the street outside. She tried to piece together a scenario of who he was and why but Tony's voice cut through her thoughts.

'It looks like I'm going to have another busy day, Kate. Seems like everyone's decided here is the place to be. You're helping my profits

12

too, by drinking so much coffee today, young lady.' When she turned to look at Tony she laughed at his exaggerated concern, with his eyebrows screwed up accusingly. His face softened and he let out a low chuckle as he asked, 'Your day's really this bad that you're going to OD on caffeine?'

'Actually. Today is turning out to be okay after all,' she replied. 'Hold the chocolate on those cappuccinos and give me two of those almond croissants as well, there's a darling. Now get a move on! You've got people waiting here!' Kate said with a grin.

'Your wish is my command,' he said. He popped the two pastries into a bag with some serviettes and swapped them for the money in Kate's hand.

She stepped back into the hubbub of the street, gingerly holding the two coffees and the bag, which was tucked under her arm. The busker was taking a break, sitting on a wall with his eyes closed and his face lifted to the sun.

Kate walked over to the street artist and handed him his drink, saying brightly, 'And as an extra sorry, I bought you an almond croissant.' She rescued the paper bag from under her arm and wrapped a serviette around one before passing it to him.

'Why, thank you very much' he said, taking a huge bite out of the warm pastry.

Kate pushed her portfolio with her foot, so that it was positioned next to him and sat on it, being careful to not let her skirt ride up too much, tucking her legs to one side.

'Please tell me.' she said to him. 'You are obviously very talented. What on earth are you doing drawing here in the street?'

He looked at her puzzled face with some amusement. He reached into his pocket and pulled out a tobacco pouch and a pack of papers. As he carefully made himself a roll-up, Kate looked back to the picture. She was so tempted to touch it but she was aware that if she disrupted the chalky surface she could smudge it and ruin all his day's work. Kate was passionate about art. She'd once been an Art Gallery junkie. She would hop on a train to London and spend the whole day wandering the vast rooms of the Tate or some museum whenever she could, soaking up the grand masters and avant-garde artists that lined the walls. She didn't claim to be an expert but she knew what she liked. She could honestly say that there was little she had seen that she liked more than this curious man's art.

When he had finished rolling a cigarette, he licked the paper and took out an expensive looking lighter from his pocket. He released the smoke from the first puff with a sigh of contentment. Kate could smell the woody aroma from his roll-up as it curled around them both. After a few more deep inhales of smoke, he looked down at his own work and began to speak.

'Art is everywhere. This is my way of saying hello to people. I don't have any other way to do it.' His words were murmured as though speaking to himself. He turned his head to look at Kate. 'Where would you suggest I draw?'

'In a studio? At home? On a canvas at the very least!' she replied, unable to keep her voice calm. 'I am truly astonished that your talent is wasted out here.'

He shook his head and said, 'It's not wasted. I get to listen to the music and I get to meet nice people like you.' As he said the last sentence he stared directly into her eyes. Kate felt herself blushing again under the intensity of his gaze.

'But won't it just be ruined when you leave? Wouldn't it be tragic if people step on it or the road cleaners wash it off as they go through tonight?' she asked.

'I cover it with plastic and mask it down. People are usually very kind,' the artist replied. 'The street cleaners tend to give me a break until they're either in a bad mood, or the head honcho tells them to scrub it all off.'

'It would be awful for this just to be lost before people see it.' she said, staring at the picture again.

'It's only a picture. It's always there in my mind and I can recreate it whenever I want. To me, that picture is like a mantra that I can draw again and again, never varying the mood, never getting bored or wondering if it's right or wrong.' He looked down at his own work again and Kate could see a small hint of satisfaction and pride in his expression. 'All the pictures that we create are only memories.'

'Memories?' Kate laughed. 'I bet you haven't ever been into a bar like that before.

'No. But in my mind, I go into a bar like that often. There is a whole plethora of thoughts and ideals scattered around the room there that most people, I think, would be able to relate to.'

Kate thought about what he had said and part of her felt like she should have known that all along, as it all made such perfect sense.

14

'Blimey, you are amazing,' she said. 'So few people actually give a damn, you know?'

'Yes, well, everyone should give a damn. They really should.' He took another drag on his roll-up and said, 'What is the point of having thoughts at all if you never share them?'

'I suppose so,' Kate replied. 'But some thoughts, I'm sure, are best kept to oneself.'

'Ahhh,' he said, his eyes briefly flickering around the street. 'Yes, we can all have thoughts that we are ashamed of, or embarrassed by, but there is no reason to suppose that they are any less valid than the ones we happily blurt to all and sundry.'

Kate bit her lip gently and quietly said, 'Maybe.'

Ern looked at her and smiled. 'It has been a tremendous pleasure to meet you, young lady,' he said as he stood up and shook his coat a little, flicking his spent cigarette onto the floor and sliding the sole of his shoe over it. 'Soon the sun will be on this side of the street and people will be able to view my work. So I really must get on. I have so much more to do and so little time in which to do it.'

'Oh yes. Oh course. I'm sorry.' Kate said, as she quickly got to her feet. 'It was really nice to meet you and …um…well, I'm sorry again.' She picked up her bags awkwardly and bent down to pick up her coffee without dropping anything again.

'That's okay.' he said, turning back to his picture and leaning down to pick up a scarlet red pastel. 'Maybe if you pass by tomorrow you will watch where you are going a little better.'

Kate felt a twinge of embarrassment, quickly followed by a flicker of anger that he had still not forgiven her. As he turned his head to look at her once more, she saw he was smiling a wicked, wry smile.

'Yeah, okay,' she grinned back. 'I'll do that.'

'Pass by tomorrow?' he asked. 'Or look where you're going?'

'Maybe both,' she said and with a chuckle she walked away. He watched her as she weaved her way between the people milling about, smiled as he saw her bump into someone and apologise profusely, only to turn around and bump into someone else straight away. He kept watching until she reached the end of the walkway, turned right and disappeared from his view.

CHAPTER FOUR

Len was sitting outside Tony's café, at one of the flimsy aluminium tables that are put outside each day. His thin coat hangs loose on his skeletal frame, his thinning hair greased down to his scalp, his legs crossed revealing that he wore no socks inside his second-hand, battered trainers. His creased skin was drawn back into a smile as he surveyed the moving pictures of life around him.

Without warning, he released an explosion of laughter, rocking his body back in the chair, his hands curled around as if to catch the joke. People snapped their heads in his direction to look and see, before they turned away again, embarrassed by his very presence.

Tony knew Len meant no harm. He saw him shuffle in each day, carefully choosing a ham and cheese sandwich from the fridge, before raising his finger as his own way of ordering one flat white, to stay. He often worried about the old fella, who always chose to sit outside whether it was rain or shine but despite trying many times to get him to sit inside, Tony had always been politely ignored.

Len would sit in his own world, his foot rocking up and down, as he muttered to himself. Tony had spent many hours watching Len tell himself jokes, argue with himself and often shed tears at some memory that perhaps broke through the fug that clouded his mind.

This afternoon, after several sips of his coffee, Len started to hum quietly, with his fingers drumming some hap-hazard beat on the metal top of the table. The hum gently increased in volume until he could just be heard singing a soft lullaby, which told of firelight dancing in some faraway place.

He stopped abruptly, thumped the table top once, before digging into his pockets and producing a pencil that had obviously been sharpened with a knife, creating a long fine tip with which to write. He started to scribble on one of the paper serviettes that had been placed under his sandwich, gently humming again as he wrote.

When he had finished, he pushed the pencil back into his coat pocket and drained the last dregs from his coffee cup. He picked up the sandwich and, to Tony's dismay, started to rip it into small pieces, tossing it to the pigeons that always stood nearby in hopeful expectation. Tony resigned himself to having to shoo the pigeons away for the rest of the day until they got the message that there was no more scraps coming their way, from outside his café today.

Len watched them flutter and fight over their surprise feast, until all that remained were the smallest crumbs. He gently pushed his foot out and the scavengers fluttered up in the air, flapping their wings rapidly before settling back down to search for the last of the food.
Putting both hands on the arms of his chair, Len lifted himself up and began his long, slow journey home; his stooped figure creating a void as he shuffled through the lunchtime crowds.

Tony went out and cleared his table, picking up the serviette and reading the old man's scrawl as he liked to do everyday. It read,

I sing to you, darlin', of the nights we shared,
warm wine mellowing our minds,
the curve shadows mirroring your hips wild roll,
before I read to you their imaginations,
conjured pearls of rhyme magicians;
smooth laudanum lies that end too soon,
chasing clouds across the waning moon.

When Tony went back into the café, he pinned the serviette onto the notice-board, next to some of Len's other poems that he had saved over the years.

CHAPTER FIVE

The sun dazzled Kate's eyes as she stepped off the bus the following morning. She was hurrying because it was nearly noon and she wanted to get to the coffee shop before all the hordes of office workers descended for their lunchtime, when they would be filling the cafes and bars with their tedious chest puffing, ego stroking and chatter of who's shagging who behind the filing cabinets.

She walked quickly to the pedestrian street and was not surprised to see it jam-packed with Saturday shoppers. The big stores had stuck 'LAST FEW DAYS OF SALE' signs in their windows but she resisted the temptation to swerve in for a rummage through their rails. As she walked further along, she could hear the clarinet player. She thought she recognized the song but the title eluded her. She hummed each note as his music became louder and clearer, the nearer she got.

The busker came into view. He was a gangly man, probably in his late twenties, with his long blonde hair pulled back into a pony-tail. His left sneaker was tapping in perfect time to the beat as he played. Kate reckoned that he was earning some money to go on his next surfing trip as his clarinet case was covered in stickers from various cafés and bars in Cornwall, using words like 'dude' and 'awesome'. Kate looked to the place where she had met the artist yesterday. A group of teenagers were blocking her view but once they had meandered by she could see that, sure enough, there he was hunched on the pavement. His grey coat was tucked underneath him and his felt hat was upturned on the pavement next to the picture she had seen him working on yesterday. There was a sign next to it. Kate squinted a little and saw that he had used a green pastel to chalk the words 'Thank you'.

She smiled and walked over to Tony's coffee shop. The door was propped open and the radio off so that the busker's music could be heard inside. There were only a few customers, sipping from their oversized cups and Tony was sitting on a barstool behind the bar, reading a newspaper. A young couple were kissing on the sofa, their arms wrapped around each other. Kate resisted the urge to whisper 'get a room' as she walked past.

'Hey Tony, two coffees, please.' She surprised herself at how bright and breezy her voice sounded. Tony's huge grin appeared from behind the paper.

'Ah, so you have someone to share your coffee time with again today?' he said, looking past her to see if someone else was there.

'I'm not sure I do yet.' she replied. She decided to change the subject quickly. 'Do you know the name of the tune that busker's playing? It's driving me mad trying to think.'

'La Mer' the barista replied. 'It's one of my favourites.'

'Jeez, did everyone's dad have a copy of Acker Bilk's LP?' asked Kate with gentle sarcasm.

Tony smiled and said, 'Not mine Kate, but he loved Jazz and Blues. He was always whistling some tune or other.' Tony put the two coffees on the bar. '£4.78 please, Kate.'

She handed him a five pound note saying 'Keep the change!' with a grin.
Tony often let her off the odd few pence here and there, when Kate had found herself short of change. More than once she'd ordered her coffee only to remember she'd left her purse at home. After much frantic scattering of the contents of her handbag and more than a few swear words, Tony had just chuckled and told her it was 'on the house'. She always made sure, therefore, that she made it up to him when she could. They'd become good friends over the past few months and Tony often sat with her for a chat if the café was quiet.

'Oh, you are too generous,' Tony said. Looking at the twenty-two pence change and dropping it into the cup next to the till. 'It'll only take me another forty odd years to get my villa in Tenerife, if the tips keep rolling in like that.'

Kate laughed and said wistfully 'One day, Tony. One day…' before she picked up the coffees and stepped back into the sunlight.

Walking over to the shaded side of the street, Kate saw an old couple standing behind the artist, their shadows stretching towards her. They were pointing at his picture and nodding. Ern didn't look up at them at first but then he turned his head and Kate could see him say 'hello'. The old couple seemed to nod and smile before moving away. Kate was disappointed to see them walk off without dropping any money in his hat.

As Kate approached, she sub-consciously started walking slightly on tip-toe so as not to disturb him. She looked at the picture that had taken her breath away yesterday. The colours were more muted under the thick plastic he had taped down but the scene was still vibrant with movement and laughter.

His voice made her jump even though he was speaking quite quietly. 'Hello.' He turned and looked up at her with a smile. 'Keep those feet well back from my chalks, won't you now?' he continued, chuckling.

'How on earth did you know it was me?' Kate asked.

'You are wearing a very distinctive scent,' he replied.

Kate quickly decided not to inform him that she never wore perfume as it might spoil the compliment. She reckoned that he was obviously enjoying the aroma of her 'ice blue' deodorant

'I brought you a coffee,' she said, bending down and placing it by his side. She caught a glimpse of the drawing he was working on, which seemed to just be a wash of muted colours.'

'Thank you very much,' he said without turning around.

'No croissant today, I'm afraid. I didn't know whether you might have eaten already.'

He made an 'Mmm' sound, slightly nodding his head as he did so. Kate was a little put out that he didn't seem more pleased. She suddenly felt stupid and arrogant for considering that he had actually meant he wanted to see her again, rather than a casual, polite 'see you around'. She moved her weight from one foot to another, trying to think of what to say to fill the silence.

'You're busy. I'm sorry... I'll go,' Kate said, trying not to sound disappointed. 'Still, nice to see you again and ... umm... at least I didn't step on any chalks this time.' The street artist kept his head down and continued to make large sweeping movements along the concrete with an orange pastel. 'Okay then...' Kate said quietly before taking a deep breath to ensure her voice sounded happy and breezy.

21

'Bye, then. Have a lovely day.' She quickly turned and started to walk away.

'No! Please… wait' he shouted. Kate turned back and saw him struggling to get to his feet quickly. 'I'm sorry. I just thought that you would sit down again. Maybe I could finish this piece and then I could join you with that coffee. It was terribly rude of me. I do apologise.'

Kate smiled. The artist was looking genuinely embarrassed and she felt silly for not understanding that he would be engrossed in his work. 'Not at all. Don't apologise. I'd love to sit a while,' she said. He nodded and said 'Thank you.'

Kate sat down on the window ledge of the nearest shop, which was just a few feet away from him and looked at the piece he was working on. It was set in the slab to the left of the first. It looked to be a general wash of purple and orange hues and from the angle that Kate was looking at it from, it made no sense. A few people milled around but mostly they stayed away as that side of the street was dark and cold compared to the south facing side. She was pleased to see that he already had a few coins in his hat. She would watch him stop now and again to take a sip of his coffee, stretching his spine as he did so. Each time, he would look up at Kate and give her a small smile before dropping his head again and getting back to work. Kate resisted the temptation to grin back like a stupid schoolgirl and held her lips together when she smiled back. She saw him start to choose slate greys and black pastels, moving his face closer to the picture to put in finer details. Time passed quite quickly and the shadows were shrinking rapidly on that side of the street, as the sun moved further to the West.

'There,' he said finally. 'It's all done. Would you like to see?'

Kate moved over and stood behind him. The second picture had the same impact on Kate as the first. From above, the picture had looked like a jumble of abstract shapes but now she could see the serene scene he had painted of a city at sunset. The colour was dramatic around a few drifting clouds, hovering up a skyline that looked eastern but again was so unspecific that Kate wondered whether that was merely her own mind's perception of it. Neither the sun nor the moon were in the picture, as though it was that magical hour where neither one rules the world and there were faint swirls that hinted at other things flying too far out to be viewed with any clarity. The city was deathly black, impenetrable at first glance but almost like magic, the longer you looked you could see that muted pastel shades had been expertly used

22

to highlight signs of bustling life. There was a hotchpotch of traffic – cars and vans – which were racing on the road that edged along the waterfront, the shoreline of which stretched across the bottom of the picture. A few windows were lit in the tower blocks, hinting at the lives they contained inside. Tiny, colourful insects speckled the water's edge and a mongrel dog sat on the bank, looking directly at the viewer… at Kate.

'Do you like it?' the artist asked.

Kate kept looking at the picture. To her, it had all the visual ingredients of some kind of meditation – a serene state of being, rather than the actual wish to be there in the scene it depicted. Without looking at him, she replied with a gut reaction. 'I love it and I hate it all at the same time.'

There was a long pause before a smile played on his lips. 'Perfect,' he said quietly. He leant down to pull a large piece of plastic along with some masking tape from his bag. 'Not that I understand at all what you mean' he continued 'but you can tell me as we drink another coffee.'

Kate's eyes smarted as she realized she had, again, foolishly opened her mouth and voiced her thoughts without giving a damn about etiquette. She bit her bottom lip hard as she waited for him to finish and let her explain.

CHAPTER SIX

Kate watched the artist walk to Tony's coffee shop. She had been surprised that he had insisted on buying the coffees and felt even more guilty when she saw him pick all but one of the few coins out of his hat before he went. He had asked the clarinettist to look after his pitch for a while, with a promise that he would return the favour during the day, so Kate had walked over to one of the benches in the sunshine and sat down. She closed her eyes as she lifted her face to the sky and enjoyed the faint warmth creeping through her jumper and jeans.

Kate always found it strange how closing your eyes in the middle of a busy place sometimes made you more a part of it. She heard people going by with tinkles of laughter, lowered voices hissing their point in an argument and the plunk of a shoe tripping on a cracked pavement; the man or woman trotting to catch up with their feet before they went on their way. She tried to imagine what her family and friends were doing at that very moment. She imagined her mum sitting with a cup of tea and a digestive biscuit in the back room, with an antiques programme on the telly and the French doors open so she could call to Kate's dad if anything exciting happened. Her dad would be pottering in the garden checking that his plants hadn't been attacked by slugs in the night. 'Blasted Buggers!' he would shout whenever he found a nibbled leaf, to which her mum would reply 'Mind your language.' Jamie would be at his desk, pretending to work whilst winking at some new secretary or other and Beth would be Beth, sitting behind the counter of the soft furnishings store where she worked, waiting for Mr Right to walk in and take her away from all this. Kate smiled at the thoughts. Even though they were all far away, thinking about them made it feel like they were right next to her.

Kate didn't hear Ern approach and was startled by his voice, even though he spoke very softly.

'Coffee, madam?'

She opened her eyes and took the cup he was passing to her, with a smile and a 'thank you'.

'I didn't know whether you took sugar so I bought the whole lot just in case, he said. She laughed as he produced every variety of brown sugar, white sugar and sweetener from his pocket, as well as two wooden sticks for them to be stirred in.

'Well, I don't have sugar because I like to think I'm sweet enough already,' Kate replied with a wink.

'Is that so?' he smiled, as he took the lid off his cup and poured in three white sugars. As Kate took a sip of the scalding drink, she watched him produce his tobacco and papers from his pocket. As he plucked out some tobacco and started to roll the cigarette, Kate noticed that underneath the fine rainbow of chalk dust, his fingernails were clean and well cared for. It was a comforting thought that he wasn't some kind of down-and-out, despite his clothes. As he put the roll-up to his lips and lit it, Kate inhaled the faint woody scent that wafted her way. Even though she was a non-smoker, she found the smell heady and comforting.

'So tell me, pretty lady. Why do you hate my picture?' he said whilst taking another drag on his cigarette, followed by a small sip of coffee.

'Can't I just tell you why I love it?' she asked.

'No. I know why you love it. I want to know why you hate it.'

Kate frantically ran through her mind for the right thing to say. She spoke quietly but firmly.

'It's not that I hate it. I hate the fact that you're wasting your talent out here when people like me should be able to see your work somewhere.' She began to feel foolish and more than a little embarrassed that she sounded like she was scolding him but she was on a roll and wanted to have her say. 'Do you know how bloody lucky you are? I would give my right arm to be able to create art like you do…' Kate stopped suddenly and realised what a ridiculous thing that was to say, so tried to backtrack. 'Oh okay, I might not give my right arm because I'm right handed and then I'd have to learn to draw with my feet or something…' She looked at him to see if he was amused, irritated or angry enough to throw his coffee over her, but his face gave no emotion away as he stared ahead at the huddles of office workers sitting around the walkway with their sandwiches. Some of them were looking her way and she became even more embarrassed as she realised that her voice had got louder as she had become more passionate about what she was saying. She quietened it down to a soft hiss as she continued, 'Quite frankly, you've got a bloody cheek. I left college with grand dreams about sitting around all day creating works of art but you see I'm average… Good old Little Miss Average and I've had to go out and get a proper job.

He arched an eyebrow and said 'A proper job?'

Kate didn't know whether to be relieved or offended to hear a small tinkle of amusement playing in his voice. She quickly snapped back, 'Yes, a proper job. I have a mortgage to pay and a cat to feed and parents who would rather say to their coffee morning friends, 'Oh yes, our wonderful daughter Kate. She's a successful blah-blah, instead of 'oh yes, our daughter Kate. Well, she tries hard.'

'You'd like to be a successful blah-blah?' he said, chuckling.

Kate felt her shoulders relax and allowed herself a small laugh. 'Okay, so maybe I'm copping out of my dream but you are copping out more by sketching here on the street when you have real talent but are just too bloody lazy or selfish to make something of yourself.'

He took another sip of his drink. Kate worried that she'd overstepped the mark and was angry that she had let herself be so affected by this man and his work. She knew that she was actually being terribly rude and that she had no right whatsoever to sit here lecturing him on how he should run his life, when her own was such a mess. She tried to think about how she could repair things a little and said,

'Of course I don't know whether you're lazy or selfish or anything,' She hadn't meant to be spiteful or intrusive. She'd just hoped he'd give as good as he got so that she could begin to understand but he was just sitting there in complete silence. It felt awkward and uncomfortable.

She tried again. She cautiously bumped her shoulder against his and said 'I'm pretty lazy myself. That's why I can't even get a blah-blah job, I suppose.' He dropped his head and seemed to be examining his coffee. He took one more drag on his cigarette and then threw it onto the pavement, crushing it with the heel of his foot.

27

Kate was suddenly overcome with embarrassment and wanted to get away as quickly as possible. She knew that she couldn't leave without trying to apologise for her outspokenness. She took a deep breath and tried to explain herself. She took a deep breath before she started talking. 'Sorry,' Kate said. 'You must think I'm bloody rude. I don't mean to be. My mouth just runs away from me sometimes. I just have never seen such extraordinary talent in real life before. I've seen it in galleries and I've seen it in books but never on my own doorstep.' She held out her hands and gestured around at the street. 'Never here in my stupid little sleepy town.'

Ern kept looking at the street ahead as he quietly asked, 'So, are you saying you hate it because you're jealous? Or because you hate me for not being the person you suppose I should be?

Kate crossed her arms and lifted one of her hands to her mouth, absent mindedly starting to chew one of her fingernails. It was a habit she'd given up long ago but occasionally she found herself regressing when she felt uneasy. 'Both probably,' she said. She took her hand away and tucked it tightly back across her chest before turning to face him. There was a pause as they both looked at each other. She again felt the same deep flip in her belly at the sight of his eyes and their frame of long dark lashes. He smiled at her and she smiled back.

'I'm sorry,' Kate said quietly.

He threw back his head and laughed. 'I don't mind,' he said. 'Really, I don't. You're the first person who's actually properly talked to me in weeks and I thank you for liking my work. I really do.'
Kate had an overwhelming urge to throw her arms around him and hug him. Every time she looked at him, she wanted to brush his floppy fringe away from his forehead or to run her finger along his jaw and feel his stubble, which was just long enough to give him a rugged, rather than a ragged look. She looked down at his lips and started to laugh herself.

'You have a milk-froth moustache,' she said, pointing to his mouth. She watched him as he took his sleeve and wiped it away. After he'd swapped his coffee from his right hand to his left, he reached out to shake her hand.

'My names Ern,' he said. 'Ernest Malley Esquire to give me my full title. My friends call me Ern.'

She took his hand and shook it gently 'My names Kate' she said. 'Kate Milton. My friends call me Kate. They've been known to call

28

me worse from time to time but for now, it's best you stick to just calling me Kate.' Kate grinned at him and he returned her smile.

'Maybe I will see you tomorrow, Kate?' he asked. 'We could perhaps talk more about blah-blah jobs and you could compliment me with some more thinly veiled insults, if you like.'

'That could be fun,' she said, smiling at him for a few moments before getting up from the bench. 'I've really enjoyed talking to you Ern. Ignore my little rant. I promise you it's just my stupid way. Mouth engages before brain does when I feel passionately about something.'

'You've been like a breath of fresh air,' he said. 'I'm glad you felt free to talk to me in that way.'

'Even so, I'll try not to make a habit of it,' Kate said. 'I'll see you tomorrow.'

Ern spoke softly, 'Kate?'

She sat down again and looked at him. He was leaning forward, his elbows resting on his knees and he was stretching his hands against each other.

'Yes?' Kate replied.

'Never give up on your dreams, Kate,' he said quietly.

Kate half-smiled and shrugged her shoulders 'I'll try not to, Ern,' she said, before leaving him there, still looking at his hands. She took a few deep breaths and forced herself not to turn around for one last look at him. She felt totally elated by their chat. It was very rare that Kate found someone who intrigued her as much as Ern did. As she passed the clarinettist, she reached into her jeans pocket for a pound coin, quickly tossing it into the busker's case. He twiddled his clarinet into a high E as way of thanks and Kate waved at him with a giggle.

Ern smiled as he watched this exchange, his eyes not leaving her until she had disappeared from view.

CHAPTER SEVEN

Kate hopped off the bus still clutching the letter that she had received in the morning post. The sky was dull with a thick blanket of white cloud and the icy air seemed to invade right through to her belly. She wrapped her cardigan tighter around her, pulling her sleeves down so that her hands could curl inside and walked with her arms crossed to try and keep warm. She had been panicking all morning, so as she walked she took some deep breaths to try and calm down. The initial elation she had felt when she had opened the letter and read that she was to be given a trial period in the job, had given way to a panic that either she or they had made a terrible mistake. Maybe she'd sold herself too high? Maybe they'd confused her with someone who hadn't thrown water all over them? Or maybe she had been the only applicant to the job and they were desperate? Kate had resigned herself to the latter being true.

She had turned out her entire wardrobe that morning, trying to see what she should wear on the first day of her new job and had sighed over the circus of colour that had exploded out of her wardrobe. None of it screamed 'take me seriously' apart from the suit she had worn to the interview. So, she decided that a shopping trip would be essential for two reasons: to make her feel better and to put some of those 'capsule' pieces into her wardrobe that all the fashion shows talked about. She headed straight into Monsoon and bought herself a black trouser suit, a grey skirt and some white blouses to go with them.

Having made the hasty decision to ditch the black stilettos after her last outing, she purchased some black boots with a square toe and a rubber wedge rise, as well as some grey flats. In order to categorically ensure that she finally felt better, she also purchased some new, totally office-inappropriate underwear, reasoning with herself that no-one would see them anyway.

On leaving the store she was about to turn right and catch the bus back home, when she heard the faint warbling of the clarinet player. 'Hey Jude' swam through the breeze and into her mind, like the pied piper calling her to follow him. The previous night she had thought long and hard about her conversation with Ern. She had mentally kicked herself a thousand times over the terrible things she'd said to him. Even by her own standards, she had been incredibly rude and had no right to speak to him in the way that she had. What on earth had she been thinking?

With the help of a family-sized Milkybar (that she had kept tucked away for emergencies), she had tried to reconcile her assumption that he was some kind of amazing genius with the more likely scenario that he was a down-and-out who was probably a closet axe murderer, drug addict or psycho. Kate was renowned for picking up 'stray puppies' as her friends would call her many boyfriends and it was time for her to change… to grow up.

She stood still in the street, her huge carrier bags hanging from one arm and went over these same thoughts again this morning. She looked up at the sky, hoping for a sign that those clouds would suddenly pelt rain to help her make a decision whether or not to go home, but they were beginning to thin out and rays of sunshine were spearing through like beacons shining down on the rooftops. She half-turned to the right and walked up the pedestrian street to Tony's coffee shop, not caring that all last night's resolve to have nothing more to do with Ern, was tripping away with each step.

She glanced over to the other side of the street before she entered the café. Ern was in the same spot, hunkered over and as she watched, she saw him stretch his spine whilst tilting his head as he pulled away slightly from his work.

She pushed open the door of the café and was greeted by the intoxicating aroma of Italian coffee beans. It was warm inside and the radio was on. The dulcet tones of Nina Simone were putting their inimitable spell on the few customers who sat quietly as they read their papers or stared blankly into space at nothing in particular. Kate spoke quietly so as not to disturb the aura of calm.

'Two cappuccinos please, Tony,' she whispered. He winked at her and set about making her coffees. Kate tapped her foot in time to the music as she waited. The music faded out and Terry Wogan chipped in with his Irish lilt mumbling about the weather and then announcing Gene Pitney, whose throaty voice shook the lull of serenity out of the window and replaced it with a cheerful twang. Tony placed the two coffees on the bar.

'Hey, you were talking to that artist guy over there, yesterday?' he asked. 'He is doing some amazing stuff! You know him from somewhere?'

'No. I don't know him really. You know me Tony, I talk to anyone,' she laughed.

'Yeah, I know that all too well Kate,' Tony laughed. He was used to her sparking up conversations with people in the café who interested her. He used to tease her that he couldn't decide whether he should be pleased that it might make people stay longer and drink more coffee, or whether she frightened them away with her total disregard for 'normal' British reserve. Most times though, it was others who started conversations with Kate. Tony reckoned that she had this friendly aura that people seemed to want to share and they all talked to Kate like she was a long lost friend, spilling their troubles or sharing a joke.

'Anyways,' Tony continued, 'I'm hoping he'll stay around awhile. Business was really good yesterday, with folk veering down this end of the street to look at his work. I could certainly do with business staying that busy.'

'Well, I'll go and see what he's up to today,' Kate replied, as she paid for the coffees and grabbed some sugars from the side.

She stepped out into the street, which was now brightening with the sunshine that had managed to soak through the clouds. The busker had begun to play 'La Mer' again and Kate smiled with the pleasure of being able to recognize it straight away now. As she approached Ern's hunched figure, she could hear him gently humming along to the music. A woman in a headscarf was standing watching him and taking a great interest in whatever he was drawing today. She looked so incredibly sad that Kate wondered if she should stop and not move any closer to her. The woman bowed her head and walked away. Kate walked up to Ern, trying to be quiet so as not to disturb him. He stopped humming and without turning around said 'Hello.'

'Hello back,' she said, flattered that he'd sensed her being there again. She looked down at the piece he was working on. It was a literal explosion of deep red tulips; their petals were perfectly rounded and glistening with a dew that had the steely solidity of mercury droplets, clinging to the blooms as they cascaded towards her like the rush of a geyser. At the centre of this explosion, was a small metal box with scratchings of tiny hieroglyphs on each side. The movement that Ern had managed to create within the picture was incredible considering the small amount of time and the limited shading that his chalks allowed. Kate knelt down to take a closer look. She put the coffee carefully to one side. 'What's that?' she asked Ern, pointing to the metal box in the centre.

'It's whatever you want it to be,' he whispered close to her ear. 'Just ask yourself what you want it to be.' Kate took a while to think.

'I would think that is a box containing a ring, perhaps?' Ern watched her as she spoke, her eyes down examining his work. He watched her smile as she said, 'Maybe that's her throwing the flowers back at him after he proposed.'

Ern gave a small chuckle, before saying, 'To me it is a machine and there is a man in there, thinking of the woman he loves. It's very sad though because he's dying.'

Kate widened her eyes in surprise. She looked again at the picture and imagined Ern's man inside the   box. 'That's very sad. Why is he dying? And why then would it be tulips? Were they her favourite flowers?'

'Maybe,' Ern replied. 'They are a symbol of their time together, memories shared.'

'Damn,' said Kate. 'It's such a glorious picture. I'm not sure I want it to have sadness hidden in it.'

'It doesn't. He's very happy,' Ern replied. 'His head is full of his wife. He finds comfort from the thought of her in his last moments.'

Kate turned her head to look at him. She felt the flutter in her stomach as his eyes met her own. She had a sudden urge to kiss him but all her thoughts from the previous night kept screaming at her. She took a deep breath before quietly saying, 'I bought you coffee.'

'I can see that,' Ern said. 'That is very kind of you. Thank you.'

Kate pulled out the sugar and a wooden stirrer from her jeans pocket and placed them on the pavement next to his coffee. 'Will you stay awhile?' he asked. There was a faint hint of 'please' as his voice lifted the last word into a question.

'If you don't mind me sticking around, then I would like that very much,' Kate replied.

She picked up her bags with one hand and her coffee in the other, walking over to the store front where there was a large low window ledge on which she could perch. Ern spent a short time adding to the picture, going over some lines and rubbing lightly over others. Then she watched him go through the routine of placing the plastic carefully over the drawing, masking it down and then pushing his hat over for people to put their coins in.

He picked up his coffee and walked over to the window ledge. Kate shuffled over to make room for him to sit down. He eased himself down and crossed his legs allowing his foot to gently bob in time with the music.

'You're very happy today,' she said, absent-mindedly crossing her legs too.

Ern was already rustling in his pocket for his tobacco and papers. Kate reached over and took his coffee for him, so that his hands would be free. 'Doesn't your bum get awfully cold and sore sitting on pavements all day?'

'Yep,' he said matter of factly, 'but you get used to it. How are you today?'

'Oh. Well, I got that job… the blah blah job I was rushing to on the day we met. I thought I'd mucked it up but it seems they're desperate. I start a week on Monday.'

'Aha!' he said, looking genuinely pleased for her. 'Maybe they think you are a very good artist. I shouldn't think desperation comes into it. You will brighten their dreary office if nothing else?' he said with a chuckle.

Kate smiled, before saying 'Maybe they just think I won't ask for a pay-rise too soon. But it's okay. It's going to be good to have some regular work for once.'

'So, you like my tulips?' Ern asked.

'I do. Very much. They're actually my favourite flowers and you have made them look so…' Kate struggled for the right word. She spread her hands out as though she only had one word to offer, '…real! I love tulips,' Kate said again enthusiastically, 'and those are amazing tulips.'

'Well, wouldn't you know it,' Ern said, as he reached behind and, with a flourish, produced a large bunch of pink tulips, which he arched in a circle in front of him, like a magician who'd just cadabra'd them from thin air. Kate was stunned and it took a moment before she realised he was actually giving them to her. She reached out and took the bouquet. 'I thought you might like them,' he said. 'The flower seller gave them to me, as a down payment for a small portrait of her grandchild.'

Kate looked at the perfect blooms that were wrapped in smooth cellophane, tied with a yellow bow of ribbon.

'Thank you so much,' she said, not really knowing what else to say. She fumbled for the right words, 'I'm touched... really. Thank you.' She felt embarrassed and totally out of control of the situation. She was always taken aback by kind gestures - whoever they were from - but this man hardly knew her and again she tried to remind herself he was most likely an axe-murderer. She looked around the street to see if anyone was watching but the few Sunday shoppers seemed to be in a contented daze as they casually wandered in and out of the stores, not minding anyone's business but their own.

'No, thank *you*,' Ern said. 'I have enjoyed my coffees with you very much. '

Kate relaxed a little as that statement had allowed her to slot the gift into some kind of reasoning - coffee for bouquets. That brought things back onto a level which she could handle. She looked at this curious man. How on earth could he be so attractive to her? She watched him smoke the last of his cigarette, still tapping his foot and smiling at the passers by. He was quite handsome but really nothing extraordinary. It was when his eyes looked into hers that she felt a rush of uncertainty. His eyes were the most amazing eyes she had ever seen. Kate realised that she was staring at him and that he'd noticed. He was staring back with a small smile playing on his Cupid's bow lips. A faint blush spread from her chest to her face and she decided that she should leave quickly before she embarrassed herself further.

She gathered up her bags and rushed out her words, 'I must be going. I have to go and ... umm... do stuff.'

'It would be nice to see you tomorrow' Ern said quietly, nodding his head to the man who had just dropped two coins into his hat. 'If you have the time?'

Kate really didn't know what to say – half of her wanted to say 'try and stop me' and the other half of her wanted to say 'I can't. I'm a sensible person who doesn't mingle with axe murderers', neither of which seemed appropriate, so she just smiled at him and started to walk away. She tossed her empty cup into a bin before piling all her bags onto one arm and reaching into her jeans pocket for some coins. As she passed the clarinettist, she threw the change into the busker's case, where they jangled against the few others that were there. Like yesterday, he twiddled a high note as way of thanks but Kate kept her head down, lost in thought. Ern clicked his fingers to the tune and whistled in perfect harmony. Once she was out of view, he went back to finishing his drawing.

CHAPTER EIGHT

Annie knew she was lucky to have such a prime position in the town centre. Her flower stall was at the centre of the crossroads, joining together the two sides of the pedestrian walkway and the wide path leading down to the sea. She had always taken such pride in making sure her stall looked colourful and stocked to the brim with the season's blooms, as well as a large selection of oversized pot plants. Even when profits were low, she had managed to scrape a small living to keep herself ticking by until takings took a turn for the better.

She had lots of stories she could have told someone but since Tom had passed on, despite having more people than she could mention say 'hello' to her every morning, she had no-one to sit down with for a good old gossip once she got home. Sometimes, she would become friendly with another stall holder but most of them moved on when they realised that their jewellery or bath potions weren't going to make them rich quick.

Annie always helped out the young lads who were buying a few flowers for a date or for their mum. She would see them twitching nervously by the carnations and gently coax them into thinking about who they were buying for and what message they wanted to give that person. Of course, the wide-boys who didn't want to seem 'wet' in front of their friends would go for a bunch they could tuck under their jackets until they had safely delivered them to the intended recipient. She would often get disheartened by the various men in suits who would buy two bouquets with some lame quip about 'one for the wife and one for the girlfriend'. Tom had never brought her flowers when they were married but Annie hadn't minded. He used to come home

with a packet of her favourite biscuits or occasionally a bar of
chocolate, which they would share as they watched the telly together.
Annie had supposed that he thought she had enough of flowers selling
them all day and she never thought to tell him that flowers bought
especially for her would be extra special. She just accepted that was
the way it was.

This woman standing by her stall today had been worrying Annie for
the past few weeks. She was always well turned out with her hair
tucked into a headscarf but her face was always drawn and pale. She
would stand and stare at the flowers as though she was asking for
answers from them. She looked so unhappy. Annie had always left her
to her own thoughts, not wanting to intrude but this morning, she
wanted to find out what it was all about.

Annie stepped quietly up to her and said 'Are you alright, luv?
Looking for something to brighten up your sideboard?'

The woman turned her head to look at her and Annie was shocked to
see that the woman had a few tears running down her cheeks. She
pulled out one of her tissues from her overall pouch and passed it to
the woman. The woman smiled sadly, took the tissue and dabbed at
her eyes, saying 'Thank you.'

'What's the matter, luv?' Annie said, touching the woman's arm
gently.

'It's silly, really. My husband always used to buy me tulips.'

Annie looked down to her fresh stock and the spectacular array of
colours. It always amazed Annie that the charm of tulips was never
diminished by them being unceremoniously dumped in large black
buckets. In some strange way it even added to their beauty. The
woman started talking again; her voice was quiet and sad,

'The first time he bought me them, was when our son was born. I
remember him walking into the hospital ward, clutching those damned
tulips and not wanting to put them down because it would mean he'd
have to learn to hold the baby,' the woman laughed gently before
continuing. 'He was so scared he'd drop him, you see? But he was a
good dad.' Another tear ran down her cheek and she wiped it away
roughly with the tissue. 'He was a good husband.'

Annie suddenly understood and said, 'He's passed away then,
luvvie?'

The woman nodded and Annie stepped forward to rub her arm. 'I'm
sorry. I know it can be hard getting used to life on your own.'

40

The woman looked at Annie and, after a moment's thought, asked her 'Do you ever get used to it?'

Annie shook her head and replied, 'Not really, no.'

The woman nodded, patted Annie on the arm and whispered 'Good bye. Thank you.'

As she started to walk away, Annie called out to her, 'Hey! Hang on! You forgot something!'

Annie quickly pulled a bunch of ten yellow tulips from a bucket and passed them to the woman with a smile. The woman looked down to them as Annie told her, 'These are on the house, luv. Never make your good memories sad, okay? You can always keep memories alive.'

The woman smiled at her and hugged the bouquet to her chest. 'Thank you,' she said as she walked away. Annie went and sat on her little stool just inside her stall. She poured a cup of tea from her flask and looked around the street as she took some small sips from the plastic cup. 'At least I'm not the only one alone,' she thought to herself. 'There's many who are more alone than me.'

CHAPTER NINE

The tulips Ern had given to Kate had made her happy. Very happy. Every time her head had tried to tell her that they were inappropriate and that she should have refused to accept them, her heart told her head to 'get a life.'

Kate had taken them home, poured some water into her one and only vase and then dropped them in without any kind of ceremony. She placed them in the middle of her small, pine table. She had sat looking at them, her chin propped up by her hand as she tried to puzzle out why she was so under Ern's spell. Her thoughts had run away with stupid Hollywood images of them rolling on sand, walking hand in hand and that one sweet, perfect, passionate, AMAZING kiss, before she gave herself a mental slap and told herself to grow up.

The phone had rung a couple of times. Each time the sudden sound had made Kate jump. She'd let the answering machine pick it up, which was very unlike her. She loved chatting with her friends and had even been known to spark up long conversations with telesales people, about anything other than the double glazing they were trying to sell her or whether she would like a new kitchen. One of the calls last night had been Beth, her best friend that she had met during a motor maintenance evening course, which they'd each signed up for at the local college. They were the only girls on the course and had both been utterly useless at changing tyres and oil changes, so had quickly formed a bond of all girls together.

Kate had listened to Beth teasing her through the answering machine and the stillness of the room. 'You out on a date, girly? Ha-ha… go get him. I'll speak to you tomorrow,' to which Kate had raised her coffee mug and whispered, 'Speak to you tomorrow, Beth.'

There was a couple of calls where they just hung up as soon as the answering machine kicked in. She resisted grabbing the phone to find out who was so intent in getting in touch with her. She got her answer much later on in the evening, when it rang again and she heard Jamie's voice fill her sitting room. 'Kate? Where the hell are you? I know when you go quiet you're keeping something from me, which is pretty frustrating to be honest.' Kate reached out her hand to pick up the receiver and stopped herself. Jamie paused before going on, 'How was the interview? Have you managed to pay that electricity bill? Have you got laid?' She heard Jamie let out a frustrated laugh. 'Can you at least ring me and let me know you're okay? You really don't want me coming around there with a few fire-fighters to break your door down do you?' Kate chuckled. 'Well, maybe you do, so scrap that.' He'd paused then and spoken more quietly to sign off, 'I love you Kate. I'm always here for you. Give me a wink to let me know you're okay… please. Bye.'

There was a hollow silence in the room after the answering machine had let out a long beep to signal the end of the message. Kate leaned over and pressed play to listen to his voice again. It was good to know he was there but she didn't want him telling her what she already knew – that she was hankering after a man who was a no-hoper: a bum who drew on streets for a living but was able to schmooze his way into any unsuspecting female's life with his gift of the gab. She knew that Jamie would patiently listen before putting his arm around her and telling her that's how it was. She didn't want that. Not yet.

So she decided there was only one decision to make that evening and that was should she drown her sorrows in Vodka or ice cream? Vodka would have the desired effect of delaying any decisions and ice cream would displace her guilt with another more fierce guilt of calorie overload. She decided on both so that she could feel guilty eating a whole tub of cookie dough before forgetting all about it with the help of some of Russia's finest. To complete the decadence, she'd put her Moulin Rouge DVD on and fallen into the arms of Ewan McGregor. It was the perfect cure-all.

But waking up the next morning, she had felt like she was cheating herself. She didn't want any unanswered questions in her life. She wanted to grab every chance she got. Wasn't that what life was all about?

Kate got up and threw on the first clothes she could find, under the pile that she had dumped on the floor in order to clamber into bed last night. She quickly fed the cat, trying not to notice the pile of dirty coffee mugs or her washing strewn on every available radiator and chair, ready for day she decided to do some ironing. She went to the hall mirror and sighed at her own reflection. Her mother had told her to smile at herself each time she looked in the mirror because it was important to remind yourself that you like what you see. She tried to smile but it turned into a grimace at how little care she'd taken with her appearance that morning. She picked up her emergency mascara (which was always left by the door in case of unexpected visitors), zigzagged her eyelashes with the brown/black sludgy cream and tried her smile again. 'You're okay,' she whispered to herself. Then she grabbed her coat from the banister, slipped into her trainers and walked out into the early morning haze.

Kate stayed on the bus for an extra stop so that she could get off at the promenade and make her way along the beach. She bought herself a watery coffee from the snack booth and strolled along taking sips of her drink.

When she was sure she had found a quiet part of the seafront, she picked her way down to the shore. Kate winced at the bone-crunching sound of the pebbles underfoot as they shifted with each of her steps. She slid her feet sideways down the steep slope which had been left by the morning tide and walked a little closer to the water, before laying her coat on the stones and sitting down. The haze had drifted back to the horizon and she looked out to see which boats and trawlers were passing by but there were none today. She lifted her face up to the sun and closed her eyes. Her mind wouldn't stop shouting questions. Those questions had become more like accusations with each hour that passed. She lay back and felt the waves send vibrations up through the pebbles; massaging her back and making her feel calmer. The sea was a magical thing, there was no denying it.

She desperately wanted to see Ern but maybe, just for today, she should try and find some of those answers. Maybe today she should look to herself rather than other people telling her what she should do all the time? Although she was reluctant to admit it, most of the problem was fear of failure and making a complete idiot of herself.

The latter she had succeeded at many times and, although she always managed to laugh it off at the time, the hurt and humiliation still ran deep. She had a failed marriage, a failed career and had pretty much messed up 'the big dream' she'd had when she'd first left college. Had it really been that big a dream? All she'd wanted to do was to be happy, to draw and paint, to be surrounded by people who she loved. But growing up, taking on the real world was something that she'd always struggled with. It had seemed the obvious Get Out of Jail Free card to get married. Martin had loved her, she had loved him, so what could go wrong? Things went very wrong almost the moment they came back from honeymoon. Whilst Martin had wallowed in moaning about the nine to five and having to shave everyday, Kate had consistently fought against consistency. She'd taken on temp jobs here and there to keep the finances ticking over but most of the time, she would be obsessively trying to expand her understanding of Art; visiting art galleries, going to seminars and pouring over huge epic books on the techniques of the Greats. Martin never liked her friends, Kate never liked his and they constantly argued about responsibilities, responsibilities, 'RESPONSIBILITIES!' which would usually result in Martin slamming out the house shouting that she was a waste of space. Looking back on it now, Kate knew that she had been just as stubborn as he had, but he was the one who had changed from the boy she loved at College; who had felt the same excitement as she did at every new film, song or picture they discovered, to a stressed out executive with no more thought than how much his next pay-rise should be. Was it really not possible to be responsible and still find the supposedly most unimportant things in life so wonderful? Was she really too naïve? Her mum and dad had been so disappointed. They had adored Martin and readily accepted him into the family. She felt guilty that it was just one more way in which she'd let them down.

Kate sat up and hugged her knees. There was now one trawler making its way over to the port and she wondered how far it had come. She forced her thoughts back to what she should do. She desperately wanted to see Ern but, at the same time, she knew that she had to get things clear in her head first. She stood up quickly and dragged her coat up from the pebbles, throwing it over her shoulder as she made her way back to the prom.

As Kate passed the wide path leading from the seafront to the town centre, she could just make out the busker crooning some love song with his clarinet but it was soon drowned out by a bus that thundered by. She walked along to the pier and crossed to the arcade. The mood was always different in here compared to the busy chain-stores in the main shopping area. The arcade was packed tightly with small shops either side, owned by art and craft gurus, jewellery makers and a handful of mystics selling crystals or magical trinkets, which supposedly set you up on a higher plane. Kate walked to the end of the tiled corridor, glancing in each window as she went by and pushed open the door to the art shop at the very end of the arcade.

To Kate, entering the art shop was exactly the same way a small child feels when they walk into the sweet shop. She could quite literally have spent hours breathing in the various scents of paper and paints, eyes wide at the thousands of colours that always made her wonder how so many colours can ever be created from just the primary colours of red, blue and yellow. She took her time, choosing carefully and piled her chosen items on the counter. The old man who ran the shop, smiled at her and said 'Someone's going to be busy,' but all Kate could manage was a smile as a reply, her mind already whirring with ideas of how she was going to fill the blank canvas she had purchased. As he rang the amounts of each item into the till she suddenly said 'Oh!' and ran to the left where she knew the chalk pastels were displayed. She ran her finger along the colour charts until she found the number for cobalt blue. She prised the front one out, allowing the others behind to roll down to close the gap and walked up to the counter. 'I nearly forgot this,' she said as she handed it to him. The old guy wrapped her purchases up in brown paper, which Kate always thought made this place even more special. When she got home, she would carefully pick the sellotape and open up the paper to reveal all those things just waiting for her to make them into something beautiful. It was so much more elegant than dumping them all out of a carrier bag. Kate tucked her packages under her arms, allowing him to open the door for her as she left. She walked along the arcade smiling with the excitement of her spending spree.

As she stepped back into the street, Kate squinted against the sunlight to look across the road to the opening of the main walkway through town. She knew Ern would be there but she shook her head, listened to her brain instead of her heart and got on the first bus that came along. As the bus passed the end of the walkway, she forced her head to stay down, inspecting her nails so that she wouldn't be tempted to look and see if she could catch a glimpse of him.

CHAPTER TEN

Kate hadn't slept well. She had stayed up most of the night, ignoring the phone again, plying herself with strong coffee and painting. She had enjoyed the adrenalin rush from creating something from nothing and as the picture had begun to take shape, she felt a pride that she had long forgotten in her own work.

This morning, Jamie had woken her up by phoning her mobile and this time she had answered it. She'd sleepily told him that she'd got the job with that company, to which Jamie whooped loudly forcing Kate to hold the phone away from her ear. She loved Jamie like a brother but she still didn't want to tell him about Ern. For now, Ern would have to stay her secret until she'd put all her feelings about him into the right boxes and sealed them up. Jamie had told her about a girl he'd met the previous night. Kate smiled as she listened to his enthusiasm for yet another bright young thing he'd met in a bar. It had taken her quite a while to get used to the dating 'scene' and how much more difficult it had become when they were out of the college environment and then how absolutely impossible it had become when she now had to present herself as a divorcee. Jamie's own marriage had broken down at about the same time as Kate's and mutual friends had introduced them to each other. After a brief flurry of them falling into each other's arms, thinking they had found their true soul-mates, bonking at every opportunity wherever and whenever they met, Kate and Jamie realised that they were both just incredibly vulnerable, lonely and in need of a good friend. So that was what they had become to each other. In truth, Jamie was more like the older brother she'd never had than just a friend. He had taken to dating again like a duck to water and Kate envied him the ease he felt in chatting to who ever without any reserve or shyness. She was fine when she was only expecting friendship or a good gossip but flirting? She was not even sure she'd know where to start.

She stepped into the shower and let the cold water run over her body, not caring that the boiler hadn't fired up properly. She felt her mind come alive with the shock of the icy blast hitting her back and instinctively held her breath. She resisted stepping out of the jet of water before she allowed herself to breathe again when warm water started to filter through. She fumbled along the wall with her eyes closed until she found the shower gel and breathed in its 'raspberry crush' scent. She suddenly realised that may be what Ern had mistaken as her perfume. She giggled at the thought of smelling like a big raspberry and squeezed a large dollop onto her hand, lathering it through her hair. After a few minutes, she started swaying her hips and singing the classic '*I'm going to wash that man right outta my hair,*' as loud as she could. She lathered more soap over her skin, washing away her goose bumps and scrubbing the memory of her restless night, whilst wishing that the yearning she felt to talk to Ern was as easily washed away.

She dressed in blue jeans and an orange baggy jumper, slipping on some trainers as she checked her face in the hall mirror. She walked out the door and slammed it hard, before tutting loudly, fishing in her bag for her keys and letting herself in again. Her coat was thrown over the banister and she dug around in the pocket for the pastel, wrapped in a paper bag. She tucked it into her back pocket and left the house again.

The bus was packed with the early morning commute, some surveying each other behind rustling newspapers and others looking out at the grey start to the morning. Kate tried to block out the coughs and snuffles that provided a background chorus to the rattle of the bus, as it trundled through the residential streets before the wider streets of the town centre.

Kate took some deep breaths as she stepped into the fresh air and held back while everyone else bustled past her and on to wherever they needed to be. She tucked her hands into her jeans and wandered along to the pedestrian walkway. The few stalls dotted around were just finishing their setting up. The flower stall woman was gossiping with the fruit seller next door. Kate caught snatches of their conversation as she walked by and gauged that it was mostly idle gossip about no-one much, followed by an update on what happened in the soap operas last night. She wondered what secrets they must have before reminding herself that sometimes other people's secrets are best not even considered.

Kate was relieved to see Ern hadn't set up yet. She went over to look at his work. The one that he had obviously drawn yesterday was a rich carpet of gold and browns. A wise sage stared back at her, a tiger curled asleep at his feet. On the shelves behind, fractured light blasted from a variety of bottles and curios. On the top shelf were dusty books where the gold embossed author's names were faintly scratched. Pearls were scattered under the old man's fingers, sirens darting from the shadows to try and steal them. The sirens mouths were open and their brows furrowed as though they were singing some warning to him. Without caring who was watching, Kate knelt down and gently touched the plastic that covered it. It was such a beautiful picture and she wanted to try and work out what linked them all, or even if there was a link. Were these separate pictures all part of a whole story? She stood up and took a step back so that she could try to view the pictures as a whole. The blending wasn't seamless but there was a common magic in each one. She just couldn't figure out what was making that magic or what the connection was.

She looked left and right, checking the street but there was no sign of him so she walked over to Tony's and pushed open the door.

'Hello!' said Tony, greeting her with a smile. 'We missed you yesterday.'

Kate laughed and said 'Oh, it's so nice to be missed but it's only been two days!' After a moment's thought, she added, 'We?'

Tony nodded. 'Yeah, that artist guy asked whether I'd seen you.' Kate smiled. She felt flattered and more than a little embarrassed. She pretended to dig around in her purse for some change and said, 'Cappuccino, please Tony. To have in.'

'No problem, Kate,' he replied.

She waited while Tony set to work preparing her coffee, drumming her fingers on the bar top. As he placed the oversized mug in front of her, he said 'He seems like a really nice guy, Kate. He said that he'll think about doing a painting for one of the walls in here. What do you reckon?'

'I reckon that would be wonderful,' said Kate quietly. She felt a little rise of panic as she made the knee-jerk decision to tell him what she was doing. 'I'm doing a painting myself, Tony. I'm doing it of the walkway actually.'

Tony looked surprised and said with a chuckle, 'Well, you'll have to let me look at that, Kate. Maybe I could have a whole wall of masterpieces?' Kate smiled at him and nodded, dropping the change for her coffee into his hand.

She went over to the bookshelves and picked out an old, fusty book of Wordsworth's poems from the top shelf. She was always pleased that no-one had walked off with it as it was one of her favourites to sit and read when she was here alone. She always made sure she put it back in the most hard to reach corner. She didn't pretend to understand poetry or any of the skill put in to each verse but she loved the rhythm and the images that it conjured up in her. She flipped to page 14 and the poem entitled 'Her eyes are wild'. It was a poem of a heartbroken woman searching for the father of her baby but there was a mix of panic and joy in nearly every verse. Kate was always stunned at the gentleness with which Wordsworth had treated his subject, even though in those days she probably would have been a scandalous woman shunned by society. Kate read more poems, turning the pages carefully, enjoying the old English spelling and the escapism of the world he was launching her into. Her coffee went cold as the leather chair warmed to her body and she sunk lower into the well worn cushions. She saw out of the corner of her eye that Tony was turning the radio off before going to the door and propping it open with the umbrella stand. The clarinet player's tune drifted in and, as she looked around, she was surprised to see that the café had become quite busy while she had been engrossed in the book.

Kate sat up and looked over to the other side of the street. Ern was now there, hunched over in the usual spot. She quickly drained her cup, wincing at the cold powdery dregs and went over to the bar to order two cappuccinos 'to take out'. Tony looked harassed and red-faced at the sudden rush of customers but as he carefully clipped the lids on her coffees, he grinned at her and said, 'You take care now, Kate.' Kate didn't know whether it was a casual remark or some kind of concerned warning as he could always tell when she was stressed out, so she just smiled and said 'I will, Tony. Thanks.'

She left the café and walked quickly over to Ern. Her voice was bright and breezy as she greeted him.

'Hello,' she said.

Ern snapped his head up and looked at her with a grin. 'Well, hello,' he replied.

'Coffee?' she asked, holding up the cups.

'Perfect. Thank you.' he said, still grinning.

She put his drink down next to him and carefully prised the lid from her own.

'Come and sit by me won't you Kate?' he said. 'It would be nice to have some company today.'

'Oh dammit, Ern' those concrete slabs look very cold today. We need cushions.' Ern smiled and after a moment's thought, removed his coat and lay it on the ground for her.

'Goodness me! What chivalry!' Kate laughed. 'You'll get bloody freezing though!'

'Oh, I'm made of strong stuff and the coffee will soon warm me up.'

Kate tucked her sweater down over her bottom and sat down. 'Ern, you really should have chosen to draw on the other side of the street where the sun is. This is madness!'

'I like the brightness of the chalks against the gloom. It helps me choose the most vibrant colours and then when the sun finally hits them…' Ern held his hands up into the air and shot them apart as he said, 'Kaboom! It's like an explosion to the eyes.'

Kate watched him work, his long fingers, with their perfectly trimmed nails, were smudged with chalk dust of different colours which stretched down to the side of his palms. She looked at the picture forming before her eyes. He worked quickly but stopped often to peruse before changing to a different colour.

She watched a young boy emerge, half asleep draped over a school desk, a witch enticing him further into his dreams. The woman wore a half-smile, which gave a hint to her being a temptress, her purple gown shimmering and cascading over the boy's shoulders. The shadows behind seemed to have faint hints of others standing in the background.

'Well, you're certainly doing something right. These are remarkable. Tony told me you might be doing a painting for him?'

'Well, if I am around for much longer I should be able to,' he said. 'You can never really tell how it's all going to go, though.'

53

Kate wondered whether to dismiss this comment or whether she should question him. Someone had once told her that you should never ask a question when you think you know the answer. She had never really understood why not, so quietly asked, 'What do you mean?'

'This and that. That and this,' he replied. 'That's all.'

Kate wanted to cross-examine him, shout at him with a 'what the hell does that mean?' but knew that she really had no right. So, she decided to change the subject quickly before she made a fool of herself again. She rose up onto her knees and pulled out the paper bag from her back pocket. She held it in her hand for a moment wondering what she should say as she gave it to him. She decided that less was best.

'Here,' she said quietly, passing the bag to him. He looked at her quizzically. 'What's this?' he asked.

'Nothing much,' Kate replied. 'Just my way of saying sorry.' Ern looked into the bag and she saw his cupid lips stretch into a grin. 'And a thank you,' Kate said. 'It's just been wonderful seeing your work.'

Ern took out the blue pastel and carefully ripped a little of the paper around the tip. He rubbed it onto his finger slightly and then bowed over his work to add some blue hints to the purple gown. He carefully blended with some black and highlights of white. The effect was to make her dress look like it glimmered with sapphires.

'Damn you for being so talented,' Kate teased. 'Tell me about this picture?'

'Now if I were to reveal that then I would not be allowing you to use your imagination, would I? That would be very selfish of me.'

'I don't know how you do it. I really don't.' Kate bit her lip gently. She was all too aware that she was gushing over this man but, despite her usual tendency to quip instead of compliment, she just couldn't help it.

'I think you do know how I do it,' he said quietly. 'You just pretend not to understand. I think you are seeing how I do it, very clearly.'

She raised her eyes and shook her head. 'There's no way I can admit that I really don't, is there?'

Ern straightened his back, glanced up at the sky as though steeling himself for what he was about to say. He spoke quietly. 'I shall be finished shortly. The kind music man has offered to stand next to my art this afternoon and collect any coins I get thrown into my hat. I know you've probably got things to do and I completely understand if you'd rather not but…'

Kate resisted the urge to scream 'spit it out, Ern!' as she held her breath for him to finish. He took another moment before continuing. 'Would you care to share lunch?'

Kate sat for a moment, unsure of what to say. 'I thought maybe the beach would be pleasant?' Ern said, looking at her face for any clue as to her answer. Kate returned his gaze before grinning at him and saying,

'Oh, that would be wonderful!' She hugged her knees as he carried on drawing. The clarinettist was playing some blues number that she didn't recognize but Ern obviously did. He started to whistle and she tapped her fingers in time, willing him to hurry up and finish.

CHAPTER ELEVEN

The pebbles crackled as Kate and Ern picked their way over the beach from the promenade. The seafront was empty apart from a few seagulls, picking up the shellfish and dropping them down onto the rocks to crack their shells.

Kate had been surprised at the lively welcome Ern had received in the fishmongers when they'd gone in to collect the picnic lunch Ern had arranged with them. They seemed to treat him with a great respect and, yet again, he had done a deal with the owner of a picture in return for two light salmon salads. Kate had looked at Ern's half of the deal, which was a drawing outside on the chalkboard that was propped up against the lamppost outside. Under the fishmonger's name, Ern had drawn a silver salmon, the skin of which was glistening with faint spectrums of colour and its glassy eye was replaced with an iridescent pearl. Ern had signed it with a simple 'E'. It was utterly beautiful and Kate had told Ern so as soon as he emerged from the shop. He had just nodded and quietly said, 'Thank you.'

They hadn't said much to each other on the way to the beach apart from a brief mention about the gorgeous weather. Kate took a deep breath of the sea air as they walked. The waves were lapping the shore almost in slow motion, the water crackling against the stones and leaving a bubbling froth as the tide receded. The winter sun was strong enough to create a glare on the iron grey water of the English Channel.

Kate kicked off her shoes and picked them up. She was relieved now that she'd made the extra effort to try and find a matching pair of socks that morning, as she often couldn't be bothered. Not that she thought

Ern would have minded, or even noticed, but it felt good to have nothing for him to tease her about. She would have been ready with the argument that socks were purely functional and as long as each were clean, it didn't matter if they matched or not.

She enjoyed feeling the coolness of the smooth stones through the thin material.

'Why are you taking your shoes off?' asked Ern. He was looking at her and pointing down towards her feet as though it was the most bizarre thing for her to do.

Kate just shrugged her shoulders, kept on walking and grinned, replying, 'It's what I do.'

'Okay,' he said, shrugging his own shoulders and trotting to catch her up. Out of habit, Kate kept her head down looking for any pebbles with holes all the way through. She had told her niece that they were fairy stones that you should put on a chain and wear for good luck. They'd shared many Saturday afternoons scouring the beach for fairy stones and crystals, carrying them home in the pockets.

Ern turned around and said 'How about here?' to which she nodded and waited for him to ease himself down with a few grunts before she sat next to him. He opened the paper bag and took out the two plastic cartons which each contained salmon with a potato and spinach salad. Ern rustled in the bag and produced serviettes and two plastic forks.

'Oh, I should have bought some drinks,' said Kate.

'Da-dah!' Ern said with a chuckle, as he produced one bottle of mineral water from each of his coat pockets.

'Do you have rabbits in there too?' Kate laughed. 'First there were tulips and now drinks!'

'No rabbits,' Ern said. 'Maybe the odd handkerchief or too but they would just be plain white and boring. If you want I could buy you another coffee after this and maybe a pastry for dessert...if I haven't scared you off by then.' He looked at Kate and she smiled back at him saying, 'You're not scary.' Kate bit her lip hard. She reminded herself that she had been in so many situations where she regarded people as old friends before she'd even found out their age or how many GCSEs they had or whether they preferred ketchup over brown sauce. Once, she had been chatting to a woman in a café for over an hour before the woman revealed that she liked the taste of blood. Kate had been polite enough and listened to the woman's tales of witchcraft and the benefits of knowing which poisons lead to a quick death and which lead to an agonizing, squirming, eyeball popping demise, before Kate decided she really should be making some excuse about having to leave. It suddenly occurred to her that she had put herself in just the same kind of vulnerable situation with Ern.

She looked at him closely. He was enjoying his meal and savouring the taste rather than wolfing it down like a man who only had pennies to buy his food each day. Kate so desperately wanted to know more about him. Maybe then she would be able to understand why she felt so attracted to him, his pictures and those damned eyes that kept looking in her direction. She tried to keep her voice casual as she asked him, 'I mean, should I be scared of you?'

'Oh, I'm not very scary.' He turned to look at her and said 'My heart's in the right place, Kate. I don't mean anyone any harm.'

Kate looked deep into his eyes and felt herself relax. 'No,' she said. 'I didn't think you did.'

'Thank you,' he said quietly. Kate wanted to lighten the mood. She popped open the lid on her salad and stabbed some potato with her fork.

'No, thank *you*,' she said brightly. 'I would have just been at home fretting about my new job if you hadn't asked me out for lunch.'

'I think everything will be alright. I think that everything becomes clear if you give it time.' Ern started to eat his lunch and she could see he was savouring the rich flavour, allowing the flavours to mingle in his mouth before he went for the next forkful.

'Do you like your towels soft or crunchy?' Kate asked with a serious face, waggling her fork at him.

'What?' said Ern, surprised.

'Soft or crunchy? If you dry them on the line and iron them they're beautifully soft and if you iron them on the radiator they're all crispy and crunchy.'

'Oh, definitely crispy and crunchy. It's got to be good for your constitution to be brutal with a hardened towel' Ern chuckled. 'What on earth possessed you to ask that?'

'I want to know more about you. Tell me about you,' Kate said, waggling her fork at him again. As an afterthought she remembered it should be a question rather than a demand so she put her fork down and added, 'Please? I really want to know.'

'There isn't much to tell. I'm here and then I'm there. I only stay where my art is. My life is uncomplicated now... it suits me.'

Kate tried hard not to make it sound like an inquisition but her curiosity was getting the better of her. 'But how do you mean now? Have you had crap in the past?'

'Haven't we all?' he replied swiftly.

'I was always told you should never answer a question with a question,' she grinned hoping that he would see that she recognised her own cheekiness.

'Oh! Why would that be?' he said with a small chuckle.

'Perhaps you would care to tell me?' she said back.

'No, no, perhaps you would care to tell me?' he asked.

'Is the sky blue?' Kate asked.

'Is grass green?' Ern replied.

'You see?' she laughed. 'Too many questions never get you any answers.'

'Too true,' Ern said. 'This is good salmon,' he continued, changing the subject and spearing some spinach with his fork.

'It is,' Kate said. 'Have you ever wished you were like me? I mean; the house, the mortgage, the cat...?'

'You have a cat?' he asked. Kate recognised he was trying to veer off from the questions being directed at him and that was okay... there was plenty of time.

'I do have a cat. I think I told you that already though.'

'What's its name?'

'Cat,' she said, wincing at the inevitable ribbing she was now well used to when she told anyone her feline housemate's name.

'Ha! You have a cat called Cat. You don't have much of an imagination when it comes to pet names then, I see.'

'Oh no, I just thought that it would be the only cat around called Cat, so it would be easier to call her in at night,' Kate laughed.

'I had a cat once,' he said gently.

'And what was your cat called?'

'Tigger.'

'Tigger? Was she a tabby? I have a tabby.'

'Oh no, she was black,' he replied.

'So why did you call a black cat Tigger?' she laughed.

'Oh, I think every cat should be called Tigger. It gives them something to aspire to.'

Kate nodded with mock seriousness as he went on, 'Cats are the perfect companion. They leave you alone when they can't be bothered with your attention and they keep your feet warm at night.

Kate nodded and said, 'You don't seem like a cat person though. I would have had you down as a dog person.'

'How so?'

'I just imagine a dog trotting beside you adoringly – I don't know why really. I suppose you seem like someone who would appreciate a loyal companion,' Kate said.

'Well, Tigger most certainly wasn't loyal. She turned up at my door one evening unexpected, looking at me with her Tigger eyes, daring me to take her on. How could I resist? She came and went as she pleased but she was never really mine. I reckon… she loved with her stomach rather than her heart. That's probably why she ran off… to find a better stocked larder.' He returned to jabbing his salad and chasing an olive around the plastic bowl with his fork.

'Oh, I'm sure that's not the case! Maybe she got run over?' Kate said with too much enthusiasm.

'That is an outrageous suggestion!' he said with a laugh. 'Let me believe she is living in front of someone's fire with fresh mackerel for dinner every evening.'

'Sorry, sorry… I say these things. I'm pretty useless really.'

'That's okay,' he said. 'I'm only fooling myself. I saw the street sweepers peeling her off the road one morning. The poor mog must have been hit with a juggernaut she was so flat.'

'OH NO!' said Kate. 'I am so sorry. I really didn't think…'

His wicked smile shut her up. 'Gotya,' he said with a wry smile.

She punched him gently on the arm. 'That is not nice.' She felt happy by the ease of the conversation but she still wanted to know more. 'Tell me more about you, Ern. What do you like and dislike? Are you just a rebel without a cause…' she winced at her own bluntness before continuing, 'or are you doing this because you just don't care about so-called 'fitting in'?'

Ern put his food down and leant back on his elbows, stretched his legs and crossed his feet. Kate suddenly noticed his shoes, which had obviously seen better days but were still stylish brown leather brogues. 'I'm doing it because I want to. I've had the house, the job and the cat. I don't really feel that they are what I want at the moment. That's all.'

61

'Isn't any part of you scared that if you decide you want those things again, you'll turn around and it will all be too late?'

Ern took a moment to think. He picked up a pebble and gently tapped it against another.

'I need to apologise again,' Kate said. 'I'm nosey. It's just the way I am. Not for the sake of being nosey but I am genuinely interested. I love hearing about people's lives. Sorry… again… I'm not judging you, I promise.'

He looked at her with sad eyes. 'I know. I used to like hearing about people's lives too because how on earth can you judge meaning in anything if you only have your own experiences to gauge it all on. But then you wake up one day and you don't really give a damn about anyone's life… including your own. Is that the ultimate success or the ultimate failure?'

He looked at her and Kate dropped her head, inspecting the pebbles. She was disappointed at the serious turn in his voice. 'It's alright, really it is,' he said. 'I suppose I've just never had to talk about it with anyone. I've always kept these thoughts in my head.'

He flicked the pebble across the beach. It landed just before the sea rolled in with a fresh wave of froth. They both watched the water retreat and the pebbles glisten in its wake.

Ern spoke quietly. 'I suppose we can all wonder about what will happen if it all gets too late. Maybe though, it was too late a long time ago. Maybe now you can live what you wanted to do before it becomes too late.'

Kate sat for a moment digesting his words before exploding into giggles. 'That makes no sense whatsoever!' she said. Ern laughed too. 'I know,' he said. 'I speak complete crap sometimes. In my mind it makes sense but then, I suppose, my mind is a curious place.' He rolled onto his side, propping himself up on his elbow. 'Tell me more about you, Kate.'

My life is pretty boring really. I had a normal childhood without any massive traumas, went to college and got my qualifications, started off climbing some huge mountain that I was never going to reach the top of, slipped down to this sleepy old town and decided to climb a more manageable hillock, instead.' Kate smiled a mischievous smile.

Ern raised his eyebrows and a lop-sided grin. A hillock?

Kate laughed. 'Yep, a hillock.'

'I think you need to aim for more than hillocks.'

Kate hugged her knees and tried to ignore the fact that the chilly breeze was beginning to make her feel icy cold. She didn't like the way she had made such an accurate metaphor of her life. She tried not to sound too wistful as she said,

'Hillocks are okay. At least it's not far to travel to the shops.'

Ern shrugged and said, 'True.'

Kate let out a quick yelp of excitement as she saw a glint on the beach to her right. She kept her eyes fixed on the dazzling shard of light and reached over to pick it up.

'Look,' she said. You don't find these too often.'

She showed Ern the grey stone that had been cracked on one side, revealing tiny crystals that had formed. As she manoeuvred it in her hand, each one caught the sunlight and twinkled like fine diamonds.

'Who would have ever though such a plain stone could hold such beauty,' he said.

Kate rubbed the smooth side of the stone with her thumb. 'But you do the same thing every day when you draw on the pavements.'

'You're too kind to me, Kate.'

'No, I'm not,' she quickly replied. 'I'm only speaking the truth.'

Kate slipped the stone in her pocket and wrapped her arms around her knees again, resting her chin on top of them.

They sat for a while in silence. The sounds around them were so peaceful with the waves rolling in, fizzing on the pebbles, before retreating again. A few seagulls became excited by some discarded titbits and Ern watched them squabble in flight as one tried to lift off with a huge portion of bread roll in its beak.

Ern spoke quietly. 'What's your favourite film, Kate? If I were to take you to the cinema what would be your dream film to see?'

'I'm a bit too fidgety for films. I think the last film I saw in the cinema was some epic 3 hour thing that bored me rigid and I left half way through. I can't understand why I don't seem to like films everyone raves about.' Kate looked at Ern but he seemed deep in thought. There was another moment of silence before he said, 'I used to watch all the old musicals when I was a kid. It wasn't my choice to. If I could have chosen I would have turned over to the football. Some of those old films though – the way they were shot and the illusion they created of this perfect world – they were intoxicating.'

Kate nodded and said, 'To be honest, I've always had a secret passion to be Doris Day.'

'Ha!' Ern laughed. 'With that gorgeous hair and those smouldering eyes, you are a Gina Lollobrigida rather than a Doris Day.'

Kate blushed. She wasn't used to compliments being thrown her way in such a direct fashion. She struggled to think of something to say but simply decided on 'Why, thank you.'

Ern spoke softly, 'My mum's favourite film... it was a show too.' The words were so quiet they were nearly a whisper.

'Really? Which one?' she asked. She put some more salmon in her mouth and savoured the peppery coating which sizzled on her tongue.

Ern turned his head to look at her and said, 'Kiss me Kate.'

Kate didn't move as he leaned forward and touched her lips with his own.

CHAPTER TWELVE

It was a couple of seconds until, Kate realised that he'd actually stopped kissing her. Her eyes were closed, her lips were very slightly open and she was completely oblivious that Ern was looking at her with a straight stare and a serious face. She opened her eyes slowly and looked at him.

There was a moment more of silence and then she suddenly came to with a shiver.

'Bloody Hell,' she said.

'Is that good?' he said, with a half smile.

'Umm, yeah,' she said, nodding slowly. 'That's very good.' Kate could feel her mobile phone vibrating in her pocket and she willed it to stop so that she could just keep feeling that tingle which their kiss had sent running through every nerve ending in her body.

Ern looked embarrassed and suddenly unsure of himself. 'I have to go,' he said, raising onto his knees and picking up some of the rubbish from their picnic.

Kate nodded and helped him clear everything up, confused by his change in mood. Ern suddenly stopped and sat back down onto the pebbles.

'Kate?' he looked at her, concern on his face. 'I'm sorry if I overstepped the mark. It's just that from the moment I saw you... well, you just took my breath away. I really do apologise if I've made you feel uncomfortable.'

She stopped and looked at him. 'You haven't made me feel uncomfortable. Quite the opposite really but that makes me feel uncomfortable too.'

He chuckled. 'I have no idea what you mean.'

'Neither do I' she grinned back.

He held his arms out either side and let them drop back to his side as he said, 'What the hell are you doing talking to me Kate?'

'I don't understand what you mean,' she replied, becoming even more confused.

'I mean what are you doing here? You could do anything, be anyone and yet you're sat here on a beach with a bum who drags himself around not giving a damn about anything or anyone and…'

Kate tried to prompt him as he searched for the right words. 'And?' she asked.

Ern looked at her before continuing, 'And you genuinely seem to like my company. Am I wrong?'

Kate looked down at the pebbles, disconcerted by the sudden intensity of the conversation. 'No, you're not wrong,' she said quietly.

'Do you see me as some sort of curio? Some sort of 'project'?'

Kate was shocked and spoke loudly, 'NO! I feel really insulted that you would think that. I know I ask a lot of questions but I'm not judging you. I'm genuinely interested. You really think that about me?'

Ern put his hands up to cover his face, pushing them up and through his hair before he said, 'No, I don't. I just can't seem to get it straight in my mind what's going on here.'

Kate didn't know what to say to that. She didn't know what was going on either.

'Do we have to have to get it straight in our minds?' she asked.

Ern just shrugged his shoulders. He looked thoroughly miserable.

Kate took a deep breath and told him, 'Ern your art is inspiring. I have never been touched by work so close to my home before. And you…' she stopped herself from blurting out just how much he had affected her. She didn't want to let him know just how much she liked him. It was too soon and just made no sense whatsoever. She chose her words carefully as she continued, 'There's just something about you that makes me want to know more.'

Ern turned and smiled at her. Kate felt relief wash over her and the tight knot in her stomach eased.

He spoke quietly to her. 'Likewise.' He let out a long, exaggerated groan and continued, 'But to be honest with you Kate, I don't need the complication of liking anyone. I'm not sure that it would be good for you or for me.'

Kate wanted to kick back with protests but instead she stayed quiet. She was upset that it had all gone so wrong when it had all just been so wonderful. She thought about standing up and just walking, leaving him to it, showing him that she wouldn't be mucked about. That was what Jamie would have told her to do and she knew that it would have been for the best. She knew that she was only just keeping it together and that if she risked moving - even an inch - it was a great possibility that it would kick-start the tears that she could feel lying in wait. There was absolutely no way she was going to make more of a fool of herself than she had done already. She chose a spot to stare at way out in the distance. She pushed her tongue hard against the roof of her mouth and willed herself to pull it all in, take a step back from it... anything, as long as it wasn't crying.

Over to the left of the beach, a little boy clambered over the groyne separating their section from the next. Kate looked at him in his bright red jumper, his face set with determination, as he ran towards the water. She opened her mouth to shout at him not to get too close, when she heard a woman's voice scream 'CHARLIE! YOU GET BACK HERE OR I SHALL BAN YOU FROM WATCHING CBEEBIES FOR A WEEK!' The little boy stopped dead and Kate could see he was weighing up the options. His mum's head appeared over the groyne. She had obviously been running to catch up with him and clearly was just plain exhausted. The little boy looked at the water and then looked at his mum. 'Charlie,' his mum said in a calmer voice. 'I mean it.' Charlie plopped himself down on the pebbles and crossed his arms defiantly looking out to sea for a few moments before looking up at his mum again, standing up and clambering back over the groyne to be greeted by a big hug from his mum. Kate smiled and looked at Ern but his face was still very serious.

Ern spoke softly, 'I don't want to feel Kate. I don't want to feel anything other than that feeling I get when I create imaginary people in imaginary places through my art. I can handle that. I'm not sure I can handle liking someone as much as I like you.'

She looked at him. He seemed lost in his own thoughts and she didn't want to say the wrong thing. His words had scratched into her head like someone dragging the needle over an LP on some old record player. It was like it had spoiled everything. She buried her head down onto her knees with her arms wrapped around and closed her eyes. She hated not knowing what to do. She heard the pebbles start to bump together as he moved and resisted the urge to look up. She felt his hands rest on hers as he moved to kneel in front of her.

'Kate?' he said softly.

She bit her lip hard before lifting her head to look at him.

His concerned expression suddenly turned to one of pain and he said 'Bloody hell, these pebbles are hard on the knees.' He fell backwards, untangled his legs and rubbed his knees vigorously. Despite the way she felt, Kate allowed herself a chuckle.

He moved back to her side and draped an arm across her shoulders.

'I thought I was making life so easy for myself Kate. Meeting you has made me question things again that's all.'

Kate felt totally out of her depth. Part of her felt that she was being manipulated by him and that made her angry. 'Should I apologise for that?' she asked. She lowered her voice a little and said, 'I m not sure what you're wanting me to say. You're confusing the hell out of me, Ern.'

'I'm sorry,' he said, shaking his head. 'And no, no, I don't want you to apologise.'

He picked up a large flat pebble and threw it hard so that it landed onto the beach with a crack before being swallowed up by an incoming wave.

'I like you, Kate. I really bloody like you.'

'You make that sound like a terrible thing,' she said.

'Oh no,' he replied. He picked up another rock and threw it even harder. It plopped into the sea, sending ripples spiralling from the centre of its landing place. 'No, Kate. You really are perhaps the most wonderful thing that's happened to me in a long, long time.'

He turned his head and smiled at her. 'You are an amazing woman,' he said quietly. 'I hope you'll forgive me for sounding like such an idiot. Like I said before, you've been like a breath of fresh air to me.'

Without stopping to think, Kate leaned forward and touched his face, running her finger along his jaw and up to his lips. 'Then let's perhaps not try to figure anything out, okay? Maybe it's just one of those things that don't have an answer.'

'Maybe it is,' he said. 'Can I see you tomorrow?'

Kate couldn't look him in eyes as she nodded. She really wasn't sure that she ever wanted to see him again but then she really wasn't sure of anything any more.

Ern carefully eased himself up from the pebbles, straightened his spine and began to walk away. Kate watched him walk back to the promenade. Once he had stepped onto the tarmac, she saw him begin to turn his head to look back at her. She quickly whizzed her head around to stare at the sea, determined not to make eye contact with him. After a few minutes, she looked back again but he had gone.

CHAPTER THIRTEEN

Steph had started her shift at the pub only ten minutes earlier and already her nose had accustomed to the fog of stale beer and the boom-boom-boom of the jukebox. The place had started to fill up with the suits who had wandered over for a pint before entering the nightmare that was rush hour on the only road that led out of town. She envied them their structured lives with a ready made gang to gossip and flirt with. The other staff in the pub always came and went so quickly that she never really had anyone to banter with. Each time one of them left, it made her assess what the hell she was still doing there. The truth was that she loved her job. She loved watching people who came in and seeing moments of their lives play out in front of her. She'd seen make-ups and break-ups, declarations of love and even the odd proposal since she'd been there. Then of course, there was always the regulars. There was Albert who could recite every landlord the pub had since the 1950s, Stan who always had to be watched because most of the time he had already had a bellyful of beer before he even left the house and Vicky, the resident matriarch who sat in the same seat, every evening, with her Zimmer frame propped up in front of her and her single glass of peach schnapps lasting the whole evening.

A young guy walked in carrying what looked to be some kind of music case and perched himself up on a stool by the bar. Steph walked over and greeted him with a smile. 'What can I get you?' she asked. 'Ah, I'll just have a pint of Harvey's Best, thanks.'

She took a pint glass from the rack and tilted it under the beer tap. 'Have you come for the open Mike night?'

'Yeah,' he said, 'some guy saw me playing in the street earlier today and asked if I'd like to come along and have a jam with his band.'

'Really? Which band?' She passed the beer to him and took his fiver before ringing it into the till.

'Chameleon. You know them?' She flicked her head around and laughed.

'Oh yes, I know them,' she said, pushing the drawer closed again and sliding his change onto the bar.

'What's so funny?' he said, not sure whether to laugh before he heard the punch line.

'Oh nothing, really. They are a mixed bunch but they're harmless enough. They do some good covers and regularly play down here on a Friday night.'

Steph flashed him another smile, wiped the bar down and opened the hatch to go and clear glasses. She felt her heckles rise when she saw that a lot of the dirty ones had obviously been there since lunchtime but pushed the feeling away quickly so as not to start the evening on the wrong foot.

As she leant over to wipe one of the tables down, she felt the hand slide over her buttocks and squeeze. She turned quickly, ready to say 'What the…' but he was quick as lightning and he changed tact grabbing both breasts with his greasy hands.

There in front of her was Art Garfunkel leering, with his eyes half closed. Of course, it wasn't really Art Garfunkel but someone who had been the unfortunate affliction of being born his looky-likey. Everyone called him Art, even though his real name was Norman. His ginger hair was receding over his moon face and his baby suckling lips finished off the look of a man who was truly revolting. She was just about to knee him in the balls when a fist flew in from the right of her vision and caught Art on the jaw. Admirably, Art did not fall to the side immediately but managed to stay upright for an impressive few seconds, before crumbling to the floor, still smiling.

She turned to look at where the fist had come from and was met by the young busker staring at her with concern.

'Are you okay?' he asked.

'Yeah, I'm fine,' Steph replied. 'But you may not be. That's the lead singer of Chameleon.'

'Ah!' said the busker. 'Probably not the best way to be introduced to a prospective new band member then,' he said with a chuckle.

'He's always drunk. He likes to play the big pop star, picking up any groupies he can and sneaking into the ladies loos with them when he thinks no-one's looking. His wife and four kids don't seem to be an issue as far as he's concerned.'

The busker raised his eyebrows with surprise and shook his head, before saying 'Arsehole.'

'Oh,' Steph replied. 'There's a lot worse than him around, I can assure you.'

Steph and the busker struggled to lift Art up. She cringed at the stench emanating from him - a mix of beer, curry and cigarettes. Grabbing him under the armpit to lift, she was already resigned to the inevitable sweat patch that her fingers would find. They propped him onto a barstool and she leaned over the bar, to use the sink, in a vain attempt to get the smell out of her palms.

'My name's Luke, by the way' the young busker said.

'I'm Steph' she replied, extending her hand to shake his, before withdrawing it in case any of Art's sweat was still on it and settling on a 'hello' smile.

A guy with long brown hair ambled into the pub, carrying a guitar case. He saw Art unconscious next to the bar and said 'She-it! What happened here?'

Luke spoke up, 'He got a little overly friendly with Steph here so I'm afraid I just laid him out.' Luke held out his hand and said, 'We met earlier in the street?'

'Yeah, yeah,' the guy said, shaking his hand. 'I remember. My name's Graham. I'm really glad you came.'

'Doesn't look like you'll be jamming tonight though?' Luke said.

Graham turned to Steph and rubbed her arm. 'I really am sorry about him, Steph. He has been having a bit of a bad time at the moment. He tends to sink his head into the bottle when he has woman trouble, as you know.'

'As long as he doesn't try to sink it in my breasts again' the words were out of Steph's mouth before she realized that it was not the most demure thing to say. She looked over to Luke who was chuckling softly at her retort. She shouted over to Alan, the Landlord.

'Hey Al, can I have a jug of water and a cup of ice please?'

Al looked at her and winked 'Sure thing Steph.'

Once the pitcher and glass were delivered, she pulled Arts jeans away from his skin (leaning back as far as possible so as not to even be tempted to look) and dropped the ice down there in one. Then she dipped the cup in the water and poured it over his wiry ginger hair. Art opened one eye, looked at her, Luke and then at Graham, before lurching forward and vomiting on his own shoes.

'AH, SHIT MAN!' shouted Graham.

'You sober him up, Graham and I'll clear that up. Although I can't promise that he'll be allowed to play down here again tonight or any other night. It's not good for business, you know what I mean?'

Graham nodded and jabbed a number into his phone. Steph heard him talking to Art's wife and agreeing to put Art in a taxi. When he had hung up, he turned to Luke and said, 'So, Luke. I know you are one hell of a clarinet player but do you also sing?'

'I can hold a tune,' Luke replied with a grin.

'Well, it looks like we'll be jamming tonight after all,' Graham said, before hitching Art up and staggering outside with him.

Steph turned and looked at Luke. She hadn't really realised how cute he was with his hair tied up in a pony-tail and his gangly surfer look. 'I best get back to work,' she said to him.

'Perhaps we could have a drink together sometime?' Luke asked quickly.

'Perhaps,' she said. 'It's not often I have my very own knight in shining armour come to my rescue.'

Luke flashed her a grin. Graham came back into the pub and he motioned to Luke to join him over at a table. 'Laters then,' Luke said to her.

'Laters,' she replied, watching him walk away to the other side of the pub. She shook her shoulders and mentally forced herself to click back into feisty barmaid role, turning her head and shouting over the bar, 'Tony, hun, you got a pavement pizza out here… you'd better clean it up quick if you don't want Vicky going A over T in it.'

As she slid back behind the bar she promised herself that tonight was going to be a very fun night.

CHAPTER FOURTEEN

Ern picked his way back over the beach. The sun was setting and the peach hue of the sky was casting an unreal tinge on the gentle lapping of the sea. He was pleased to see that a thick blanket of cloud had rolled in during late afternoon. That meant that he wouldn't get too cold this night. He didn't want to check into the Bed & Breakfast where he'd been staying because he had too much to think about. He didn't want to be able to hear the couple next door having sex, or the man above shouting and ranting at the TV. He just wanted quiet. So, he'd gone to his room, grabbed his old sleeping bag from the bottom of the bed and told the landlady he'd be back in the morning for a shower. She had looked at Ern as though he was crazy but he was getting used to that look. It really didn't matter what anyone thought of him anymore. He'd reluctantly admitted to himself that it was becoming increasingly important what Kate thought though.

The seagulls were lined up on the beach and he had half a mind to run along through them flapping his arms screaming at them, just so that he could release some of his frustration. Instead, he tossed them the leftovers of his greasy chips and waited until they had devoured the last of the scraps before leaning down and taking the paper back up and rolling it into a ball. Scavengers were always making him assess his own life. Was that what he was doing? Begging for money from complete strangers to keep him alive? Was he really providing them with some form of entertainment and some sort of escape from the humdrum or was he as bad as those seagulls? Most of the problem was that before he met Kate, he wouldn't have cared either way but now she was making him care. He wanted to be someone for her. He wanted to make her happy because, no matter how much it pained him to admit it, that would make him happy. He had gone over their lunch date again and again in his mind. He had no grand illusions about being some desirable 'catch'. So what was it about her that liked him? How could someone as wonderful as Kate look at him and think that he was worth spending time with?

Ern felt certain that it would probably change when she knew the whole truth. Kate had a good heart and she would not be able to reconcile his past with who she wanted him to be. He'd spent too many months leaving that person behind that it was a huge risk now to bring him back, but how on earth was it fair to keep letting Kate believe he was someone he wasn't?

He found the boat which he had checked out earlier and lifted the tarpaulin. He knew it wasn't going to be a particularly comfortable night but part of him knew that it was his own way of pushing things to the boundary. He wasn't going to start getting complacent about everything until he had it all straight in his mind. He had tucked the items that he considered to be most personal and important into the pockets of his coat. He remembered to pull them out before he climbed in so that he wouldn't crush them. He dropped them gently down onto his bag before he tugged on his sleeping-bag and carefully stepped in, trying not to let the boat rock too violently. Once he was lying down, he pulled the tarpaulin over and made sure it was tied down above his head. He got the torch out of his bag and flicked it on. The dim ray of light made him feel even lonelier and heightened his fear of being discovered – not because of any threat of being beaten up or mugged but he simply wouldn't have been able to take the shame of discovery. No matter how low he sunk, he desperately wanted to not have anyone give him false pity. They had to know that he was choosing to live like this.

Ern shone the light down onto the bag and picked up his mobile phone. He jabbed it on and said a silent prayer that there was enough battery left to make at least one call. He turned off the torch as the light from the phone cast a glow on his hands. One bar came up on the battery and he saw that he had 24 missed calls. They were all from his sister. He pushed the return call button. He watched it dial and flash 'connected'. As the seconds ticked away, he could here his sister on the other end 'Hello? Is there anyone there?' He felt a great temptation to hang up but he knew that he had to put her mind at rest. He put it to his ear and quietly said 'Hello, Maureen.'

His sister's voice came through as a scream 'Ern! Is that you?'

'Yes, Maureen. It's me. I'm really sorry it's been so long.'

'Where are you? Why the hell haven't you called? We are SO worried about you! James has…'

'Maureen I don't have much battery left. I just wanted you to know I'm okay.'

'Oh great,' his sister's voice was heavily loaded with sarcasm. 'You're okay so that makes everything alright does it? What about us here worried sick about you? What about me having to tell mum not to worry all the time? What about John having to pick up all the crap you left behind when you decided to up and leave without so much as a 'see you around'?'

'I'm sorry, Mo,' Ern said. His heart sank as he heard her start to cry.

'Maureen, please listen. I just need more time out. I've been going through the motions of getting on with business for years now. I've just reached the lowest point maybe.'

'Ern, you've got to let it go…'

'No, Maureen. I don't need to let it go. I need to learn to live with it. Right at this moment, I just need to accept that I can't ever change what's happened and I possibly will never remember the truth. Do you realise how depilating that is? I don't know whether I'm fooling myself or you and it's all just waiting to spill out. It's like being in no-mans land just waiting.' His voice had become angry and frustrated. He tried to calm himself and said, 'I am absolutely sick and tired of waiting for some kind of answer that might never come.' He closed his eyes and waited Maureen to speak. He knew it was impossible for her to understand fully.

After a few moments of quiet, Maureen simply said, 'I know.'

Ern could feel his own tears welling up. He hated the burden he had been to his family. He hated how much he had let them down and shamed them. When Maureen started to talk again, he imagined her straightening her back, jutting out her chin to try and play the big sister card. He loved her dearly but their sibling hierarchy just wasn't going to cut it this time.

'Ern you need to get a grip on this and move on. We have all tried to help as much as we can.'

'I know. That's what I'm doing now. I promise you, I will be back soon.'

'Ern, you must…'

The battery cut out and plummeted him back into a silence that was almost unbearable. As he struggled with the emotions, his head filled with a searing white noise that burned his eyes and the back of his throat. It was a reaction that he knew was his mind's way of screaming the pain away. At first he had thought he would go insane from that noise but now he saw it as part of a release from him doing anything more drastic.

Switching on the torch again, he reached into his bag, pulling out a diary and a small box. He opened up the box to retrieve his pen… but stopped as soon as he saw her face looking back at him. The photo of his daughter was beginning to suffer from its long journey and curl at the edges. He held it against his cheek and waited until he felt the glossy paper warm slightly. As he brought it back into his lap and shone the torch directly at her smiling face, he couldn't hold back the tears anymore. He looked at her blonde hair, held up with a red ribbon and her polka dot dress, which had made her look like some picture book child from a fairytale. He touched the photo with his forefinger and slowly swept it along the line of her forehead. 'I love you,' he said aloud. 'I miss you.' He inhaled suddenly, determined not to stop himself from sobbing.

Ern swallowed hard and continued with his nightly prayer to her, 'I hope you are warm. I hope you are at peace.' He placed her photo back in the box and pulled the other blanket over himself, flicking off the torch as he did so. He lay back and watched the tarpaulin billow in the freezing breeze that was blowing in from the West. He felt around for his hat and placed it over his face, closing his eyes and listening to the sea crashing into the pebbles as he tried to drift into sleep.

CHAPTER FIFTEEN

Kate had been up half of the night painting. She had mooched around the house examining in her mind every detail of the conversation during her lunch date with Ern. Her emotions had swung each and every way, leaving her totally exhausted with the ambiguity of their relationship. Could she even call it a relationship? Wasn't that jumping the gun a little? She had tried to ring either Beth and Jamie by phone, but both of them were out and she hung up without leaving messages for them. She didn't want to leave a short quirky message and sound as though everything was alright. She wanted to have them sympathise with her and then make her laugh about something or nothing, just so that for one moment she could forget about it all and have a joke with her friends.

As Kate had been so unable to settle, she decided that the only thing she could do was to use that energy positively by splattering it all onto her canvas. If Ern thought he could escape life by creating imaginary people in imaginary places then she would go one better and create real people - people that she knew were there, just behind the crowd, who deserved to have their emotions and lives captured, as much as anyone else did.

She worked furiously, painstakingly recreating the walkway in her own unique style, never quite sure if she was creating a true replica or whether this was only her perception of the place. If it was merely her perception, then she hoped that love would shine through. She wanted the painting to be alive with movement, music and snapshots of people's lives by the look on their faces, or the way they held themselves or the people they were with. Much of the time Kate would stand back allowing herself to be absorbed and inside the picture she was working on. She knew that she had to be a part of it as an unseen observer, in order to absolutely make it come alive. The initial idea was growing into a master plan as she worked. There was no consistency with the way she indulged her artistic flow - sometimes leaving an area having only drawn a brief outline, other times concentrating on one small patch, filling it with minute detail. At times, she felt overwhelmed with the responsibility of making this a tribute to her town - her people – and she tried to ensure that each and every person was placed with care and love.

She didn't know exactly what time it was that exhausted, in both mind and body, she finally gave in to tiredness and flopped, fully dressed, onto her bed. She swung the duvet over her body and pushed her legs out to kick the few bits of clothes that were lying on top, down onto the floor. Cat jumped up and nestled next to her. Kate put her hand on Cat's soft fur and before her mind could stumble back to thoughts of Ern, she fell asleep.

A few hours later, the shrill tweep, breep, of the telephone shook her from her dreams. Kate wondered whether it was part of her dream at first and tried to roll over to push herself back into sleep. But the phone kept ringing and she opened her eyes to see that the morning light was streaming through her half-open curtains. She groaned and slowly reached across the bed to lift the receiver.

'What, who and why on earth are you calling me at this ridiculous hour of the morning?' she said, in a drone, assuming it would be one of her friends.

'Kate Milton?' a plummy voice asked.

'Um… yeah.' Kate tried to think her drowsiness away before asking 'Who is this?'

'This is Artslinks Ltd.'

'Who?'

'We've just sent you a letter advising of your recruitment to our staff?'

'Oh shit! I mean, yes, sorry…' Kate lifted up onto her elbows and swung her legs over the side of the bed. She let her feet search for the slippers, as she quickly tried to stop sounding like a complete idiot.

'We wondered if it would be possible for you to come in for a few hours today for some induction. We need you to bring your P60 and your National Insurance number. We'll walk you through the office procedures etc., as you'll be starting on one of our major projects first thing on Monday.'

'Oh yes, of course. What time would you like me there?'

'No later than 10am, please. All our staff are in a meeting from 12pm.'

'Oh okay, see you then.'

Kate fell back down onto the mattress as she clicked the phone off. She rolled over and let thoughts of Ern fill her head. She was still reeling from his kiss - her head tumbling with the sense of happiness it had engulfed her in. Of course, she couldn't remember the kiss without remembering all the other things he'd said. Kate rolled her eyes to the ceiling and said aloud, 'And I thought I was high maintenance!' Now that she wasn't so tired, she could see the irony of the situation and how delicious that irony was. She had been ridiculous to expect some spectacular love story and for now, she would just go with the flow and see what happens. She smiled and rolled over the other way to stare at her alarm clock.

'NO!' Kate sat bolt upright when she saw the time: 9:07am. She threw the duvet off and jumped out of bed, quickly opening the wardrobe and staring blindly in to see what she should wear. She slammed the doors shut again and went to start the water for her shower.

Cat blinked at her each time she ran past in various stages of undress. First she was just in a towel with her hair dripping down her back. Then she hopped by with one leg in and one leg out of her knickers. She paused for a moment of concentration while she twisted her arms around to do the clips on her bra before trying on one, two three, four, five different outfits before she finally settled on her new grey skirt and a pale pink shirt, with some low kitten heels that she'd bought in some sale or other. Going to her dressing table she blasted her hair with the hairdryer, scrunching her curls with a silent prayer that they wouldn't decide to go frizzy today and then she quickly put some mascara on as well as a barely-there lipstick. Her favourite part of the whole getting ready process was always rooting through her bowl of knick knacks - bangles, beads and rings that she collected like smiles. Even the sound they made was pretty, as they chimed together when she scooted them around in the bowl to find her choice of the day. She chose a couple of hefty silver rings, three wooden bead

81

bracelets and slipped her shoes off again so that she could pop a toe ring on for luck. She turned and looked in the mirror. With a little bit of effort she forced her smile wider and whispered to herself 'Relax, you're doing just fine.' Cat meowed at her and Kate leaned over to tickle her chin. 'C'mon Cat,' she said. 'Let's get some breakfast.'

When Kate walked into her kitchen she glanced through the window and at the painting, which was just visible in the conservatory. She had worked so hard on it the night before but it looked different today. Kate couldn't relate to the painting actually being her own work because it was so unlike anything she had painted before. Cat meowed again and the sound snapped Kate back into action. She opened a sachet of cat food, tapped it into a saucer and grabbed a couple of digestive biscuits from the tin. When she opened the front door she could see heavy, grey clouds on the horizon, so she flicked her yellow Mac off the coat peg and threw it over her shoulders.

Kate's ankles kept wobbling on her heels as she ran for the bus but luckily there was a bus just arriving at the stop as she turned the corner. She ran daintily up to it waving at the bus driver so that he wouldn't pull away before she got there. She sat herself down on the first seat available and closed her eyes to try and force herself to relax a little. It always rattled her nerves when she knew she had to make an impression on someone. Strangers, that she would probably never see again, were no problem, but to be introduced to people who you would see everyday, work with and probably come to blows with from time to time, was a terrifying prospect. Kate knew that she was one of those people that you either loved or hated at first sight, with never much in the middle. She hoped they would like her. Not that it was necessary of course but, yes, she hoped they would like her.

Kate glanced at her watch as she jumped off the bus in the town centre. She had ten minutes to get to the offices. She cursed under her breath and started running again.

She smiled at the clarinettist as she trotted past and then ground to a halt behind Ern's hunched figure.

She tapped him lightly on the shoulder. He turned to look at her and immediately his face curled into a grin. 'Hello, lovely lady. You are early today.'

'Yep. I've had a call to go in and learn the ropes in this office that

I'm starting work in on Monday. I'm really not looking forward to it.'

'Will you be free for lunch?' he asked.

'Oh, definitely,' Kate said, nodding. 'It should only take a couple of hours.' She looked over his shoulder at the first outlines he had made of the picture of the day. Faint tones of rose pink and silver grey looked to be swirling around creating a spiral. 'Hey, your picture matches my clothes today,' she said with a grin, twirling around quickly to show off her outfit.

He grinned at her and then looked back to his work. He nodded and said 'Ah yes, there is nothing quite so satisfying than synchronicity.' He looked back at Kate and said 'apart from that absurd yellow mackintosh. You're not really intending to wear that are you? It will make you look like Fireman Sam!' Ern chuckled at his own joke and she rewarded his cheekiness with a gentle tap with her foot against his behind. 'I don't mean to be rude,' he said 'but it upsets the aesthetics of your beauty. Leave it with me and walk to work looking like the gorgeous, stylish woman you are.'

'You're on,' she said with a grin. 'If it rains, though, I shall blame you for me getting wet. I won't look gorgeous at all if that happens.'

'Oh, if it rains we are all in trouble' he said. Kate didn't give his words a second thought as she dropped her Mac on the window ledge in front of him and looked at her watch again.

'Crikes, I must go,' she said. 'So, I shall come back later to see you, okay?'

'I'm counting on it, Kate,' Ern said. 'I would like to buy you lunch again.'

Kate leaned down and without hesitating, she kissed his cheek, whispering 'That would be delicious. Thank you.' She started running again, shouting over her shoulder, 'I'll see you later… you want me to pick up some lunch on my way back?'

'No. Leave it all to me,' he called after her. 'Have a fantabulous morning.'

'Thanks Ern,' Kate shouted. 'And you!'

Ern turned back to his drawing and picked up a lighter pink pastel to the one he had been using. 'Sweet as candyfloss,' he said.

Kate opened the door and stepped into the warm interior of the office. It was 9:59am and she breathed a sigh of relief that she wasn't

83

late. It was an old Georgian house that had been converted into offices and inside there was the most breathtakingly beautiful architecture. The high ceilings were framed with the most wonderful plaster mouldings. In the centre of what was once the front room, there hung a huge chandelier set into an internal dome. The office had been furnished with minimalist oak desks and leather sofas which, although thoroughly modern, blended in beautifully with the feeling of opulence. The receptionist that she had seen on the day of her interview was sitting at her large desk, with the phone clasped to her ear.

Kate went up to her, leaned in towards her and said very quietly 'Excuse me. I'm...'

'Ssh!' said the receptionist as she quickly held a finger in the air, as a clear indication to Kate that she would have to wait.

Kate stood up straight and tried not to look put out. She swayed slightly from one foot to the other as her shoes were starting to pinch. She reckoned the woman was in her mid 40s although her severe Princess Di haircut made her look much older. She was wearing what was obviously a very expensive cashmere twin-set, in duck egg blue, and a double row of pearls around her neck. Kate browsed the immaculately tidy desk and came across her name plate - Mrs. M Howe. Mrs Howe was obviously agitated as she kept stabbing her notepad vigorously with the point of her pen.

Kate tried to guess what the M in her name stood for. She decided that the woman didn't look like a Mavis or a Maud. It was more likely that it would be Margaret or a Marjorie.

The Receptionist's voice suddenly cut through the silence of the office like a razor blade cutting through butter.

'Mr Jones. This is Milandra Howe from Artlinks Ltd.' Kate's eyes widened as the woman's shrill voice reverberated around the office. Kate's eyebrows shot up as her mind took in this information. 'Milandra! Oh my, that's a perfect name for her!' The receptionist continued with an extremely agitated tone,

'Yet again, I find myself in the difficult position of having to contact you with a 'situation'.' She said the last word heavily laced with sarcasm, drawing it out by slowly pronouncing each syllable succinctly.

Kate decided that she should move away a little so that she wasn't accused of eavesdropping, but the woman's voice was so loud that it was impossible not to hear, as she continued,

'Mr Jones, if you please. I asked for a good selection of meat and vegetarian finger food, of the highest standard and instead you send me three catering size pork pies and a pineapple.'

Kate opened her handbag, pretending to look for something inside, so that her smirk would remain hidden. The receptionist continued,

'I know we have had our differences in the past, Mr Jones, but I really think that some professionalism is imperative for our continued business relationship.'

Kate could just hear the man's voice blaring through the end of the telephone.

'Mr Jones! There really is no call for language like that. You know as well as I, that last time I complained I was perfectly justified. The butter was salted rather than the specified unsalted, low fat spread and the cheese was sliced rather than grated.'

Kate was beginning to have an insight into just how their 'professional' relationship had been conducted in the past. She did a quick calculation as to how many catering companies there were in the town and came to the conclusion that no matter how many there were, they probably all would have fallen foul of Ms Howe's impeccably high standards.

'Crusts off! Crusts off, Mr Jones! One should never present a plate of sandwiches with the crusts on. They take too much time to chew which makes polite conversation totally impossible.'

There was a brief pause and then she spoke again, her voice raised to almost a shout...

'Mr Jones. If I ask for doilies I expect white doilies, not gold doilies only fit for a tart's lock and key party.'

Kate was finding it very hard to suppress the giggles.

'No, Mr Jones. I have never actually attended a tart's lock and key party and yes, I am sure that they are probably *very* civilised affairs.' The last word was said with such scorn, Kate would not have been surprised if the doodles Milandra was furiously scratching into her note pad, were depicting a short fat caterer, being butchered with a blue ball-point pen.

'Mr Jones, can I presume that I will receive the correct order within the next two hours - a discreet and appetising selection of vegetarian and non-vegetarian sandwiches, accompanied by some crudités and bite-sized custard pastries as a dessert.'

The receptionist sighed and deliberately tried to calm her voice…

'Yes Mr Jones, I will try not to complain that the crudités are too crude.'

Kate couldn't hold back and snorted loudly, quickly turning it into a pretend sneeze. The receptionist threw her a look that would have withered fresh daisies.

'So I will see you back here before 12pm then Mr Jones? Thank you, Mr Jones. No, Mr Jones I am not available for a pint at lunchtime. Yes, Mr Jones maybe another time.'

The receptionist slammed the phone down, dropped her pen on the pad and muttered 'Over my dead body, you disgusting little man.'

She straightened her cardigan over her shoulders and looked directly at Kate.

'Now. What can I do for you?'

Kate stood up and extended her hand 'I'm Kate Milton. I'm here for some induction… you called me earlier.'

The receptionist looked at Kate's hand but instead of shaking it, she picked up her pen once more, using it to jab in an extension number on the phone, whilst saying…

'Ah yes Ms Milton, I will call for someone to take you up but I do believe that you were asked to be here by 10am and it is now…' She glanced at a delicate 9ct gold Rotary on her wrist. '… 10:04am. A little greater heed to punctuality may be prudent, if you wish to make a good impression. We are expecting clients at lunchtime and our schedule must be adhered to.'

Kate opened her mouth to protest but quickly decided to shut it again. She had the feeling that this was one woman she might like to keep on the good side of. Ms Howe picked up the phone again and pressed one button. After a brief pause, she said 'I have a Ms Milton here for you.' As she said the words, she gave Kate a long look up and down. Kate crossed her arms and tried not to look intimidated.

'They'll be down in a minute, for you. Take a seat,' Milandra said.

Kate sat down on the sofa, trying to ignore the butterflies in her stomach. She went over in her mind all the pep talks she had given herself about being as good as anyone else, a bright smile, kind heart and excellent taste in underwear.

One of the men that had interviewed her, burst through the door and walked quickly over to Kate, holding out his hand. 'The name's Harper. Good to have you on board,' he said, with no hint of a smile.

Kate stood up and shook his hand firmly. 'Yes, thank you,' she said, following him as he turned around and walked back to the door of the main offices. Kate glanced at Milandra before she left the room and could see that she was back to stabbing her pen on her notepad, with the phone receiver to her ear. Kate smiled, stepped through and closed the door behind her.

As they walked through the offices, what had seemed cold and sterile when she had come here for her interview, now seemed lively and exciting. Although everything was neat and tidy, she noticed that each person had personalised their workspaces with little mascots or photos from home. There was a notice board next to the photocopier that was full of cartoon strips and what she presumed were office jokes, dotted between the other official notices about important meetings and deadlines. She was introduced to what seemed like hundreds of different people, forgetting their names the instant she was told them but liking the fact that each person stood to shake her hand and welcome her. One woman said that she would soon get the hang of the place and if Kate had any problems, just to ask. Kate was shown the coffee machine, which seemed to be the place to hang out as a few people quickly scuttled away when they saw her approaching with Mr Harper.

They walked to the end of the corridor and Mr Harper said 'You've got this space, Kate, which I can tell you they've all been fighting for back there but the rules are that whichever one is vacated is taken up by the new person on board. So you got lucky with the best view in the house.'

Kate peered around the side of the partition and gasped at the sight of her new office. A clean white drawing board was set up at the window which had the most spectacular, clear views out to sea. It seemed as though you could see all the way from East to West. She slowly scanned the rest of her space and tried to take in all the new and wonderful things that were there. Beside the drawing board was a tall trolley that was neatly stocked with every colour, shape and size of stationery knick-knacks a girl could require. There was also a desk with a bright red office chair and a computer which swirled it's standby screen, 'Artlinks Ltd.' Under the window there was a low cabinet with glass doors, that was full of various coloured papers, inks and tools for Kate to use on the graphic presentations she would be asked to do in her role. She immediately tried to do a mental check-list of which bits and pieces she should bring from home to make it hers, before she scrubbed them all out and decided that she loved it here just the way it was. 'I'll leave you alone for a moment so that you can get a feel for the place,' Mr Harper said, to which Kate just nodded.

Once he had disappeared around the side of her partition, she sat down on the chair and whizzed herself around on it several times, smiling and not quite believing how excited she was. She opened the drawers of her desk and saw neatly stacked pens, envelopes and printer paper, as well as some business cards that they had printed in her name. Everything was so neat and new that Kate made a silent promise to herself that she would keep it that way and not have it messed up like everything in her new house. Unfortunately, Kate made that promise to herself so often that it had become a bit of a joke.

Kate turned her chair around and looked out at her view. She could see a car trying to fit into a parking space that was too small, the driver becoming more and more frustrated. She could see the fish shack, where people could get fish that had been freshly caught that morning, direct from the fisherman. She could see a woman walking her dog, with her chin tucked into her scarf to protect her from the morning chill. Kate was so excited that she would still be able to see life passing by her window even when she was at work. This job really was going to be alright.

She wondered what Ern would say if he could see this office, everything so neatly stacked and perfect. His tin of pastels and concrete canvasses were all very well but wouldn't everyone want this, if they could? She swivelled back around to her desk and rested her head on her hands. She gave it some thought and admitted to herself that no, not everyone would want it. Ern wouldn't want it. She would just have to accept that.

CHAPTER SIXTEEN

Ern looked down at the picture he was creating. Usually he repeated the same images that he had kept in his mind for years by recreating them with subtle differences each time he drew them, enjoying them growing older and changing just as he was with each passing year.

Today's picture was nothing like he had ever drawn before. The picture was looking down on a pier which stretched out to the horizon. There was a candyfloss haze in front of the scene, lending it all a sugary rose-tinted feel. The pier was old and dilapidated but two young lovers were walking, hand in hand, along the seemingly never-ending planks. There were cracks in some of them through which the icy cold water lay still as though frozen, with no froth, no swell of a wave. Above the pier, a flock of starlings danced and swirled like fortune tellers' tea-leaves, as they searched for a roost in the twilight.

Ern couldn't deny that Kate had changed everything. Even though he was resentful of not being able to just plod along, doing what he was doing without a thought, he felt honoured to be shown that there were still true, genuine, moments of happiness possible in his life.

He twisted his head to look around at the street. It was a quiet day and in any other town he would have thought it was time to move on. He looked over to the clarinet player who was sitting on a bench, his case open by his side, a pretty girl chatting to him. Ern watched them both suddenly lift their heads and laugh at the same time. Their laughter made him smile and long for Kate to be there by his side too. Further along the street, he could just make out the flower seller, sipping a mug of tea and saying hello to people as they walked by. He wondered what it must be like to have been somewhere so long that you know everyone's face, their routines and be able to tell their bad days from their good.

Ern looked down again at his drawing. He put his hand up to his face, sliding it from his cheek to his temple where he pushed in circular motion with his fingers to ease the tension he could feel beginning to knot his brow. In a sudden rush of activity, he snatched up a purple pastel and started to shade the water underneath the pier. He scratched in violent sweeping motions, before taking a black pastel and making the sea look even more sombre. When he had finished, he threw the few scattered pastels back in his tin and slammed the lid back on.

He was just about to cut the plastic that would be taped over it, when he felt a light tap on his shoulder. Ern jumped a little and snapped his head up to see who it was.

'Hey, sorry man. I didn't mean to scare you,' the clarinettist laughed. 'Just wondering if you'd like a cup of coffee as time's getting on?' Ern inhaled deeply and tried to push his black mood away as he exhaled. He was finding it easier to stop depression sinking in but it was always there, hovering, waiting for any opportunity to slam him down. He looked up at the busker and nodded with a smile.

'That would be wonderful thank you, Luke. I've nearly finished here and then I have some preparations for my lunch date.'

'Hey, me too! I had a gig at the pub last night and got talking to Steph over there. Maybe we should pair up?' Luke said the last sentence with a laugh and Ern grinned back at him, before saying.

'Ah now, I don't think either of us would really want that, eh?'

'No man,' Luke said. 'Sometimes you've just gotta say these things though, right?'

'Right,' said Ern, laughing.

'Coffee then. White and four sugars wasn't it?' Luke started rooting around in his jeans pockets for some change but Ern quickly dipped into his coat and produced a five pound note, saying, 'Oh, I think I'll manage with three sugars today.'

'Quite right too,' Luke said, taking the money and walking over to Tony's coffee shop.

By the time Luke returned with the coffees, Ern had taped down the plastic and put out his 'Thank you' notice next to his hat.

'Hey man, I've just thought. As I'm on a date myself, I won't be able to look after your pitch today. I'm really sorry.'

'Oh, it doesn't matter at all,' Ern replied. 'Town's pretty quiet and it's not going to come to any harm. It's not really very important when it compares to taking a beautiful woman for lunch on the beach.' Ern winced inside at the cliché of his own words but Luke just whistled and said 'Well then man, you'd best get changed... put your best bib and tucker on.'

'You think?' Ern hadn't even considered the idea. He looked down at his creased trousers, his navy blue jumper that had just started to unravel around one cuff and his scuffed shoes. 'Maybe I should,' he said quietly.

'Whatever you do, man, have a good one,' Luke said, as he walked away. Ern watched him walk up to Steph and she stood up, linked her arm through his and they went on their way, smiling at each other. Ern stood up, picked up his coffee and went over to sit on the window ledge as he drank it. He thought about how he really shouldn't have to change. Kate knew him as he was and if he was going to dress it up into something else then what would be the point? He took another sip of the coffee, placed it by his side and took out his tobacco and papers. He watched the people strolling by as he rolled the tobacco, wondering why he was making life so difficult for himself. As he lit his cigarette, inhaled deeply and savoured the dull sensation it gave him, he got his answer. Kate was why he was making it so difficult. He knew without any doubt that she was worth it too.

Ern stubbed his cigarette out on the ground and picked up his hat, putting it lightly on his head and buttoning up his coat as he strolled towards the department store. When he walked in, he was surprised at the fusty, close air that seemed to be at odds with the sparkling newness of all the stock, which was laid out neatly on various counters and shelves. He saw the stairs over on the left, by which was a list of where each department was. Ern eventually found the Men's Clothing Department listed on the second floor. He thought it would save time to take the lift next to the stairs but when the door opened he saw that it was obviously the original lift from way back, with the iron gate that you pull back and carpet up the walls. Ern stepped in, pulled the gate closed and turned to see a tiny, old woman, sitting on a stool next to the buttons.

'Where would you like to go, young man?' she asked.

Ern was completely taken aback. He cleared his throat and said 'Second floor, please.' He watched her turn a key in the wall of the lift and then press 2. She looked at him and smiled, revealing a glittering pair of false teeth that looked completely out of place set into her deeply lined face. She was incredibly small and Ern could see she was wearing several layers of clothes. Her thin hair was styled in big, soft curls that were a curious apricot colour. He smiled back at her and asked, 'Do you sit here all day?'

'Every day for the past seven years,' she said in a broad Sussex accent. 'I've been working here since I was twelve years old but my legs can't really take all the standing around you have to do on the shop floor any more.'

'Have you ever thought about retiring?' Ern asked.

'No, ducks,' she replied. 'They'll have to wheel me out of here in a box.' At this, the woman let rip a frightening laugh that could have come straight out of the witches' scene in MacBeth. Ern smiled nervously at her, unsure whether he was supposed to laugh as well. The lift pinged and the lights above the gate showed they had reached the second floor. Ern pulled back the gate and stepped out. 'Thank you,' he said to the woman. 'Should I close this gate again?'

'Yes ta,' she said. 'It won't be long before someone else calls me and they're the divvil to get shut when you've got arthritis, like this old bird has.' She waved both her hands with a royal wave and cackled another cheery laugh. Ern smiled broadly at her.

'Okey dokey. Have a good day,' he said.

'Ta, ducks. And you.' the old woman said as she gave him a final wave goodbye.

Ern pulled the gate over and walked away shaking his head. No matter how bizarre his own life would get, he couldn't imagine sitting in a lift for the rest of his life.

He turned his head slowly and looked around at the signs hanging down from the ceiling. Each one seemed to mention some designer or other, with a few SALE notices dotted here and there. Ern absolutely detested shopping for clothes. He had often thought that there should just be a bag ready at the checkout, for men like him, that contained one pair of jeans, one t-shirt, one pair of underpants and some socks. Men don't care if something's a little too big and they don't particularly care who made it, just as long as they have the basics. There could just be three kinds of bags, colour coded in black, brown and blue. Ern reckoned that would keep the majority of the male population satisfied. He walked to the left where he could see a massive wall sectioned up for jeans of every size and colour. The assistants were watching him warily. As Ern walked past, he was sure that he had overheard one of them suggest they get security to throw 'the old bum' out. He picked up a pair of blue Levi's and put them up against himself to see if the size was okay. He knew that he'd lost a lot of weight over the past few weeks but reasoned that he could always slip one of his belts on if needs be. Then, Ern wandered over to some rails on the other side of the aisle and chose a new navy blue jumper with a cowl neck, as well as a white t-shirt to go underneath.

He walked up to one of the assistants and asked 'I wondered if you had a shoe department in here?'

The girl's face contorted into a sneer. Ern looked at her. She couldn't have been older than nineteen; her face was plastered in make-up and her hair was styled with so much hairspray that it looked rock-solid. Ern imagined any boyfriend could lose a couple of digits if he tried to run his fingers through her hair. The girl opened her pink glossed lips, lifted a single, perfectly plucked eyebrow and contorted her voice into some bizarre impression of Lady of the Manor whilst saying,

'Sir, you do know that those will have to be paid for?'

The second assistant sniggered behind her and the girl threw her a smile of victory.

'Actually I was rather hoping to steal them,' Ern said finding it hard to conceal his irritation. The girl's mouth dropped open with shock and before he knew it, a security guard was at his shoulder, frogmarching him down the escalators and pushing him out into the street, causing him to stumble and fall.

Ern heard the security guard shout 'We don't want to see you in here again, alright?' Ern lifted himself up, dusted down his coat and turned in order to give the guard the two fingered salute. After a moment's pause, he thought better of it and instead flourished into an extravagant, low bow, pretending to applaud the guard as he stood up again.

He heard a chuckle behind him. Turning swiftly, he saw Kate standing there.

'Have you been causing trouble, Ern?' she said with a broad grin.

Ern was angry and embarrassed that Kate had witnessed him being humiliated. There he was trying to improve his appearance for her and all he'd achieved was make himself look like even more of a bum. He looked at Kate still smiling at him. She was not judging him at all. He spread his arms wide and said, 'People just do not realise when they have a genius in their midst.' To ensure that she was aware of him exaggerating his arrogance, he winked at her and bowed again.

She laughed loudly, took his arm and kissed him lightly on the cheek. 'I'm starving. Are we still on for lunch?'

'Why of course, madam,' I had hoped to dress for dinner but unfortunately the arseholes in there…' he turned his head and shouted loudly over his shoulder '… do not know the relationship between natural style and natural indifference.'

Kate giggled as she said 'Ssh!' and they strolled back to his drawings in silence. The sunshine had filled his side of the walkway and the colours rebounded in the light. Kate knelt down to look at his new picture closely.

'I love it,' she said.

Ern walked to the window ledge and picked up a brown paper carrier bag. There was a note attached to it, which he read, before peeling the sticky tape off and popping it in his pocket.

He held out the crook of his arm and said 'Shall we?' Kate looked at the picture again and back at Ern. Ern wondered what on earth she was thinking as she just stared intently at him. He raised one eyebrow as if to reiterate his question.

Kate stood up and said 'Yep. We shall.'

As they walked, Ern felt like something was missing. He realised that it was so much quieter without the clarinet playing in the background. As they reached the end of the walkway, Ern started to hum La Mer.

'I can name that tune in one!' Kate said, before humming along with him as they walked in step with each other.

CHAPTER SEVENTEEN

As Kate and Ern approached the promenade, it became obvious that they were not going to enjoy the solitude of their last date. Old age pensioners were sauntering along; the ladies in their colourful Mac's and the men wearing caps of varying colours of brown and grey. Although it was cold in the town, the glare of the sun radiated off the sea, warming the people who were on the prom or further down on the beach. Kate whispered to Ern, 'It's special prices at the fish and chip shop on Wednesday's. They all come out for cod and chips when it's cheap.'

'Cheap as chips?' said Ern with a grin. Kate groaned and punched his arm.

'Shall we have chips today?' she asked.

'If you like, although I did have something a little healthier in mind,' Ern said.

Kate smiled at him and said 'Are you going to produce a four course banquet out of your pockets?'

'Ha! Not today. I've just got some nice bread rolls and some brie in this bag,' he said, holding up the bag and shaking it.

'Oh, yum! Perfect,' Kate said.

They joined the prom and walked past dozens of people dozing in deckchairs or gossiping on the benches. Some had brought their own folding chairs and were just sitting quietly next to each other, gazing out to sea. There were quite a few cars parked and many of them had their passenger doors open with elderly couples sitting inside, eating cheese and pickle sandwiches, drinking steaming tea from a flask.

'At least you'll always feel young living here, Kate,' Ern said, with a chuckle. 'You are a mere child by comparison to all these people.'

'It's only like this in the daytime really. Have you been out into the town at night?' she asked, suddenly realising that she couldn't imagine what he did in the evenings.

'No. Nightlife and me don't really mix,' he said.

'Well it's a whole different place at night. Sometimes people catch the train into the city but there's enough here to keep any age happy.' After a pause she continued, 'I like seeing the old folk strolling along anyway. It's nice to see some of them holding hands and enjoying each other's company. It makes me believe that there is such a thing as true love.'

'Do you really believe all these people still love each other?' Ern asked her.

Kate looked at him and reckoned he was gently teasing her as a smile played on his lips. 'Yes, I do. And I believe in the tooth fairy and leprechauns and Father Christmas and not one damned person is going to make me think otherwise. Okay?' She squeezed his arm hard as she spoke.

Ern laughed. 'Okay, point taken,' he said.

They walked along in silence. Kate's mind kept flicking back to her new office and she wondered whether she should tell Ern all about it. It was quite possible that he would dismiss it all as bourgeois nonsense and she didn't want anything to spoil how good she felt about it. She was so deep in thought, that she didn't notice Ern was getting visibly uncomfortable; tensing his shoulders and frowning. When she turned to look at him, she was quite shocked at how unhappy he suddenly looked.

'What's the matter?' she said, stopping and tugging him around to face her.

'Shall we walk along a little faster and see if we can find a quieter beach?' he asked quietly.

'Why? Not a crowd person, huh?' Kate replied, hooking her arm back through his. She wasn't appreciating just how upset Ern had become.

He unhooked his arm from hers and this time it was him who turned her around. He held his arms out to his side and looked down at himself, then back to Kate. His face was a mix of frustration and sadness as he said 'Kate… Look at us!'

'What?' said Kate, totally bemused, trying not to smile at the sudden change in Ern's mood. She was too happy to let his grumpiness bring her down.

'We must look ridiculous! Haven't you seen the way people have been looking at us? Haven't you noticed them muttering? We must look like…' Ern struggled for the right things to say, whilst Kate just stood there, not really taking his concern with any seriousness. '… Like bloody Lady and the Tramp!'

Kate burst out laughing. 'Well, that's fine by me! Lady was a cutey with those long eyelashes and droopy ears.'

Ern didn't know what to say. He looked at Kate's happy face and how she genuinely didn't seem to give a damn what other people thought and allowed himself to laugh with her. 'Yeah well, the tramp was no stud.'

'Oh, I don't know about that,' Kate said, hooking her arm back through his yet again. 'Now, let's go and find that beach. Okay?'

'Okay. Sounds good.' Ern said, pushing his hands into his pockets to make the loop of their arms close, as they began to walk again.

'Oh, for goodness sake, Ern,' Kate continued. 'Who cares what people think? You might be able to fool them, but look at your hands for instance…' Kate pulled his hand out of his pocket and held it in front of her face '… beautifully kept fingernails, soft skin, no calluses. Your clothes might be tatty but they can't make you someone you're not.'

Ern smiled at her and began to relax, as Kate wittered on, 'For all I know you are a secret millionaire running away from your riches to find yourself or something, like some hippy movie where everyone dies at the end.'

Ern chuckled and said, 'I can assure you I am not a millionaire and I am most certainly not a hippy.'

'Phew!' said Kate happily. 'That's alright then. The hippy part, I mean. It would have been a wonderful fairy story if you were a millionaire. Mind you, not many of them seem to be very happy either. Now I come to think about it, it's probably better to be a hippy than a millionaire.'

Ern smiled and looked at her. He wanted to stop and kiss her but he couldn't shake the feeling of being so conspicuous, despite Kate trying to laugh it off.

'And you schmooze so well' Kate exaggerated each word with a sing-song tone, enjoying her opportunity to be cheeky. 'Look how much intelligence you show when you speak and when you draw.'

'Ah, you are just easily fooled,' Ern chuckled. 'I am nothing more than a heathen to all sections of polite society.'

'You've been very polite to me,' Kate said, her voice quietening.

'Yes. I have. But you are very special,' he replied, looking at the beach. They had walked quite a long way and there was finally no-one else around. Ern stopped and gently tugged at Kate's arm.

'Shall we eat here?' he said 'It looks quiet and peaceful.'

'Perfect,' said Kate.

They started to pick their way over the pebbles. Kate stumbled slightly and Ern grabbed her arm to stop her from falling over. Ern kept hold of Kate's hand as they walked down closer to the shoreline. He stroked the back of her hand with his thumb as they walked. They stopped before they reached the line where the beach was still drying out from the morning tide and Ern took off his coat, laying it down and motioning to Kate to sit.

'You haven't got any pastels in those pockets, have you? Or Tulips? Or Rabbits? I wouldn't want to crush anything more of yours,' she said with a wink.

'No, my pockets are bare,' Ern said, sitting down and opening the bag that contained their lunch, before saying with surprise, 'Unlike this bag which is full of wonderful things!'

'Who did you do a deal with today?' Kate asked as he produced the Brie, a wonderfully rustic looking round of bread and a fresh apricot.

'The nice woman who owns the bakery. She was jealous of the fishmonger's drawing, so I drew some cream cakes and currant buns on her own notice board.' Ern chuckled as he said it.

'You have your own currency going on there, Ern,' Kate said, genuinely impressed.

'It's never happened before. It has been wonderful to meet such kind people,' Ern said.

'I think you're giving them as much as they're giving you. It's the perfect transaction, VAT not included.'

'True, true,' Ern said with a smile. He took out a small knife which had been wrapped up in a wad of paper napkins, which he spread out to cut the brie. He ripped off some bread and placed the brie on top before slicing some apricot and tucking it under the cheese. 'Try this,' he said, passing one piece to Kate.

She took a bite and closed her eyes, savouring the tastes. Ern watched her until he was sure that she was enjoying it, before picking up his own and taking a large bite.

'Oh Ern, this is gorgeous,' Kate mumbled with her mouth half-full.

'It is, isn't it?' Ern replied. He put his lunch back down on the serviettes and looked into the bag, from which he pulled out two bottles of iced tea. 'You like this too?' he asked, holding it up for Kate to see. 'We have bottled water but this is such a quintessentially English thing to have with a picnic, don't you think?' Kate laughed and said, 'Oh yes, and I do like to be quintessential sometimes.'

Ern twisted the top off one bottle and passed it to her. The dry, woody flavour of the drink was perfect with their lunch and they both sat munching in contented silence. Once Kate had finished she lay down on her back and crossed her feet. Ern cleared some of the bits and pieces away, before lying down next to her and closing his eyes against the sunlight. Kate edged her hand across until she found Ern's hand, curling her fingers between his.

'Ern?' she said.

'Yep?'

'I still want to know more about you. I know I shouldn't be so nosey. I just really want to know more about you.'

'I understand,' Ern said quietly. 'That is why we are here today. I promise you, I shall answer any question you have, as long as you allow me to do the same.'

'It's a deal,' said Kate.

'Ten questions for you and then ten questions for me... how does that sound?' said Ern.

Kate swallowed hard before replying 'Ten? Is that all? I'd better make sure they're good ones.'

Ern forced himself to relax. It looked like this was going to be crunch time for him. He tried not to think about the possibility that she would walk away from him today and never want to speak to him again. If that was the way it was going to be, then he just had to accept it.

'Do I really only get ten?' said Kate.

'Fraid so,' Ern replied.

Kate exaggerated a deep sigh and then said, 'okay. I'm ready.'

99

Ern pushed away the doubts in his mind and forced himself to smile. 'Uh oh,' he said, trying to keep his voice light. He took a deep breath and then he said, 'okay. Fire away.'

Kate rolled onto her side and propped her head up on one arm.

'Question number one,' said Kate, joking in a stern Anne Robinson voice.

'Y-es,' said Ern, wondering why she was now sounding so casual about the whole thing.

Kate screwed up her face and said, 'Have you got any chocolate cake in that bag? I really think we need dessert.'

'You're really going to make that one of your questions?' Ern said, sitting up and chuckling.

'No! I haven't started yet. Even if it was, chocolate is important!' Kate replied with a serious face. 'I thought it might help me think of good questions. You have to get your priorities right.'

Ern reached into the bag and took out a white card box. He lifted up the lid and tutted loudly, while shaking his head. A grin played on his lips. 'No, I'm sorry there is no chocolate in here.' He turned the box around and Kate saw that inside there were two heart-shaped strawberry tarts. She laughed and said 'Ern that is SO cheesy!'

'Well you did say I was good at schmoozing,' he said. 'I have a reputation to live up to.'

Kate took one of the tarts and picked off the strawberries, before taking the pastry out and biting into the golden yellow custard tart underneath. 'This is delicious,' she said when she'd finished chewing.

Ern closed the lid on the box and said 'I think I'll save mine for later. C'mon,' he said. 'Ask me those questions. I promise that I won't evade the answers.'

'Maybe I don't really want any answers,' Kate said quietly, folding the foil case in half, then half again and tossing it into the paper bag in front of them.

'That's kind of irrelevant now, Kate. You need to ask them and I need to answer don't you think?' Ern said, looking at her intently.

'Okay,' said Kate. 'Can we lie down again? I don't know why but it just feels right somehow.'

Ern took hold of her hand and they lay down next to each other. He put one arm under his neck to prop his head up and closed his eyes.

'C'mon Kate. You wanted to know,' he said. 'Fire away.'

CHAPTER EIGHTEEN

'Is Ern Malley your real name?' Kate asked.

'Yes, it is,' Ern replied. 'Unfortunately. When you're born in a small town in Ireland, like I was, you are named after the last aunt or uncle that's just died. Uncle Ernie died four weeks before I was born.'

'You're lucky it wasn't an Aunty Mavis, I suppose,' Kate said with a grin.

Ern chuckled. 'Yes, I suppose I was.'

Kate squeezed his hand slightly. She didn't really want to ask all those questions anymore. She just wanted to lie there and feel as though they knew everything there was to know about each other. She didn't want anything to spoil it. Ern squeezed her hand in return and gently said, 'C'mon. Next question.'

Kate sighed and said, 'How old are you?'

'Thirty-seven.'

'Ha!' she said.

'Ha what?,' Ern asked.

'Just Ha! I was right because I had you down for nearly forty,' Kate replied.

'I am not nearly forty,' Ern said emphatically. 'I have three years until I'm forty! I prefer to think of it as being just over thirty-five.'

'Whichever way you want to dress it up,' Kate said with a giggle.

'I don't mind growing old,' Ern said. 'I think grey hair will suit me.'

'I'm sorry to burst your bubble but you've already got one,' Kate said.

Ern sat up quickly and looked down at her, 'Where?'

Kate pushed herself up, pinched her fingers around the hair which was sticking up to the left of his forehead and quickly plucked it out. 'There!' she said, showing it to him.

'Holey Mackeroney!' Ern said with no amusement in his voice whatsoever. 'That's not funny.'

'Oh, I don't know about that,' said Kate, lying down again with a grin on her face.

'Okay, so I am nearly 40,' Ern conceded as he lay down beside her. He grabbed for her hand again and said, 'Next question.'

'Did you really have a cat?'

'That's another wasteful question,' Ern laughed.

'No, it's not. It tells me a lot.'

'Okay, okay. If you insist then yes, I really had a cat and its name really was Tigger.' Kate smiled. She had long held the theory that if you lived with a cat then there was no way you could be cold-hearted. Cats expect attention only on their own terms, so to keep a cat around you have to love completely selflessly. She had come to the conclusion that often it was the owner who needed the cat more than the other way around.

Kate took in a deep breath of the sea air. She liked how comfortable they were with each other today. All the angst and worry that Ern had shown last time they talked seemed to have disappeared.

'You were born in Ireland. Do you still call that home?'

There was silence for a second or two before he quietly answered 'I have a home in Glenagearie, Ireland.'

Kate was surprised. She hadn't expected him to say he had a home. 'Then why are you here?'

'To draw... relax...' Ern said, before adding 'to breathe.'

Kate sat up and studied his face. He still seemed relaxed but that answer had thrown a thousand more panicked questions into Kate's head.

'Does anyone live in your home with you?' she asked quickly. She could hear her pulse banging against her skull. She desperately wanted him to say 'no' and that he lived alone, but Ern just lay there with no discernable expression that would give Kate a hint to his reply. She wanted to nudge him, either verbally or physically to make him answer quickly. She suddenly went cold when she realised that she would not know how to react to him if he suddenly told her he had a wife or a girlfriend waiting for him back home. She kicked herself for being so

102

stupid to not have even considered it before.

Finally Ern answered. 'No. No-one lives with me anymore.' His words came out cold and emotionless. Kate took a moment to let the information sink in.

'Is that why you're here?' she asked. 'You left home and decided to drift around because you lost someone close to you?'

'Not because I lost them, no. That all happened many years ago and I've only been on the road for three months. It's more because I didn't know who I was anymore.' Ern sat up and gazed out to sea. The sun was already starting to go down and the moon was faintly staking its claim over in the East. The sea seemed even calmer than before, with barely a sound as it gently lapped into the pebbles. Even the seagulls seemed to have settled down, with only the odd lazy call to each other.

Kate didn't like the silence between them but she didn't want to push Ern into revealing more than he wanted to. She wanted him to feel like he could tell her anything. When he eventually spoke, he sounded as though he was annoyed with himself. 'I know it sounds ridiculous but I just didn't feel like I was anywhere at all. It was like I'd ceased to exist in my own head.'

Kate knew that the next questions should be about who he lost, why he lost them, how he lost them, but only one question came into her mind that she genuinely wanted an answer to.

'And how about now, Ern?' He turned his head and looked into her eyes. She asked again, 'How do you feel now?'

'Happy,' he said, nodding and looking down at their joined hands. 'I just feel happy, that's all.'

Kate leant forward and kissed him. For the first time, he put his arms around her as they kissed and she slid her hands under his coat, wrapping them around his back. They held each other for a short while before Kate spoke again in a sleepy voice.

'How many questions have I had?'

'Seven,' Ern said quick as a flash.

Kate pulled away and looked at him suspiciously. 'Are you sure?' she said. 'I'm sure I haven't asked that many.'

'I'm sure,' Ern said with a smile.

'Dammit,' Kate said, hugging her knees close to her and laying her chin on them as she thought of the next question.

She didn't want to spoil the light mood with any more heavy questions. About a year ago she had a girly, drunken evening in with

Beth, where they were both drowning their sorrows over flash-in-the-pan relationships that had gone belly up the week before. They'd made up a tick list for all future boyfriends and Kate rattled her brain to see if she could remember any of the points they had decided on. She decided that the number one question would not be appropriate as it was 'do you have any sexual diseases?' Kate smirked at the memory of her and Beth rolling on the floor, giggling until their stomachs hurt, as they discussed whether you should ask that on a first, second or third date. Beth had made it a *Law of Beth and Kate World* that it was vital it was to be asked within the first five minutes of meeting someone. She decided on question two instead.

'Do you prefer Ketchup or HP Sauce?'

Ern looked at her with a 'you-cannot-be-serious' look before straightening his face and answering,

'They both have distinctive qualities but if I was looking for a catch-all condiment, I would have to choose Salad Cream'

'Oh, good answer!' said Kate, pleased that he'd entered into the spirit of it. 'Do you have any GCSEs?'

'I have eleven GCSEs, four A levels and a degree in architecture,' he said smugly.

'Bloody hell,' said Kate. 'Eleven GCSEs? Are you sure?'

'Quite sure, thank you very much,' he said.

'Architecture?' Kate said, suddenly catching on to what he'd said. 'You're really an architect?'

'No,' said Ern. His face had become serious again. 'I'm really an artist. Always have been.'

Kate nodded and thought about what he'd just said. There was obviously a hell of a lot more to learn about Ern but if she were honest, she really didn't care about anything other than the way he made her feel when he kissed her, or when they held hands… or when he looked at her.

'Okay then,' she said quietly. 'I just have one more question.'

'You're not allowed any more questions,' Ern said jokingly.

'What? Why not?'

'You've had ten.'

'Nine! I've had nine!' Kate said emphatically.

'No. You said 'Architecture?' and that counts as a question.'

'Oh, it so does not,' Kate said, putting her hands on her hips.

'Rules are rules,' Ern said with a chuckle, lying down on the pebbles.

'Oh well.' Kate said with an exaggerated huff and laid back down next to him. 'Your loss.'

Ern rolled over onto his side, brushed Kate's cheek with his hand, before gently moving her face towards his and kissing her again. He rolled over onto his back and hugged her close so that her head was resting on his chest. She could feel the vibration of his voice as he spoke. 'How is it my loss?' he said.

'Well, you'll never know will you, 'cause you won't let me ask my last question,' Kate said.

'Was it a big question?'

'Medium sized perhaps,' she replied with a smile.

'Oh,' said Ern. 'Never mind.'

Kate knew he was teasing her but she didn't want to lose this one. 'Yes, never mind that you won't get to hear my best question and that you won't get to gain the benefit.'

Ern looked down at her. 'I get benefit?'

'Yep,' she said.

Ern whispered, 'Go on then. You can have just one more.'

Kate closed her eyes tight and let the words come out in a rush. 'I don't know how long it's been since you've had a home cooked meal or anything and I shouldn't really be asking you because my house is in a terrible mess but…' Kate paused when she felt him hold his breath for a moment. His chest softly started rising again and she quietly said, 'Would you like me to cook you dinner tonight, at my house?' She desperately didn't want him to assume that she was planning to seduce him. Just dinner. For now. 'I do a mean Spag Bog…' she said, '…and I think I have a bottle of salad cream somewhere.'

Ern didn't answer. Kate lay very still, willing him to say yes. He moved his hand up to touch Kate's hair, finding a curl and twisting it loosely around his finger. Finally he said, 'Spag Bog, huh?'

'It's either that or cheese on toast,' Kate replied. She felt Ern's chest rock up and down as he chuckled.

After a few more moments of thought, he gave her his answer, 'I would like that very much, Kate. Thank you.'

CHAPTER NINETEEN

Kate burst into the coffee shop flushed with excitement and a huge smile on her face. Tony had put one of his Blues cds on the stereo and there was a cosy, warm feeling as couples huddled together, deep in conversation.

'Hiya, Tony!' Kate said to his back.

He turned around and she was shocked by how tired he looked.

'Well, hello there. How are you today, little lady?'

'I'm good thanks… but a cappuccino will make everything better,' she grinned at him. 'You look knackered, Tony. Are you okay?'

'I'm fine, Kate. I suppose I'm just finding these longer opening hours a little tiring but I've got to compete with that new Italian chain that's opened up over by the Prom and they stay open till eight every night.'

'Oh, you've got me as a customer for life, Tony,' Kate said. 'It's been really busy in here though. You don't need to worry, surely?'

'Business is good, don't get me wrong. I was thinking I might get someone in to work part-time to help me out.' He spooned the milk froth onto her coffee and placed it on the bar.

'I think that would be a good idea. I have been working really hard on that picture for you Tony. I really hope you're going to like it. You're under no obligation whatsoever and I totally understand if you don't want it but…'

Tony held up his hand to stop her jabbering and said, 'Kate, I would love to see it, really. I love those doodles you leave lying about.' He pointed over to the notice-board and Kate saw that he'd pinned up a few of the pages that she'd ripped out of her sketch pads. 'Oh my goodness, Tony. I didn't mean for you to keep those. I'm flattered. How come I've never seen that before?'

'Because you walk around in your own world, Kate,' Tony laughed and held out his hand for the money.

Kate dropped a note into his hand and looked at the notice-board more closely as he got her change. There were other doodles besides her own and there were also poems written on serviettes, some children's drawings and even a caricature of Tony, which was a really good likeness with Tony's trademark grin. Kate was thrilled to see so much talent lying undiscovered in her town. 'You see Tony?' Kate said. 'That Italian place doesn't stand a chance. People love coming here.'

'I hope so, Kate. I really do. I'll put a notice up in the window for an assistant and so that I might give myself time to put my feet up now and again.'

'You do that. See you later, Tony.' Kate walked over to the bookshelves and sat down in a chair by the window. The sun's rays were intensified through the glass and Kate decided to just sit quietly rather than read.

Ern had gone back to his pitch and they had arranged that she'd meet him in a few hours. Kate had to make a decision whether to go to the supermarket for the stuff they needed for the meal or to go home and clear up the house a little. As far as she could remember, her lounge wasn't too messy, so if she could just keep Ern in there for a while when they got home, she could whizz around and do a quick tuck-n-hide job on the rest of the house. It also meant that she could sit for a while and gather her thoughts. It had been a hell of an emotional day.

Kate looked at the two women sitting at the next table. They looked so close that it gave her a sudden urge to speak to Beth or Jamie. She wanted to tell someone but knew that Beth would be overly enthusiastic and Jamie would be the completely opposite. Both reactions would force Kate to be defensive about it all and she didn't want that right now. She just wanted to wallow in this lovely feeling for a while. She closed her eyes and took a sip from her coffee. She could hear the girls on the next table talking.

'... I'm so lost. I feel as though everything's just stopped and I have to kneel down on the floor, rocking, waiting for it to start again.'

Kate half-opened one eye so that she could just see them as they chatted. The one who was talking looked huddled up and thoroughly miserable. She had no make-up on and was wearing clothes that Kate could relate to as 'comfort clothes'. It looked as though she'd been crying. Her friend looked calm and relaxed, leaning back into her chair with her long legs stretched and crossed in front of her. She was extremely glamorous and was wearing a bright yellow coat, as well as a purple beret. She was sipping on an espresso, whilst her Plain Jane friend had a hefty mug of cappuccino.

Purple beret woman spoke up. 'You can't. He may not love you anymore but so many good people still love you to pieces.' They were sharing a blueberry muffin and took turns in breaking off small bits of the sponge as they talked.

'I know,' says Plain Jane, stabbing her fingernail into the sponge and digging out a blueberry, which she pushed onto the rim of the plate. 'Tell me how to stop it hurting?' she said quietly.

Purple beret picked up her coffee and shook her head. Her voice was kind but firm. 'I can't. It won't stop hurting until you have worked through it... until you realise that it was the only thing that could have ever happened... or at least until the memory fades.'

'But I've been going on like that for weeks. I can't keep trying. I can't.' She paused before continuing, 'I'm sorry. I know I'm being pathetic.'

'No, you're not. I know how you feel... I really do.' Purple beret leaned forward and softly touched her friend's arm. She sat back again and looked into her cup. 'Well, there is one thing you can do but...'

'What?' said Plain Jane, leaning forward attentively.

Purple beret put down her coffee and sat up straight. 'I was feeling just as bad as you after Mark. You remember?'

'I just remember you telling me you were ok.'

'Well, I wasn't darlin'. I was completely devastated. I felt like I wanted to die.'

Plain Jane looked shocked. 'Why didn't you tell me?'

'Because I couldn't. I was too ashamed because I knew he was a complete arse and that I should never have loved him.'

'I'm so sorry. So, so sorry. You should have talked to me.' Purple Beret shook her head. Plain Jane spoke again, 'So what did you do? What can I do?'

Purple beret leaned forward and wiped fresh tears from her friend's eyes.

'You have to realise that I would only tell you this in an absolute emergency. You have to promise me that you will believe me.'

'Ok-ay,' said her friend slowly, her eyebrows arched with suspicion and the beginnings of a smile curling her lips.

'When did you last shave your bikini line?'

Her friend snorted loudly before sighing and flopping back into her chair.

'Why?' she said loudly, causing a few people to turn and look at her. Purple beret had a very serious look on her face.

'When did you last shave your bikini line?' she repeated firmly. She had a wicked smile on her face.

Plain Jane screwed up her face as she tried to remember. 'Ummm, about three weeks ago, I think.'

'Ok, so you have the perfect timing. Tomorrow, go down to that beauty salon by the arcade and get a Brazilian.' After a moment, her friend's shocked face exploded into laughter. Other customers turned to stare and Kate stifled a giggle as she watched the girl try to regain some composure. Finally Plain Jane had her giggles under control and said,

'That's your solution? How on earth is a Brazilian wax going to help me get over a broken heart?'

Purple Beret sat forward and said firmly, 'Because I swear to you, it works. You walk to that salon and you know you're doing something for yourself. If you like you can put some pop psychology on it like you're ripping him out of your life. Put your sexiest, skimpiest underwear on and let them put you through twenty minutes of hell.' She rested back in her chair again and said, 'I have no idea how it works but while you're in pain, you don't give him a second thought and afterwards you just feel so stupid, brave and wonderful that you walk home with a smile on your face.'

Her friend laughed and said 'Even though you're walking home like you've been riding a horse for a week?'

'Yep,' Purple Beret replied with a grin.

The two ladies smiled at each other and each took a sip of their coffee. Plain Jane put her mug down and moved out of her seat to give her friend a hug, saying 'Thank you for being my friend.'

Purple Beret hugged her back and as they stood up, she gave her a wink and a click, click with her mouth, saying 'That's ok, grasshopper. C'mon, we've got some serious shopping to do.'

Kate watched them leave and walk out of view. She opened her handbag and pulled out her mobile phone, which was flashing two missed call. They had both been from Jamie. She looked at the screen for a moment before smiling and hitting the call-back button.

'Hiya Jamie,' she said when he answered. She kept her voice dipped so as not to be overheard.

'Finally! Where the hell have you been?' he said jokingly. 'I've missed you stalking me on my phone every five minutes.'

'I've been busy. I went to look at my new office today and oh! It's wonderful! I've got a full sea-view and a red chair and it's just gorgeous!' Kate leant back in her chair and put her feet on the one opposite, before remembering Tony scolding her once for doing that and putting them back down on the floor again.

'Excellent,' Jamie said, sounding genuinely pleased. 'What about your new office mates? Are there any hunky, single millionaires waiting to be swept off their feet?'

'I didn't get a chance to look properly but I shall keep the radar up,' Kate replied.

'Good girl,' Jamie said. Kate knew he was smiling and happy by the tone of his voice. She wanted to tell him about Ern. She really wanted to tell him about Ern.

'When do you start the new job?' he asked.

'I start Monday. I've bought myself some new no-bullshit boots to show them I'm serious.'

'Sheesh, any excuse,' Jamie said with a chuckle. 'Are we still on for tonight? The band are supposed to be really good and I was hoping you wouldn't mind if I brought along this girl I've met.'

Kate groaned inside as she realised she had completely forgotten that she was supposed to meet up with him that evening, to see a band in their local. Jamie took her lack of response as a sign of disapproval and said, 'You'll like her, Kate. She's a good laugh and knows all about you and me being best mates.'

Kate didn't mind at all that he was taking someone. She was used to a string of pretty things following Jamie around and she often let the girls cry on her shoulder when Jamie tried to let them down gently with a 'perhaps we would be better as friends' line.

'Jamie, I've sort of got something going on at the moment. Do you mind if I rain-check?' she said, crossing her fingers that he wouldn't blast her with a thousand questions.

'What do you mean you've got something going on?' Jamie said, clearly irritated. 'Kate if you'd rather I didn't bring her then...'

Kate interrupted him quickly, 'No, it's not that, Jamie. I've...uhm...' Kate squeezed her eyes shut and crossed her fingers as some kind of defence against any white lies she was about to tell. 'I've sort of met someone.'

'Heeey... don't say you've gone and got yourself a date?' Jamie said. 'That is fantastic! Who, what, where and does he have a sister?'

'It's complicated,' Kate bit her lip as she said the words. Half of her wanted to tell Jamie everything and the other half of her knew that she would be blasted for being an idiot.

'Ok-ay,' Jamie said warily. 'Complicated can be good sometimes. He's not married is he?'

'No, he's not married' said Kate with almost certainty. 'I just think I like him too much.'

She heard Jamie whoop at the other end of the line before he said, 'That sounds perfect. Truly Kate, it does. It's about time someone shook you out of your spinsterhood and showered you with attention.'

'Jamie?' she was going to spill...

'Yep?' he sounded so happy for her.

Kate stopped herself. 'Nothing,' she said. 'It's alright. I've gotta go. You'll call me tomorrow though, right? Maybe we could meet up for a coffee or something?'

'I'll come around to yours,' he said. 'I'll see you there about lunchtime. Who knows maybe your luck will rub off on me and I'll score tonight too.'

'JAMIE! You're already going with one girl!' Kate said with a giggle.

'Yeah but you never know what's just around the corner, eh Kate?'

Kate nodded slowly and smiled at the truth in his words. 'No, you never know what's around the corner,' she repeated. 'See you tomorrow, Jamie. Love you.'

'Love you too, babes. Have an amazing time,' he said.

'I think I will. You too,' Kate replied and pushed the end of call button.

She looked out of the window and at Ern, who was chatting to a young couple as they looked at his work. She quietly repeated Jamie's words to herself again with a smile, 'You never know what's just around the corner, Kate.'

CHAPTER TWENTY

Ern saw Kate watching him through the window of the café and waved at her. He picked up his hat and tipped out the coins that were inside. Kate was able to see that he had a few notes in there too, which he pushed into his back pocket. He put his hat on his head and walked over to the coffee shop.

As the door opened, Kate felt a flurry of nerves and excitement in her belly. Ern smiled at her before walking over to Tony.

'Hey Ern, how's it going?' Tony said to him.

'It's going good thanks,' he replied. 'How has your day been?'

'Put it this way,' Tony slumped his shoulders as he spoke. 'I'll be looking forward to hitting the sack tonight.'

Kate's ears went on full alert as she panicked about Ern saying something crass and blokey about how he was going to be hitting more than a sack but Ern just nodded and changed the subject.

'I wondered if you'd like me to start on that picture for you in here. It would be my gift to you as way of thanks for the coffees and friendship you have shown me.'

Tony pointed over to Kate and said 'Well, that's the second good offer I've had today on that score.' Kate blushed and looked down at her coffee. Tony smiled and said to Ern, 'I would love that. Thank you, Ern. You want a coffee?'

Ern looked over to Kate and raised his eyebrows as a 'shall we?' Kate nodded.

'Yes. Two cappuccinos would be wonderful, thank you.'

'I'll bring them over to you,' Tony said, smiling directly at Kate.

Ern sat down on the chair opposite Kate and looked out of the window as he spoke. 'You still want to cook me dinner?'

'That's the plan,' she said. 'I picked up a bottle of wine too.' Ern nodded slowly but said nothing. Kate wondered if he was having second thoughts. 'It might disguise the taste of my Bolognese if nothing else,' she joked, trying to get a reaction from him.

Ern smiled at her but she felt as though she'd said something wrong. The silence was broken by Tony bringing their coffees over.

'Do you want any pastries or muffins?' Tony asked.

Ern answered him. 'No, thanks Tony. This beautiful lady has offered to cook for me tonight.' As he looked back towards Kate he smiled warmly and she felt herself relax. She didn't notice the concern suddenly flash over Tony's face. Tony spoke quietly, 'Well then. You two have a lovely evening.' He walked back to the bar and watched them as he loaded the washer with some mugs.

'So,' said Ern. 'You're painting a new picture?'

'Yep,' said Kate, embarrassed. 'It's not going to be a patch on yours of course but I've loved doing it.'

'It's a good feeling isn't it?' Ern said, tapping the side of his mug with his finger. 'Creating people, I mean and making them come alive.'

'I'm different to you, Ern. To me those people are already alive and I'm just capturing how I see them.'

'That is because you walk around in a different world to me. I prefer to keep my head down and let them all get on with it. Most of the time they're not worth a second thought,' Ern replied with a dismissive wave of his hand.

Kate laughed at his cynicism. 'Oh not everyone's like that,' she laughed.

He smiled and said 'I know. It's just easier to believe they are.'

'Oh, I don't think so. I think it's much better to believe everyone is nice until they prove you wrong. When - or if - they prove you wrong then you have permission to kick yourself but there's not point walking around scared to bump into someone,' Kate said, slowly realising that she could just as easily have been talking about her first introduction to Ern.

'That's a nice way to be Kate,' he said quietly.

She decided to change the subject and pointed over to the bookshelves. 'Do you read?' she asked.

Ern looked over to them and said 'Oh, I used to. I used to read all the time, every moment I got but not so much now.' He leaned forward and smiled at her. 'Tell me what you like to read?'

Kate wondered whether she should try and impress with a list of classics but instead she just replied truthfully, 'I like everything. Really I do. If I'm sat in here for any length of time, I like to read poetry but to be honest, I'm just as happy with a Jackie Collins.'

Ern nodded as though he had already known the answer. 'I like some poetry too,' he said. 'It's all connected don't you think? Art, writing, music... they're all bound together by the same passion. No-one has ever quite managed to achieve all three at the same time though. It's like without one the other can't exist but if you crammed them all in to the same room, they would suffocate.'

'That's a strange way of putting it,' Kate said, intrigued. 'I've never thought of it like that before but yes, I suppose that's true.' She looked down at her bags and said 'Damn, we should get a move on or we're going to be getting botulism or something, from this beef mince sweating in the bag.'

Ern laughed and said, 'C'mon then.' He drained the last of the coffee from his mug and stood up, picking the shopping bags up from Kate's side. She waved at Tony and they walked into the crisp, misty air that was coming down with the early evening.

'Do we walk?' Ern asked.

'Oh, let's catch the bus,' Kate replied. 'Cat will be scratching my sofa to bits as penance for not getting her dinner down in time.' She looped her arm through Ern's and they walked out of the pedestrian street to stand at the bus stop.

It got dark quickly as they waited and when the bus finally turned into the street, they were relieved to see it all lit up like a haven from the harsh wind that had blown in with the evening. Kate got the tickets and held onto Ern's hand as they walked along the gangway to find a seat. As they sat down, Kate could tell that Ern felt uncomfortable being closed in with so many people. She thought that and the way he had talked in the coffee shop earlier was such a huge contradiction to how well he got on with people on a one-to-one basis. Tony obviously liked him and all the others who he'd done little pictures for. She squeezed his arm and they stayed quiet for the entire journey.

Kate pushed the bell for her stop and nudged Ern to let him know it was their stop. They fought their way past people standing in the gangway, before stepping out into the harsh cold air. Ern looked around to take in his surroundings. There was row upon row of beige brick houses, which were all identical apart from various flower baskets and window boxes that some had dressed theirs up with. Most of them were tiny terraced houses and Ern could see there was a large population of children in the area, as there were bikes and footballs discarded on several front lawns.

'Not quite suburbia,' Kate said, sounding apologetic. 'It was all I could afford after the divorce.'

Ern looked at her with surprise and asked, 'You were married?'

Kate nodded and said, 'Not for more than five minutes. I have been known to be impetuous.' She grinned and Ern smiled back at her. 'You don't say,' he said. They walked along to Kate's row and she led him down the path of number 21. Ern could see Cat on the other side of the glass door, waiting for Kate to open it.

As she slid the key into the door, she felt a flurry of nerves rumbling through her stomach. She told herself to push them away and just relax. As the door creaked open, she looked over to check there wasn't piles of underwear on the stairs ready to go up but it looked remarkably tidy in her hallway for once. Cat was sitting, blinking at them slowly, as they walked in.

Ern immediately went over and ran his finger over the mog's head. 'Cush cush,' he said quietly. Kate opened the lounge door, stuck her head around to look in, yelped and then quickly slammed the door shut again. She turned around with her back against the door and her hand still on the handle. She forced a bright smile and took a step towards Ern.

'Ern, could you just wait here for a moment?' she said, wringing her hands together. Ern took off his coat and put it over the banister. 'Of course,' he smiled. 'I'll sit here with my new best friend.' He sat down on the stairs and Cat jumped up onto his lap. Kate nodded her head and went into the lounge, slamming the door quickly behind her.

Kate stood for a moment, silently mouthing a scream as she ran her hands through her hair and tugged at it. Her front room was in a terrible mess with dirty coffee cups, dvd cases scattered everywhere and the odd socks lying discarded on the floor. She ran through the adjoining door to the kitchen and grabbed a carrier bag, before running back, getting down on her hands and knees and scooting all the cd and dvd cases under the sofa. She put everything else that was on the floor into the bag, which she hid quickly behind a pot plant in the corner. She leaned over the coffee table and clinked all the coffee cups together, picking them all up at once, walking carefully to the kitchen in order to dump them all in the sink. When she saw the sink was full, she opened the back door with her elbow and put them down on the doorstep. She shouted 'I won't be a minute, Ern' and ran back into the lounge, plumped up some cushions, closed the curtains, turned on a table lamp and then looked at her room again. With a satisfied grin, she congratulated herself on still being an expert at hiding her sloppiness. The only person who knew the truth about just how slovenly she could be was her mum, who had spent several years trying to teach Kate about 'everything having its place' without success.

Kate smoothed her hands over her hair and opened the door to the hallway. 'Come in, Ern,' she said. 'Make yourself at home.'

Ern got up from the stairs and walked into her living room, looking around and smiling. Kate had painted two of the walls bright pink and the other two were orange. She had seen it as a bit of a rebellion when she first moved in. This was her place and it was going to be as girly as she wanted. There were scarves draped over the back of the sofa and several Indian cushions were scattered over it. Some of Kate's pictures hung on the walls and Ern immediately saw that she had a distinctive style even though she used a variety of mediums with which to paint and draw. 'This is nice, Kate. Very you,' he said.

Kate was pre-occupied and quickly said 'Thank you. Now will you sit down and not move for a moment? I'll uhm…' She thought about how best to tackle the mess in the kitchen. '…put the kettle on,' she said, before running out of the room and closing the adjoining door behind her.

The kitchen wasn't as bad as she first thought and she piled all the dirty crockery into the washing up bowl. Once she'd cleared all the sideboards of wrappers and half-empty jars and tins, she heaved the bowl out of the sink and put that out in the garden too.

After taking three deep breaths, she filled the kettle and flicked it on, shouting 'Kettle's on!' She quickly ran up the stairs as Ern replied

117

'Okay.' She piled all the dirty washing that was draped over the banisters into the linen bin, although she had to sit on the lid to make sure it all fitted in. Then she pulled the cord on the bathroom light and sighed with relief when she saw it was pristine. It was one of those things that she could never explain but while the rest of the house went to rack and ruin, Kate took such pleasure in having all her porcelain in this room gleaming and screaming 'take a bath, shower in me, pamper yourself!' There was just one towel still on the floor from her shower this morning, which she scooped up, threw in the laundry bin, before pulling the light off again and running back down the stairs.

When she walked into the living room, with the two cups of tea, Ern was sitting on the sofa with Cat lying on his chest.

'She likes you,' Kate said.

'Ern sat up properly and begrudgingly Cat jumped down onto the floor. 'She's probably thinking I'll feed her,' he said with a smile.

Kate went to jump up again, 'Yes, I'll feed her…' but Ern grabbed hold of her arm and said 'Won't you sit for a moment? I need to tell you something.' Kate sat down again slowly. Ern put his mug of tea down on the table and turned to look at her. His face had changed dramatically, worry lines wrinkling his forehead and his eyes were heavy.

'I know you want the full story, Kate,' he said. 'I really think you deserve to know, but I really want to ask that you hear me out, okay?'

Kate nodded. She didn't like how sad he looked. She wasn't sure that she wanted to hear what he had to say. Panic thumped in her head and her skin prickled as she waited for him to talk.

'I was married. I had a daughter,' Ern said quietly.

Kate looked at him. His head was bowed and he was looking down at his hands. My daughter, Phoebe, died when she was only three years old. I was accused of her murder.'

Kate shifted in her seat. She felt her face redden with the confusion. The shock and disappointment she felt was so immense that she wanted to throw him out of the house there and then. There was a startled silence, neither of them moving a muscle.

Kate almost whispered when she spoke, 'Did you?' Ern didn't move or give any indication that he was going to answer. Kate asked again, 'Did you murder your daughter, Ern?'

Ern sat back and rested his head on the back of the sofa, looking up to the ceiling. She could see that he was fighting back tears. 'I don't think so,' he said quietly.

She looked at his face. He suddenly seemed vulnerable and desperately lost. Kate didn't know what to do.

She slowly stood up and without looking at him, said, 'You'd better tell me everything, then.' She spoke to him without any emotion in her face or in her voice. 'I'll start dinner and you can talk while I cook.'

CHAPTER TWENTY-ONE

Vicky let the young man open the door for her and then carefully positioned her Zimmer frame so that it would fit through the wooden doorway without scratching the varnish. She knew that it was a silly consideration but this place meant a lot to her and she would have done anything not to make a nuisance of herself.

'Are you okay from here?' the young man asked.

'Yes, thank you dear,' she said. 'Have I seen you in here before?'

'I've only been in town a short while. I've been playing my clarinet in the walkway to get some cash for my next trip down to Cornwall.'

'Ah yes,' she replied. 'I heard you playing yesterday. You're very good,' she said, tapping him on the chest.

He smiled, thanked her and then went over to give Steph, the barmaid, a kiss on the cheek.

Vicky followed him and said 'Steph! You have a new beau, I see.'

Steph just smiled and said, 'What can I get you Vicky?'

'Just the usual, please love.' she replied and saw with more than a little satisfaction that Steph went straight to her favourite tipple of Peach Schnapps. They were always so kind to her - never minding that she would sit with the same drink for hours.

'I'll bring it over to you,' Steph said as she filled the measure.

Vicky moved over to the corner, put her Zimmer frame in front of the fireplace and eased her aching body down onto the threadbare

121

cushions, which offered little comfort to her arthritis and her poorly hip.

She looked around at all the young things, laughing and joking with their friends and lovers. She let thoughts of years passed flash through her mind. She knew they probably all thought she should be sitting at home with her feet up, in front of the telly watching some soap opera, but Vicky had been coming to this bar for thirty years and it was all she could think to do each evening.

She had started coming here with her husband, Gerry, but it wasn't such a different place back then. There had still been bands playing but it was more folk music and jazz. The drinks were the same apart from the introduction of those Alco-pops she now saw all the young girls drinking. She had thought how wrong it looked that they were drinking out of the bottle with a straw.

The toilets were in the same place, the old bell that the Landlord would ding and shout 'Time Gentlemen Please!' was still hung at the back of the bar, next to the mirror that had captured every night of the pub since it was put up on the very first day of its grand opening, long before Vicky ever moved into the town.

She and Gerry had fallen in love at the Isle of Wight festival in 1967. The music had brought them together and she loved him for that and for everything else besides. They'd drifted most of their lives. They bought a VW camper van and would go from one town to the next, staying in makeshift camps with other travellers.

Then she had fallen pregnant and Gerry dealt with the shock of impending responsibility by organizing the rest of their lives in a single evening. Suddenly he wanted nothing more than to be a husband and father, with his family safe in a two up, two down in suburbia. They hadn't quite made suburbia but the council had put them in a nice terraced house on the outskirts of town and it suited them just fine.

One baby quickly led to another and it was almost as though before she had even blinked, she had three children who had all grown up, gone to college, got married and made her and Gerry grandparents. She often sat here thinking about how her life had just disappeared.

People seemed to understand that this was her seat. It was the same seat that she and Gerry would sit on all those years ago, although it had been re-upholstered more times than she cared to remember. She remembered how they would sit, holding hands, listening to the hippy tones of Led Zeppelin cover bands and even the odd Jimi Hendrix pretender. She thought about what happy, simple days they were. She blinked back tears at the memory of Gerry. The cancer had taken him quickly. She had noticed him losing weight before anyone else gave him a concerned glance. She had been so upset when she saw that his eyes were losing that mischievous spark. One visit to the doctor had led to another and then their whole life was taken up with hospitals and syringes. Chemotherapy meant that he finally had to lose his long hair. Before then, Gerry had vowed that he would never take a job where he had to cut his hair. His hair had been his last symbol of rebellion, as it represented his love of music, of nature, of life. As clumps began to fall out with the treatment, Vicky would collect them all and tie them with a blue ribbon. Then she would carefully weave them in with the wisps he had left, giving him a long trail of silvery hair in a perfect plait down his back. She gave him a cowboy hat, which was to become her last birthday present to him and even though it was against pub rules, the landlord had let him wear down here. He was so pleased that no-one would see his baldness. It wasn't because he was vain but he just didn't want people to keep asking him about his illness… 'Life is for talk of life, not of death,' he had said.

Vicky's own hair, when she was younger, had been a strawberry blonde. She would sway it in time to the music, swinging it from side to side and sometimes putting a flower in a Kirby grip, to symbolise her love for the life that she had cherished. Like Gerry, Vicky had never once cut her hair, even though the kids had pulled it and given her tangles with their sticky fingers. Nowadays she pulled it back into a tight bun, securing it with the same Kirby grips, but her will to place any flowers in her hair had long since gone. The hairstyle and her fierce refusal to wear any colour other than black since the day Gerry died, had been why everyone had so quickly identified her as Queen Victoria, before it was then shortened to Vicky. She didn't mind. She'd never particularly liked her real name anyway and she hadn't bothered to correct anyone as the years went by. It felt more like her real name now than any other.

Vicky looked around the pub as it was now. The paint had been stained yellow with nicotine and the wallpaper had taken on an aged look. Posters new and old had been put in ancient gilt frames and fruit machines flickered from every nook and cranny. The music was just the same though. She often wondered at how it had all come full circle

123

and would sit there even now, listening to the new Led Zeppelin cover bands and impressive Jimi Hendrix impersonators. The men singing were younger of course, but the music was timeless. She would close her eyes and let them transport her back to her youth and to those days with Gerry. Nothing could have persuaded her that an evening in front of the telly was as wonderful as reliving those evenings she had spent with him.

She looked over at Steph and the young busker, who were chatting and laughing with each other. They looked so much in love. She mentally said a prayer in their direction. 'Love each other and cherish each other before it is all gone' she thought to herself. 'It goes so quickly.'

Vicky was feeling very tired. She told herself that maybe it was best that she had an early night tonight. She waved at Steph, beckoning her to come over. Steph walked up to her and said, 'You okay, Vicky? You look a little pale tonight.'

'I'm just tired, Steph. Would you mind calling me a taxi?' Vicky replied.

'Of course, I will.' Steph looked at Vicky with concern. It was unlike her to be so serious and quiet. 'You stay there and I'll help you outside when they get here, alright?'

'Thank you, love,' Vicky said. 'I'm sure I'll be feeling better after a good long sleep.'

CHAPTER TWENTY-TWO

Kate poured out the food from the shopping bags onto the kitchen worktop. She picked up the minced beef, dropped it down on the kitchen side top and tugged a drawer open quickly. She took out a very large chopping knife and swiftly pierced the film over the meat, cutting a slit along two sides. Leaning down to the cupboard underneath the worktop, she grabbed hold of the handle of a frying pan and yanked it out, sending other things tumbling inside the cupboard with a crash. She slammed it down hard onto the oven, kicking the cupboard door closed with her foot.

'Kate, please,' Ern said. His voice was pleading with her, slightly panicked. 'I didn't mean to scare you.'

Kate sparked the hob and swivelled the gas knob to full. 'You didn't scare me. It's just bloody typical isn't it? I find a man I like and Woohoo! Well done Kate! He might just be a murderer! I don't know how I do it!' Kate was waving the knife as she spoke. 'I'm also more than a little pissed off that you chose to wait until now to tell me. I know it's not something you exactly drop casually into conversation but even so.'

'That's not fair. I thought you agreed you would hear me out,' Ern said quietly.

Kate drizzled a little oil into the pan and turned on the heat, banging the oil back down onto the shelf. The irritation in her voice was heavily laced with sarcasm. 'It's fine… really. Go on. Tell me.'

Ern pulled over a stool and sagged down on to it. He loosely clasped his hands in front of him and took a deep breath.

'I was fourteen when I met Ally. We were at the same school. We were the most popular kids in the year, each and every year from then on. It was obvious that we were going to be boyfriend and girlfriend. She was academically brilliant and utterly gorgeous. I was not a bad-looker…' Ern raised his eyebrows and physically tutted at the memory, '…and the best artist that the school had. I'd paint the scenery for all the plays. They even commissioned me to paint an entire wall of the playground in anti-drug pictures and slogans.'

Kate threw the mince into the pan and the fierce sizzle drowned his voice out. She turned the heat down a little and returned to the fridge, snatching out tomatoes, basil and a clove of garlic, slamming the door shut again with a bang. Ern raised his voice slightly as he started to speak again.

'We both excelled in our GCSEs and A levels. Mine were all on the Arts side but I also had a skill for maths. Ally learnt four languages fluently and pretty much passed everything she did with flying colours. We decided to go to the same college. I took a Foundation Course with a view to moving onto Fine Arts and she went for a Business Degree. It was in that first year at college that my life changed so much.'

Kate thumped the chopping block down on the worktop. Picking up the basil, she started to chop it swiftly with the same sharp knife. 'Is this relevant at all?' she asked.

Ern decided it was best just to keep telling her everything from the beginning. 'Her father owned an architectural firm He was a pretty high-flyer by all accounts. He won a lot of work for new government buildings and the influx of commerce into Ireland was making it rich pickings for small Irish businesses that had big ideas. Ally - my girlfriend - she changed at College. She was suddenly not the brightest or the prettiest. She was resentful of all the attention my art was getting, when she had been reduced to another face in the crowd. But we loved each other…'

' Like I said, is there a point to all of this?' Kate asked, taking a clove of garlic and crushing it with one almighty blow of her hand, against the flat of the knife.

'Yes, there is. Please be patient with me. I've never told anyone the whole story before.' Ern tilted his head to try and get her to look at him, but she kept her head down as she cooked. 'Please?' he asked gently.

126

Kate felt the tears well up and stopped for a moment, holding onto the edge of the worktop and staring out of the window to the black night. 'Ok,' she said quietly.

She knew the only way to hold back the tears was to keep busy so she quickly started to move again, pushing the garlic into the pan and reaching to the shelf for an onion.

'Please don't cry,' Ern said to her.

'I'm not crying. It's the onion,' Kate replied stiffly.

Ern looked at her and, despite the tension between them, he couldn't help but smile. 'You haven't started chopping it yet.'

Kate laid down her knife and dropped her head. 'Please just tell me,' she said quietly.

'Her father persuaded me to forget about Fine Arts. To take a degree in Architecture instead, go in to the family business… and marry Ally. I loved her so much that I didn't even question it. I just agreed and that was the next four years of my life mapped out. Well, it was actually my entire life mapped out from the age of 19. I worked hard, passed with Honours and went to work at her dad's firm. Within six months of leaving College, Ally and I got married. I didn't even think about whether it was what I wanted. I just accepted that it was the way things were meant to be. The business became intense. I was so eager to please her father that I worked, twenty-four hours a day, seven days a week. I started drinking too much, trying to drown out how desperately dead I felt inside. Ally and I barely spoke. She spent all her time shopping, lunching with the 'in' crowd and whenever we were at home, I was either working or asleep.'

Kate gently pushed the chopped onions and tomatoes into the pan, sprinkling in some basil with them. She slowly wiped her hands and pulled down a tin of passata from the top shelf. She slid the drawer open quietly to retrieve the tin opener, barely making a sound.

'We went on like that for a few years and then Ally got pregnant. I couldn't even be sure that the baby was mine, but that really didn't matter. I was over the moon. I made promises to myself that I would cut back on work, cut back on the drink and devote myself to my family.'

The sieved tomatoes sizzled slightly as they were poured over the meat. Kate turned the heat down a little more.

'Her father, though, had other ideas. He worked me harder, piling on the feeling of responsibility that I had a family to support now; we must take the business to new heights, etc. I got carried away with his dream… I missed all the ante-natal appointments. I was even too late to see her born. I'd been in a meeting with some guys over from England. It was a toss-up between securing a contract for a tower block in London and seeing my baby born. I chose the tower block.'

Kate made no reaction. She went down to the cupboard and pulled out a saucepan, turned on the tap to fill it with water and then gently lit another gas ring.

'Phoebe was just beautiful. She was such a happy kid. Ally couldn't cope though. She'd been spoilt for too long and couldn't handle being 'just' a mum. She hired in a nanny and then there were three people in our family who never saw each other. Looking back, I know just how awful it was.' Ern drained his tea and put the mug down on the side heavily so that it hit the worktop with a bang. It made Kate jump as everything else was gently bubbling. She took a deep breath and snipped open the pasta, easing it into the pan.

'Ally came home one day and told me she was in love with someone else. She also informed me that she was leaving me… that we were over.'

Kate glanced at him. She couldn't gauge anything from his expression but an intense determination. Ern continued, 'I barely even protested as she grabbed Phoebe out of bed, put her in the car and drove away. I just thought that was it. Finished. She'd just gone. I didn't even watch them as they drove away. I went into the kitchen, took a bottle of whiskey down from the cupboard and started to drink. I drank… well, God knows how much… and I passed out.' Ern dragged his fingers through his hair before continuing. 'The phone woke me up. It was the hospital to tell me that Ally and Phoebe had been in a car accident. They told me that the police said Ally swerved the car to avoid a stag and ended up in a ditch. They were both okay but Ally would have to stay in for observation.' Ern looked up at Kate. 'They asked me to go and get Phoebe. Obviously Ally was too out of it to make any objection, so I grabbed my car keys and went down there. I don't remember driving there, I don't remember parking and I don't remember what I said once I got there. Christ knows why they let me take her - I must have stunk of whiskey - but they let me take Phoebe home. I put her to bed and I sat on the edge of her bed, watching her sleeping. She had a small graze…' Ern lifted his hand and touched his temple. '…just here on the side of her head, but even so she looked just like an angel. I sat by the side of her bed all night, with yet another bottle of whiskey, trying desperately to block out the feeling of failure. I must have fallen asleep for a while but I woke up just as the sun was coming up.'

Ern stood up and walked over to the back door, looking out to the garden. 'I was almost out of my mind when I realised that Ally would probably leave hospital and come to take Phoebe again.. I went and got my sketch pad out of the study and gently woke Phoebe up. In my hazy state I had reasoned that I was going to sketch some landscapes from the sea. We went down to the marina and took out the small dinghy that Ally had bought for me a few years back.'

Kate turned around and said 'But you must have still been so drunk!'

Ern walked back to the chair and slumped down into it again. 'I know. I was a seasoned drunk though. It had become so normal to continue doing everyday things whilst completely out of it. It was just something I didn't even consider.' He shook his head as he said the words, his face dragged down into the dark memories. 'I don't really know what happened. I have lost all memory of that boat trip. I have beaten myself up a thousand times trying to remember but it just won't come. I was found half-dead further out to sea. A fishing boat had found me and brought me back to shore. When I came to, I started screaming about Phoebe and they managed to get me to explain that she was my daughter. It was only then that they looked for Phoebe.'

'And that was when you were accused of murder?' Kate asked, not really knowing which way to place her sympathies. She felt totally confused.

'I'd left a note for Ally. I'd torn a page out of the sketch book and written that no other man was going to be a dad to Phoebe. I'd written that she'd never see either of us again.'

Kate took a moment to absorb the information. She spoke slowly, 'So they assumed you had done it on purpose? A suicide and the murder of your daughter?'

'Yep. I was arrested and charged. It was splashed all over the papers and Ally had a field day, doing interviews and crying in front of the cameras.'

Kate looked at him and said harshly, 'She'd lost her daughter. I think she had every right to be distressed.'

'Yes. Yes, she did. It's just I didn't know what to think, Kate. I wasn't allowed to grieve for Phoebe. I was caught up in the whirl of people shouting and accusing me. It was perverse but all I could think to do was to mentally block off from it all.'

'That's understandable, I suppose,' Kate said. 'So I take it that you went to court?'

'The captain of the trawler that picked me up was called as a witness. He gave testimony that there had been a surge into the mouth of the marina by a Russian liner that had veered off course. He said that it had nearly turned their boat over and so it was possible that was what had happened to our boat. Apparently the trawler was within a hair's breadth of my boat and they saw it flip over. They saw me go in but...' he stopped talking and swallowed hard, 'They didn't remember seeing a child at all.' Ern stopped and closed his eyes. ' I don't know what happened to her. No-one could even prove that she had been on the boat, as all tests on the wreckage were inconclusive. I just really can't remember and Phoebe's body was never recovered.'

'So there was no evidence at all to convict you?' Kate asked.

'No. I was originally found guilty of misadventure but that was thrown out at appeal. It was ironic that Ally's father paid for the best lawyers to defend me. I think he saw it as some kind of personal embarrassment to his family. Ally was furious and as far as I know, they still don't talk to each other. As soon as it was all over and the furore around it had died down, her father sacked me. Not that I'd actually done any real work for him for God knows how long. I lost the house, of course. I'd lost my daughter, my home, my work and it really felt like that my entire life had been wiped out. That was when the hell in my head just settled in like a permanent fixture. '

Kate interrupted, 'It must have been terrible but...'

Ern quickly talked over her, 'But nothing. I was a waste of space. No more than a useless drunk that had caused my daughter's death. Whether I had killed her by accident or on purpose, she was dead because of me. I drank some more, went off the rails, living my life in seedy clubs, not giving a shit and finally ended up in prison with a conviction for drunk driving. Ha! The irony!' Kate could see that Ern's eyes were glistening with tears.

'When I came out of jail, my sister took me in. I set up my own firm, taking on smaller projects like loft conversions and so on. For six years, I threw myself into it, blocking out all emotion, all grieving, all hope for the future and just worked. I gave up the booze, which was easier than I had expected... perhaps because the loss of my daughter

130

felt greater than the loss of alcohol. Two months ago, I walked out of my office and caught a ferry to England. I've searched my mind and asked myself a lot of questions.' Ern sighed before continuing, 'I've reached an acceptance that sometimes there will be no answers. I'm back to nearly being 'me' again. The 'me' that I was before any of this happened. Any of it.'

Kate looked at him. He had slumped down so that his elbows were on the counter and his hands were clasped together in front of him. He was staring down onto the shiny surface of the worktop. Kate tentatively reached out and stroked her hand along the top of his head, smoothing his hair. She felt the tears well up again and pulled her hand back to wipe her eyes.

Ern kept his head down as he said, 'I don't expect you to accept any of this, Kate. I really don't know why I feel like I do about you. I'm sorry.'

She closed her eyes and tried to calm all the emotion. The silence in the room was cracked by the timer on the oven going off.

Kate let it ring for a while before she pushed the button. She spoke quietly, 'Dinner's ready. I'd best dish up.'

CHAPTER TWENTY-THREE

Kate dished up the spaghetti and sauce onto the plates and got two forks and two spoons from the draining board. She passed the cutlery to Ern before picking up the plates and saying quietly, 'Come and sit down.' She walked around Ern to the double doors that led out to her little conservatory. She pushed down the door handle with her elbow and went through to the gloomy interior.

Ern stood at the doorway uncertain of whether he should stay or go. He could see Kate's shadow as she put the plates on the table with a light clink, before she moved over to the wall to flick on the lights. Ern's head snapped up as a cascade of multi-coloured fairy lights lit up around the roof of the room. They were reflected and multiplied so many times in the wall-panels of glass that it looked like there were thousands of coloured sparks against the black void outside.

Kate sat down and waited for him to join her. The tulips he had given her earlier in the week were standing in the middle of the table, in a pale blue vase. The colour of the petals had begun to fade; a few had already fallen and were now scattered on the tabletop.

Ern sat down opposite her and looked at her sad face in the pale glow of the lights. He again thought about how beautiful she was and how different the whole evening could have been if he'd chosen not to tell her. The steam from his plate snaked up towards him and he breathed it in, wishing they could go back to the way they were. He put his face in his hands. His head felt heavy as though there was a fug of self-pity and resentment in his mind that wouldn't clear. He wanted to try and repair this in whatever way he could. He dropped his hands back down to the table and spoke to her.

'Won't you say something, Kate?' he asked.

There was a moment's pause before she replied 'What can I say?'

'Do you want me to go? Are there no questions you want to ask me?'

'No. You don't have to go. But, there is nothing I can ask you. You have already said that there are no answers.' She sounded empty. Ern was having trouble relating her to the person he had come to know. There was no laughter in her voice, no chuckle behind each sound.

'In the absence of answers, one can only be left with an opinion. Do you not even have an opinion?' He immediately regretted his tone. He knew he sounded irritated and impatient, which was ridiculous considering that he had caused her all this anxiety.

'My opinion?' Kate laid her fork back down on the plate, placed her elbows on the table and circled her fingertips against her forehead. With a shake of her head, she stood up and went back into the kitchen. Ern heard her open a drawer and slam it shut again. She returned with the bottle of red wine and a corkscrew in one hand, one glass in the other.

Ern put his hand out for the bottle. 'Let me open that for you,' he said.

Kate looked at the wine for a second before passing him the bottle. 'Well, if it doesn't worry you? I think I just need a drink.' Her voice was clipped, as though challenging him.

'It doesn't worry me at all. Your silence though… that worries me,' he said, as he twisted the corkscrew into the soft wood and pulled. The cork eased away with a soft pop, as it was pulled gently from the neck of the bottle. The sound resonated for a moment until Ern chinked the side of the glass with the bottle and poured Kate some wine. Kate lifted it up and tasted it. The musky dryness of it dulled her mouth and she was pleased to have the rich taste momentarily distract her.

She picked up her fork and started to eat. After a few mouthfuls, she said 'You should eat too.'

Ern had no appetite but he was determined not to run away this time. Kate was too important for that. The sweet tomatoes and mince took away the dryness in his mouth as he savoured the taste. He toyed with the idea of trying to lighten the mood with a compliment or a joke about it being better than cheese on toast… but he knew he couldn't risk making matters worse. He had lived with his story for years whereas Kate was still trying to take it all in. He decided to just continue eating until Kate decided that she wanted to talk some more.

Kate put her fork down and took a large gulp of wine. She kept her eyes on the wine as she spoke. 'My opinion is that yes, you probably are fucked up. Your story is terrible... sad... extreme. Your behaviour was inexcusable. You'll have to live with the consequences for the rest of your life.'

'I know all of that,' Ern replied, again cursing himself for sounding so annoyed.

'Yes, you do.' said Kate. The distance between them was growing by the second. She could feel all the happiness of the past few days slipping away. She closed her eyes and remembered the beach, his drawings, his words. She lifted her glass again and took another sip of her wine.

'Kate, do you want me to go?' Ern asked. 'This is awful. I'm so sorry.'

Kate put her glass down too quickly, causing a little wine to splash and form a small puddle on the table. Kate looked at it and her mouth contorted slightly, her own irritation now beginning to surface. 'I'd begun to know the man you are now. Tonight, you have thrown at me the man that you once were and it's almost like you're asking me to choose.'

'That's not the way it is. They are both me.'

'That's crap. I'm sorry but it is. So you fucked up. You fucked up big time. You say yourself that you went on to fuck up a little bit more and that you are using this time to get your head straight. By your own admission you are not that man anymore.'

She avoided looking him in the eye. There was silence for a few minutes but Ern was acutely aware that he was totally unable to find the right words to try and make her understand. Kate was the first to speak again...

'Don't tell me that they are both you. Either there is the 'you' I know, or there is a 'you' that you haven't shown me. Which is it?'

'I don't know. Everything's changed since...' Finally, she lifted her face allowing him to look into her eyes. He didn't want to sound crass but there was only one truth and that was that everything *had* changed because of her. '... since I met you.' he continued.

He saw her eyes glisten and as she picked up her fork and started to eat again.

Ern could tell that Kate was deep in thought. He wanted to speak up - to justify himself in some way – but he knew he had to respect that there was no justification for his actions. He just had to wait and see how Kate was going to deal with it.

They finished their meals without another word. Kate left the table and returned with a glass of water, which she put in front of Ern. He thanked her quietly. She sat down and cradled her wine glass in her hand, still deep in thought.

Ern looked around the room. The conservatory looked very old but Kate had draped scarves over the curtain rails and there were various crystals and mobiles hanging down. He could imagine her sitting there in the summer with the doors open and the chimes softly ringing as they brushed against each other. He could see a canvas, propped up against the wall by the door out to the garden. Her easel was behind it and a huge tool box that was overflowing with paints and brushes. He wondered how on earth she could see to paint in there until he saw that there was a small office lamp plugged in to one side. He tried to imagine her sitting cross legged with a determined face as she painted. It was too dark to see what the painting was of, but Ern could just make out a central figure and…

'MEATBALLS!' Kate said aloud, with a laugh.

Ern looked over to her, totally confused. 'Sorry?' he said.

'Meatballs. That's what they had on their first date but they had spaghetti just like us!' Kate said enthusiastically. Ern could hear her soft laughter in each word again but didn't have a clue what she was talking about.

'Uhm… I'm really not following you here,' he said cautiously.

Kate smiled at him. 'The Lady and the Tramp. That's who you likened us to down on the beach today and they had spaghetti with meatballs on their first date! The manager of the restaurant sang to them.' Kate chuckled at Ern's surprised face. She quietened her voice a little and looked down at her empty plate, realising unfair it might be for her to have changed the focus from the big issue of the night. Nonetheless, she continued talking. 'It was just the train of thought I was on. He played the violin while they ate and Tramp pushed a meatball over to Lady with his nose and they nibbled on the ends of the same string of spaghetti until their noses met in the middle.' She

136

looked up at Ern again and after a moment of them looking at each other, she smiled.

Ern couldn't resist smiling back. 'That Lady… you were right when you said she was drawn to be such a babe, with those long eyelashes and all,' he said.

'And the Tramp… he was quite a smooth talker,' Kate said, cautiously allowing her voice to become lighter again.

Ern reached across the table and gently took her hand. 'I like it when we laugh,' he said.

From the other room, the telephone started ringing. They both looked at each other but Kate made no attempt to move. On the sixth ring, the answering machine picked it up and the mechanical voice told whoever it was to leave a message. Kate held her breath through the long beep, before Beth's voice shouted excitedly on the other end. 'Kate? I'm down the pub and it's brilliant! Where are you? Jamie's over in the other bar with some woman draped all over him and so I don't think I should disturb him,' she dropped her voice and said conspiratorially, 'if you know what I mean.' Beth launched into one of her fits of giggles, to which Kate smiled, pleased that her friend was having such a good time. Beth continued, 'Anyway, I was just ringing to see if you were around and fancied a drink. Call me, ok? We may need to amend that tick list because it's really not working for me.' There was another snort of laughter and Kate tried to hide a chuckle. 'Bye babes! See you soon!' Beth said.

There was a click and then another long beep as the machine signalled end of message. Kate looked at Ern's face, wondering what to do next. She reached across the table and took his other hand with hers. She looked down as she spoke. 'I wish none of that had happened to you, Ern. I really do.'

Ern went to speak but she put her finger to his lips, wanting him to let her finish. 'All I know is that you have made this huge impact on my life over the past few days. I find you intriguing and not because of what you've done or where you've been but because inside of you there's all these thoughts, all these pictures and emotions that are so…' Kate looked at him before finding the right words, '… so bloody gorgeous.'

Ern smiled at the bluntness of the end of her speech but shook his head.

'They *are*,' Kate insisted. 'I don't know whether it's you or me or what, but when I met you,' she stopped herself and decided to clarify, 'or rather the second time I met you, I just knew that you were someone important.'

'It's you that's important, Kate. You're remarkable.' Ern said.

Kate stood up and without letting go of his hands, walked around to his side of the table. Ern pushed his seat out a little and she sat on his lap. She let go of his hands and wrapped her arms around him. Ern breathed in her scent and held her, enjoying the closeness and warmth. Kate sat up, cupped his face in her hands and they kissed.

When Kate spoke, it was no more than a whisper. 'My bedroom is as messy as the lounge. I hope you don't mind?'

Ern didn't react to her words. Kate sat still, her arms wrapped around him and tried to control the nervousness she felt that he would reject her.

He squeezed her tight before moving back slightly, so that he could look into her eyes but Kate wouldn't look at him. He stroked her face and said, 'I had no idea.'

Kate tilted her face against his hand, enjoying his touch. She wanted desperately to lighten the mood. She thought for a moment before forcing her voice to be bright and saying, 'What? That my room was a mess?'

Ern smiled and said, 'No. I had no idea that you would want me to stay.'

'Neither did I,' she replied.

They just sat for a while; Kate rested her head on Ern's shoulder and he had his arms loosely clasped around her. Ern knew he should say something but he wanted to choose his words carefully.

'Kate, I think you're amazing and I'm sorry. I just hope you realise that I had to tell you.'

Kate put her finger on his lips and hushed him. She stood up and took both of his hands, tugging him gently so that he would stand up too. They kissed again before she moved over to the door, keeping hold of one of his hands. She flicked off the light switch so that the conservatory was once again plunged in darkness. Kate led him through each room, turning off the lights as she went. As they reached the stairs, Ern released his hand from hers and put his arm around her waist so that they walked up side by side.

They reached the landing and Kate turned to kiss him as she pushed the door open. They shuffled together into the room. Still kissing him, Kate felt her hand across the wall and flicked on a switch that turned on a small lamp by her dressing table. Ern squinted one eye open whilst they were still kissing and looked through Kate's curls at the bedroom. He saw that Kate hadn't exaggerated about the mess. A rainbow of clothes was piled high on a chair and they were spilling down onto the floor. There were books and magazines stacked haphazardly by the window, as well as three or four open books on each bedside table. Every surface seemed to be full of jewellery and little bottles of every shape imaginable. He couldn't stop himself chuckling even though his lips were still clamped to Kate's. She pulled away quickly. 'What?' she said. 'You weren't exaggerating,' he said, nudging his head towards all the mess. Kate smirked, 'No, I wasn't.' They started kissing again but then, as if to prove the point perfectly, Kate's foot stepped on a discarded shoe, causing her to lose her balance and they both went crashing to the floor. They both started giggling like children and Kate shifted her bottom up to pull out the shoe from underneath her, which she then threw up and over the bed, where they heard it hit the floor with a thump.

Ern rolled over onto his back laughing and wincing as he pulled his arm out from underneath Kate. He looked up at the ceiling and his eyes opened wide. 'Oh you are joking!' he said, amazed at what he saw. Kate shifted over and put her head on his chest, so that she was looking up at the ceiling too.

'Isn't that gorgeous?' she said cheekily.

Ern looked up at the huge poster of Johnny Depp smouldering with his shirt unbuttoned to the waist.

'I can't say it would be my first choice of what to have on a bedroom ceiling!' Ern said.

'Oh, I think it's rather lovely to have him be the last thing I see every night and the first every morning. I must admit though I hadn't actually thought about how it might affect any man coming up here,' Kate said with a chuckle. 'He must be very intimidating for you.'

'Intimidating? Oh, we'll see about that,' Ern said and stood up, taking hold of Kate's hands and hauling her up off the floor before leaning in to kiss her again. Kate pushed him away a little and whispered, 'Shall we just forget all the film star stuff about clothes effortlessly gliding off and just take them off ourselves like normal people have to?'

Ern ignored her and moved his hand around to unbutton her blouse. The first button pinged effortlessly but, no matter how much he tried, the second one was not budging.

He sighed with mock indignation. 'You are a very wise woman,' he said quietly.

'I'm well known for being very wise,' Kate replied, chuckling. 'They design women's clothes to be especially resistant to men's fingers. It's a stern reminder to us women to play hard to get.'

'Hmmm, is that so?' said Ern, standing up and hauling Kate to her feet. 'Perhaps you should have a few words and tell them they should play fair.'

'I'll call them in the morning…' Kate said softly, brushing her lips against his as she unbuttoned her blouse with one hand. She took a step away and watched Ern remove his jumper. Kate wasn't surprised that he had a very hairy chest and she reached out, running her fingers over it. Ern looked up at Johnny Depp and winked.

'That's a real chest, Johnny-boy,' he said.

Kate giggled loudly. Ern slid his fingers under the strap of her bra and gently moved it over her shoulder, feeling the soft skin beneath his touch and leant in to kiss her shoulder. As he moved back, he suddenly went cold inside. A blast of panic exploded in his head as he realised that this was going to be the first time for nearly twenty years that he had sex whilst sober. He couldn't be sure how it was going to be or how the hell he was going to handle that much intensity.

'Are you alright, Ern?' Kate said. 'You're trembling.'

He studied her face, tucked a curl behind her ear and forced himself to pull it all back and take control of it. He promised himself that drink, grief or self-pity weren't going to take this night from him. 'I'm fine, Kate. I'm with you and that is just incredible. That's all.' Ern felt Kate relax against him; a sign of trust that he had not experienced for many, many years. He moved his head down to kiss her neck, running his hands down her back and inside the back of her jeans. He heard Kate sigh so softly that all doubts he had were overtaken by desire for her.

They fell back onto the bed together, giggling again, narrowly missing Kate's tabby cat who had been curled up asleep on the duvet, twitching with dreams of sun soaked window ledges. Cat lifted her head and looked with disdain at the pair who were kissing and fumbling with each other's clothes. Cat stood up, stretched up on all fours, arching her back, before shaking her fur indignantly and exiting the room with her tail held high.

CHAPTER TWENTY-FOUR

Ern's mind shifted out of his dreams and slowly began to drag him back to the here and now. He opened his eyes very slightly and saw that it was just beginning to get light. He opened his eyes a little more and Kate's bedroom started to come into focus.

Panic suddenly seized him as his thoughts flitted to his confession and the awkwardness over dinner, before all the tension went away with their making love. He could feel Kate's warm body lying against his. Her arm was draped across his chest and he could feel her breath against his back as they lie spooned together. He felt a flash of guilt as he remembered the deep emotion that the impact of his story had on her. He was angry at himself for having put her in that position but, even in the cold light of day, he knew that keeping it from her had not been an option. He couldn't have gone on without letting her know his past and without letting her choose whether to be involved with someone like him. Her obvious disappointment in him having such a complex history had hurt him. It had hurt deeply. Ern knew better than to expect immediate acceptance but he just wanted someone to see and understand how much he wanted to feel there was a clear way forward. He still didn't know whether Kate understood or accepted it all. Last night was wonderful and the depth of their feeling for each other was undeniable but maybe she would feel differently this morning. He closed his eyes again and breathed in deeply.

Ern carefully lifted the sheet and then Kate's hand, sliding away from her slowly so as not to wake her. He rested her hand down onto the mattress and sat up, turning his head to look at her. Her curls were fanned over the pillow and Ern gently swept a couple down with his finger, resting them over her shoulder. He wanted to kiss her. He wanted to lie back down and move her against him. He wanted to make love to her again. But guilt was pushing him all the while to give her space and time without feeling any kind of misplaced loyalty to him. He lightly kissed her shoulder and quietly eased himself up from the bed, laying the duvet back down as he went so that she remained undisturbed.

'Finally he's awake.' Kate couldn't hold her breath any longer so released it slowly through the slightest parting of her lips. 'His touch is so soft. Wake me up Ern. I've been lying here waiting for you to wake up for what seems like forever. Wake me up and make love to me again.'

He sat on the edge of the bed looking around the room. He smiled at the chaos. It was even worse than the night before as the books had been tossed from the bed and their clothes from the previous day lay scattered on top of others. He leant down and picked up his jeans, sliding them on in one swift movement as he stood. Without doing up the zip, he left the room and padded over to the bathroom. It had astonished him, when he'd gone into the bathroom the night before, to see that it was the one room of the house which was immaculate. Candles were lined up along the back of the bath along with various potions and bath salts, all with different bizarre names and colours - 'DAMNED SEXY Bath milk', Bitter Lemon Salt scrub, Soothe-me Softly Suds & Soak and many more with even more unfathomable names or potion mixes. Thick white towels were neatly folded over the towel rail along the side of the loo. Ern lifted the seat, careful not to let it hit the back of the cistern and read the notice Kate had pinned up above the loo, which read 'If you sprinkle, when you tinkle, please...' She'd then scribbled out the next two lines and written 'piss in someone else's house, Dumb-ass'. Ern smiled as he looked at it again and quietly said, 'I love you, Kate'. He gently lowered the toilet seat and flushed. The sound making him wince as he so desperately wanted her to continue sleeping.

'What do I do? Do I ask him to come back to bed? Do I make love with him again? Do I cook him eggs? Shit... I didn't buy eggs. I am so

144

useless.' Kate didn't risk smiling at her usual forgetfulness. Instead she kept her face still and tried to keep her breathing light. 'I don't know what he wants. I don't know what I want.' She heard the bathroom door chink closed. 'He's going to the loo... did I hide my contraceptives? He might hate that I made him use a condom. He might just see it as me not trusting him.' Kate kicked her foot out of the duvet as she got a cramp in her foreleg. She swore in her mind 'Ouch! Shit!' and flexed her toes upwards trying not to make a sound. As the cramp eased, she pushed her leg back over the duvet and let the edge of the cotton rest between her knees. 'I really don't want him to go. Oh Kate, you really don't want him to go.'

Ern walked back along the landing and pushed the door to the bedroom open slightly. He could see that Kate had curled her leg outside and around the duvet but was still fast asleep. Her skin was pale and smooth against the white cover. He picked his way over to find his jumper amongst the heap of clothes, pulling it over his head and pushing his arms through. He heard his shoulder click a he did so and repeated his daily cursing of his old bones. As he looked back at her lying asleep, he noticed a small tattoo on her leg above her ankle; a small shooting star that was simple perfection against her milky skin. Ern very gently leaned over and kissed it softly. Kate didn't flinch. He watched her for a few moments more before leaving the room, slowly pulling the door closed behind him.

He padded his way down the stairs on the balls of his feet, trying to be as quiet as possible when his foot landed on something soft and a piercing, pained yowl echoed around the hall. 'Shit!' Ern hissed, as he quickly lifted his foot again, releasing Cat's tail. She raced down the stairs in front of him and into the kitchen. 'Dammit,' he muttered. He followed her into the kitchen, only to see her back end disappearing out the cat flap. He turned on the tap and filled the kettle up, flicking it on at the wall before he went back to the hallway. He rummaged through his coat pocket and found his tobacco and papers. The kettle was still straining to warm the water as he walked back through the kitchen. He unlocked the back door and stepped out into the garden.

'Hell. He stepped on Cat. He'll know that would have woken me up, won't he? What do I do? He might just slip away and I'll never see him again. I couldn't bear that.' Kate opened her eyes and sat up. I'll

go and talk to him.' She winced at the brightness of the room. 'Holy shit, this room's a mess.' She flopped back onto the bed, turned on her side and closed her eyes again. 'He likes my mess. It makes me who I am. Who am I? I'm NOT someone who has sex with just anyone having only known them for a few days. He doesn't know that. Oh no! He probably thinks I do it all the time!' Kate turned over and pulled the duvet up over her head. 'I must stop being ridiculous. People have sex with people every day. It was way overdue to be my turn. Grow up, grow up, grow up, Kate.'

The icy air hit his face and Ern shuddered as it quickly went through his jumper to his bare skin underneath. He scanned the garden quickly to see if he could see Cat but all he could see was a pile of dirty crockery in a bowl that had been dumped unceremoniously on the patio. He chuckled and rolled himself a cigarette once he'd sat down on the back step. He could see Cat eyeing him suspiciously from behind a bush and he stopped rolling the tobacco to click his fingers in the hope that it would tempt her over. By the time he had finished his cigarette, she was brushing against his legs and purring. Once he was back in the kitchen, he fed her and quickly found two mugs to make tea.

'If he does slip away and I never see him again... surely it would be just easier? Do I really need an ex-alcoholic, fucked up man complicating my life? 'She pulled her leg back under the duvet and hugged it close. 'I don't want him to just leave and never see him again but... perhaps that would be easier for both of us?'

Ern walked into the conservatory and over to Kate's canvas, squatting down to look at it properly as it rested against the wall. Her style was different to his but, aesthetically, the result was the same. The 'vanishing point' was dead centre of the canvas and the linear perspective warped into it on a curve. It was a simple scene of the walkway where they had met but the shops and benches were bounding and swelling to the music, the pedestrians limbs slightly distorted so that they curved into a simple waltz, whilst the only thing standing straight was the busker, dead centre, whose clarinet looked to be entrancing the crowd like a snake charmer playing his pipe. The pale pastel colours of the busker's surroundings contrasted starkly to the black clothing and the top hat, which Kate had chosen to paint him in. Tony was standing at the door of his coffee shop, arms crossed, laughing and the flower seller was throwing roses up in the air so that they cascaded down over passers by. Ern could see himself, sitting hunched down in one corner, his art in front of him. She had replicated his first two drawings and his hat was placed upturned to one side, in which there were gold coins piled up and flowing over the brim. Ern smiled, taking every detail in and examining her technique. 'You are amazing, Kate,' Ern said to the empty room.

'What if he doesn't like me? What if last night was too much? What if I was too unpredictable... too dismissive of his past? He probably thought I was going to murder him when he saw me crush that garlic with one blow! What if he walks away and never wants to see me again? What if he thinks I'm rubbish at sex?'

Ern walked back into the kitchen and took a slurp of his tea. He saw a pink pad with lined sheets, each one printed with a header that read 'Things to Do (If you can be bothered)'. Ern ripped off the top sheet, picked up the pen and wrote:

**'You look like an Angel as you sleep.
I must go and give you some time to think, maybe? x
p.s. Cat forgave me for stepping on her tail
because I filled her dish with food.
She is as beautiful as her mistress.
Your picture is wonderful.
X'**

He tore it off and folded it in half before pushing it into the back pocket of his jeans. After another sip of tea, he picked up Kate's mug and walked quietly back up the stairs. He pushed the door open and put the mug of tea down on the bedside table. Kate was still sound asleep. Ern looked up at the poster of Johnny Depp and smiled, then got the note out of his back pocket and placed it on the pillow next to her.

'Come back to bed. Come back to bed. Please come back to bed. Or just go and never see me again. Both options are fine but please just come back to bed.'

Ern reached out and almost touched her face. He could see her eyes flicker and he swiftly took his hand away. He watched her for a few more minutes until her eyes had settled again. He took another quick glance around the room and then left, pulling the door behind him and walking back down the stairs. He picked up his coat from the banister, leant down to give Cat a quick tickle under her chin and then walked out of the front door.

'He's gone! Where's he gone? Hell!' She sat up quickly and grabbed the note, reading it once and then reading it twice more. 'Give me some time to think? I don't know what to think. What do I think? Oh, for chrissakes, Ern. What the hell am I supposed to think?'

Kate flopped back down onto the pillows, still clutching the note. She tried to make a plan but the only thing that came to the top of the list was 'Have sex with Ern again' and 'Tidy up!' She sighed, sat up and plumped the pillows behind her, lifted the mug from the bedside table and took a sip of the lukewarm tea.

It was then that she remembered Jamie was coming for lunch. 'Shit,' she said aloud. She pulled her knees up to her, cradled the mug in both her hands and worked out how she was going to tell him about Ern.

CHAPTER TWENTY-FIVE

This was Tony's favourite time of day. It was barely light outside and the only movement in the street was the stall trader's setting up. Even though he had the flat upstairs, this was where he felt most at home. He pressed play on the stereo and Louis' trumpet led the way for Ella Fitzgerald to sing Tony 'Summertime'. It was a ritual that he looked forward to each morning. He would get all the chairs down from the tables, wipe everything down and check for any crumbs that didn't get caught when he cleaned the floor the night before. He flicked on the neon light in the window, which proudly declared this was 'Tony's Coffee Bar and Deli.' He unlocked the front door and picked up the delivery of milk and pastries for that day's customers. He took them behind the bar and rested them down. He had already been up for two hours making the sandwiches and slicing the slabs of cake that the bakery made up for him. If ever there was anyone who took their job as host seriously, it was Tony. Once people were sitting at the tables, sipping their coffees, it felt like their retreat and he was there to make it so. That was just the way he liked it. He put the milk away in the fridge and left the pastries to one side while he finished setting up. As Ella stepped up with Louis and their voices soaked into every corner of the room, Tony slid around the bar and swerved around each table taking down the chairs in time to the music, humming along to her sultry voice. He went to get his spray and cloth, dancing back to the tables and wiping them over, raising his voice and singing loudly in harmony as he cleaned. He stopped for the finale, stood facing the bar and lifted both his arms as he hushed the baby and told it not to cry, in his deep, mellow voice.

He froze when he heard someone applaud behind him. He twisted his head to look over his shoulder and there stood a woman, smiling at him and clapping his performance.

'Oh! Hello,' he said with a shocked expression on his face. 'I didn't hear you come in.'

'I saw you through the window first,' she said. 'I wanted to come in quietly so you would finish your dancing.'

'Ha!' Tony said, deeply embarrassed. 'I shall have to remember to keep the lights off next time.' He moved around and behind the bar, where he began to unpack the pastries.

'That would be a shame,' the woman said. 'They were some fine moves you had going on there.'

'You think?' Tony said.

'Absolutely!' she smiled and Tony grinned back at her. 'I was actually here because of the sign in the window. You're looking for help?' she said.

Tony took a moment to realise what she was referring to before he remembered the notice he'd put up in the window just after closing last night. It had been a tough decision because the person had to be absolutely right. He or she had to know that this was more than just a coffee shop. Tony didn't want a moody teenager wimping about the place, nor did he want some kind of straight-faced unsmiling efficiency. He just wanted someone who knew what this place was all about and who would 'get it', whatever 'it' was that he had managed to create here. He looked at the woman to see if there was any sign that she would appreciate that. She was probably early forties, small and slight, with a nervous smile. Her black hair was carefully pulled back into a pony-tail and Tony could see the odd, stray grey hair was beginning to show.

'Ah the sign, right,' he said. 'It's only a few hours a day and the pays not much but…' he made a sweeping motion around the bar area with his arms and continued, 'there's as much coffee as you care to drink.' He picked up a mug and asked 'I was just about to grind the first beans of the day. Would you care for a cup and we can talk about what I'm looking for?'

150

'Well, I don't know whether this is going to work against me,' the woman replied, biting her lip and awkwardly grinning before completing her sentence, 'but I don't drink coffee.'

'If I was a businessman, I would say that makes you perfect for the job,' Tony chuckled.

'Are you not a businessman?' she said surprised.

Tony tried to choose his words carefully. He'd tried to explain it to himself many times and rarely got it right. 'Yes, I'm a businessman, I suppose. Really and truly though, I'm just part of everything that happens here.' He pointed out to the street as he said it. 'I'm not going to get rich running a coffee shop but then sometimes that's not what it's all about.'

The woman nodded. 'Well, that's a nice way to think,' she said. She looked around the café taking in the bookshelves and the deep leather chairs with small coffee tables between. 'It's not often you actually find someone who cares enough to think like that.'

Tony looked at her and said, 'Let me get you some orange juice, you take a seat and we'll talk about this job then, okay?'

'Perfect,' she said. 'My name's Liza.' She extended her hand over the bar and Tony smiled as she shook it firmly.

'My name's Tony as you might have gathered from the name of the place,' he chuckled.

Liza smiled and went to sit down at the table next to the bar. Tony busied himself grinding beans and finishing laying out the pastries in the baskets, before popping them into the glass cabinets. The door opened and Ern walked in.

'Hey Tony,' Ern said with a serious look on his face.

'Ern! Nice to see you! Cappuccino?' Tony asked. He remembered that Ern was going to Kate's last night and, as much as he liked Ern, he felt protective towards Kate. They had shared many heart to heart chats and although Kate liked to make out she was as tough as old boots, Tony knew better.

'Make it a black Americano, if you wouldn't mind, I'm trying to wake my head up a bit.' Ern replied.

Tony dropped his voice and asked 'Did you enjoy your dinner at Kate's last night?'

Ern pulled some coins out of his pocket and pushed them around in the palm of his hand as he spoke, 'She's an amazing lady, Tony.'

Tony tried to gauge a better answer by studying Ern's face but the artist looked too deep in thought to be reacting to anything Tony might ask him. 'Do you think Kate will be in today?' Tony asked, which was his way of asking if everything was alright with his friend.

Ern looked up at him and smiled, 'I hope so, Tony. I really hope so.' Tony took this as a good sign that there had been no dramas between them and set to making Ern's coffee.

'Tony, I'm still really keen to do that picture for your wall over there,' Ern said, pointing to the bare wall to his left. 'I've just got nowhere to do it. Do you have a back room or something I could set up a board in? It shouldn't take me more than a couple of hours.'

Tony nodded and said, 'Well there's my flat upstairs. You could always use the spare room. There's good light coming in there and nothing much else to get in your way.'

'That sounds perfect. I was thinking of doing an interior of the coffee shop so it will be good to be close to all of this and able to pop down to take a look at the layout.'

'The coffee shop? That would be amazing! Thanks Ern,' Tony said with a grin.

'I saw Kate's picture,' Ern said. 'Now, THAT is amazing. I will try and compliment hers with mine.' He turned and looked at the wall. 'It would be lovely to have them side by side.'

Tony passed Ern's Americano over the bar and said, 'Just let me know when you want to set up.'

'How about tomorrow? I could do with a break from sitting on concrete all day,' Ern said passing the money over.

'Keep your money, Ern. It's going to be great to have my own picture up here of the café. From now on the coffees are on me and I'll see you tomorrow.'

Ern smiled his thanks and took his coffee over to the window to sit down in one of the brown leather chairs. As he was doing so, the door opened and another customer came in. Tony greeted them with a nod of his head and told them 'I'll be right with you.' Then the door opened again and before he knew it, Tony had a queue of five customers waiting to be served. Liza appeared at his side. 'How about I just get stuck right in?' she said.

'That sounds like a fine idea,' Tony said. 'You take their orders and money, I'll make the coffee.'

Liza greeted each customer like an old friend and always asked them if they wanted any pastries with their coffee. Tony decided that their chat wasn't necessary. She was perfect for the job.

Ern was sitting quietly and ignoring all the chatter behind him. He hadn't wanted to go back to the B&B straightaway, skulking in and having the landlady make some wise crack about him staying out all night. He reckoned that she would be busy making the bacon and eggs for the other guests in about half an hour and then he could slip in unnoticed. He looked over to his patch. A couple of people were stopping to look at it. He liked that in their race to get to their work in time, they could spare a moment to take in his drawings. He wanted to do a special picture today. He had no idea what he was going to do but he wanted to capture this calming aura of contentment and happiness that he felt. He closed his eyes and breathed in deeply. He tried to imagine Kate still lying in her bed, the duvet wrapped around her legs and her curls splayed on the pillow. He tried to remember her smell, the laughter in her voice and that amazing spark in her eyes.

Ern looked out into the street again and saw the flower seller had lifted up the shutters on her stall. She had a new delivery of tulips and he watched her carefully put them into the buckets. Then he watched her as she opened a large box and took out several cellophane wrapped bouquets of pristine white lilies. She stood up with them and put them in a tall bucket at the back. She leaned over and Ern could see she was breathing in their scent. 'Lilies,' he whispered.

Once he had drained his coffee, he stood up, thanked Tony and left for the B&B. He wanted to get his shower and collect his chalks quickly, now that he knew what he was going to draw. He whistled as he walked back down the walkway, unable to remember when he had last felt so happy.

CHAPTER TWENTY-SIX

It was an hour after Ern had left her house, before Kate began to drag herself out of bed. She couldn't come to terms with how disappointed she felt that Ern had gone without them talking - or making love again - for even a little while that morning. She hadn't wanted the wonderful feeling of the night they'd shared to go away so quickly but the moment she heard the door close behind him, she started to question whether she had done the right thing over and over again. She'd lain there, going through the words and events of the night before, trying to see how she would react if it was her best friend. What advice should she give her? But then that was impossible because nobody who looked at Ern would see the things Kate saw. She was convinced that what they shared was something special. As all the thoughts tumbled and juggled in her mind, Kate knew that she would go dizzy with it all if she didn't get moving and do something normal. She went downstairs and flicked on the kettle. She looked at all the pans and mess from the night before and went out into the garden to collect the washing up bowl. As she walked back into the kitchen, she heard her mobile phone buzz with a text from the other room. She popped a tea bag into a mug, filled it with water and then went through to the other room to get her phone. The message was from Jamie asking if 1 o'clock was okay. She glanced over to the clock on the shelf and replied, 'Meet me at greasy spoon on the prom, 1pm, xxx'. She didn't want Jamie coming here, not only because it was such a mess and he was such a damned stickler for neatness, but also because she wanted neutral territory. It was inevitable that Jamie was going to have a lot to say about Ern. He knew her too well to be impartial about the whole thing. She went back into the kitchen to do the washing up and try to figure out the best way to tell him everything.

Jamie and Kate had been best friends for many years but like all friendships, it often ebbed away for a while before some crisis or event would make them seek each other out again. Kate hoped this wouldn't be another catalyst of him ebbing away from her because whatever he said, she knew that she wanted Ern.

Whenever Kate and Jamie had a big talk planned, they would meet in the Greasy Spoon. It was actually called The Sea View Café but everyone who lived hereabouts called it by its nickname. They did every combination of breakfast fry-ups known to man. The café was dark and bleak but Kate was determined not to have Jamie bump into Ern before she had explained everything to him. It was situated down on the prom and as Kate walked around the corner to the seafront, she was blasted with strong winds that seemed unrelenting. on the edge of town and she regretted instantly not trying to find somewhere nicer. The hard wooden chairs and the coffee splats on the wall had not given her the perfect backdrop for such an emotional outpouring. She had told Jamie everything (except for the finer details of their lovemaking), ignoring his sighs and tuts, looking down into the cup she was cradling until she had finally come to an end with her story. Instinctively, Kate held her breath waiting for a response. Jamie didn't say a word. She looked over to him and saw that he was staring out of the window. The silence was uncomfortable. She let out her breath slowly and waited for him to gather his thoughts. It was several minutes until his response, which when it finally came, took her completely by surprise.

'Bloody hell, Kate! I always knew you were kooky but this is bloody insane!' From the expressionless face Jamie had as he had taken in Kate's words, he now looked furious as he spoke. He banged his coffee cup down on the table. Kate was completely taken aback by his extreme reaction. She quickly scanned the café and saw that it was full of teenagers, sipping their cappuccinos and sniggering at Jamie's outburst.

'Keep your voice down, Jamie. People are looking,' she whispered.

'I don't give a damn. I can't believe you've been so stupid,' he said but, to Kate's relief, he dropped his voice slightly. She hissed her words quietly to him, 'How nice to know that I can count on my best mate's support.' As she took a sip of her coffee, she winced at the taste. Tony's superior blend had spoilt her and this tasted like gnats piss by comparison. She tried to reason with Jamie. 'Can't you at least be considerate that finally I've found a man who makes me feel happy?'

'Happy? You're being pathetic. You've told me yourself that you were devastated by his past… and Kate, for goodness sake, he's hardly someone you'd take home to your mother now is he?' Jamie was really agitated and sounding a little spiteful. Kate immediately regretted having told him anything. She knew that Jamie would be protective of her but she hadn't expected quite this level of opposition.

'My mother wouldn't give a damn who I brought home, as long as he had all the tools intact to give her grandchildren.' Kate gave a weak smile with the words but she was under no illusion that Jamie was suddenly going to be able to laugh about things with her.

'Don't try and play this down, Kate. I was seriously hoping you were going to give me some big love story and instead you give me a bloody murder mystery starring some old drunk, with my best friend as next in his firing line.' Jamie was beginning to calm but Kate knew that he wasn't going to let it drop. She spoke slowly and deliberately to him,

'Why can't you believe that there is more to him than that? I've got to know the man inside. We all have baggage Jamie…' she looked at him sideways and held his gaze for a few moments. Their shared history had no secrets and she knew that he would not argue the point. They'd often quipped that, between the two of them, they both 'handled more baggage than Gatwick Airport'. When Jamie spoke, his voice was slightly deflated but angry all the same,

'Our baggage is purely superficial by comparison, Kate. This is big stuff. This is complicated. This is not something that anyone could just brush under the carpet.'

'This is scary enough for me, Jamie. Please try and understand.' Kate absolutely hated herself for it but she couldn't stop her eyes from welling up. Her desperate need for approval was laid bare on the table and he was making her feel stupid. She found herself wishing that Jamie would just back off and let her make her own mistakes, all the time knowing that he was just being a good friend. Jamie was staring out the window, voicing his thoughts loudly as Kate struggled with forcing back the tears

'You want me to understand?' He held up his hand and spread the fingers, pointing to them in turn as he made each point. 'An artist? Great stuff. Enigmatic? Fabulous. A bum living on the streets? Okay… well that's interesting. Then you hit me with 'Oh and by the way, he's also a child killing ex-alcoholic!' Jamie sat back in his chair and put both hands down on the tabletop in disgust. 'And you want me to be happy for you? I…' Jamie looked at her and finally saw how upset Kate was. He moved his coffee cup to the side, put his elbows on the table and put his face in his hands. Jamie forced himself to calm down before he spoke again. His voice was now quieter and more caring.

'Kate, you are the only person in the world that I have ever been able to rely on. You are perhaps the only person in this shitty world that I care about to any extent. You are my best friend…' He reached over and took her hand in his before continuing, '… my very best friend… I love you and that is why I am telling you that you deserve better than this. You deserve the very best. I will support you whatever you do but please, please just realise that his is going to cause you nothing but grief.'

'I haven't felt like this since Martin,' Kate said quietly. 'I want to be with this man so much that is physically hurts when I try to imagine never seeing him again.'

'Martin was an arsehole. You only saw him through rose-tinted glasses. We've both talked about that so many times.' Jamie let go of her hand and sat back in his chair.

'I know but you understand that I loved him. Even if I was deluding myself that he loved me back… it didn't stop me loving him. This is the first time that I've had those feelings since. You've got to understand. I'm not like you. I don't want the cheap fling. I want the real thing, Jamie.' Kate immediately regretted her words. Any other time, Jamie would have been happy to joke about his easygoing attitude to relationships but they both knew that he wanted more too. Jamie had just found it easier to believe that he would never find it and that was why he hid behind a façade of easy come, easy go.

Jamie hunched up and put his face down to the table. He spoke without looking at her. 'You pick up lame puppies, take them home and they just reward you by pissing on your carpet and chewing on your furniture, you've got to…' Kate began to talk over him, 'Cut out the crappy metaphors, Jamie. I'm not in the mood.' He looked up at her and she threw him an icy glare. She was angry at having to justify herself so much but at the same time she did not want this to escalate into a full blown row. She picked up her handbag and started throwing in her phone and purse from the table. Jamie continued talking…

'Start this new job on Monday. Meet new people. Get on with this next stage, without this guy giving you a head-fuck. Just go easy on yourself… please Kate.'

'I'm going,' she replied.

'No, Kate. Listen…' Jamie reached out and grabbed her arm. Kate shook it away from him.

'No, Jamie. I've heard your opinion. I'm going and I'll call you tomorrow.' As she stood up to leave, Jamie stood up too. They looked at each other and finally Kate put her arms around his waist and hugged him. 'Jamie, I don't want to fight with you. Please just be my friend.' She spoke into his chest and gave him a gentle squeeze.

'I'll always be your friend,' Jamie said, kissing her hair. 'That will never change and that is why I will never stop wanting the best for you.'

Kate pulled away and walked out the café, without responding. As she passed the window, she looked in at Jamie. He waved his hand with a sad smile on his face. Kate waved back and carried on down the street, fighting back the tears again.

CHAPTER TWENTY-SEVEN

Ern kept glancing over his shoulder all the while he worked. He kept hoping that he would see Kate walking along and up to him, with a big smile on her face. A couple of times, he thought he had seen her approaching and a tingle of excitement had run through his hands but each time he had been wrong. As lunchtime came and went, he began to accept that she might not come to see him today. He looked down at the picture which he had just completed. The white lily was in full bloom with its petals spread out to fill most of the slab. It was shaded with the subtlest variations of cream to give each petal depth on the tips and the shading increased as they expanded, reaching down to the stem. The stamen were a dazzling gold and, for the close observer, Ern had applied his trickery. Each one of the pollen clusters was shaped to depict a resting butterfly, with their filigree wings almost closed. In the very centre of the lily there were the shapes of two people, which were tiny in comparison to the rest of the picture. Neither figure had a discernible gender as their bodies were so closely entwined they had become one. Ern took three different shades of green pastels out of his tin and started to work on the stub of stem that could just be seen between the two bottom petals. He extended it out in tendrils, separating as they went down and along to each corner at the bottom of the slab. Each tendril became swollen and morphed at the end into a screaming, tortured face. Once he was satisfied that he could do no more, he put all the pastels back in his tin and began to tape down the plastic.

Ern leaned over and dragged his hat over to him. He was pleasantly

161

surprised to see it had been a good day and many people had dropped coins in as an appreciation of his work. He always tried to acknowledge people with a thank you but once he got involved in drawing, he would often enter his own bubble which nothing and no-one could penetrate. He hoped nobody had thought him rude by not thanking them personally. He tipped the coins into his hand and then poured them into his coat pocket. It was mid-afternoon and the busker had only just turned up. Ern went over to him as he sat down on a bench and took his clarinet out of its case.

'Hey man,' Ern said, slapping him on the shoulder and sitting down next to him. 'You're late today. I didn't see you at breakfast in the B&B either.'

'Yeah, I had a big night,' the busker said. 'I've been seeing the barmaid from the pub over there.' He nodded his head in the direction of the old building Ern had tried to avoid looking too closely at. 'She's agreed to come down to Cornwall with me when I leave next week. It's going to be a blast.' Ern looked at the young lad's grin and smiled back.

'Ah, I'm pleased for you,' Ern said. 'If only everyone's love life could be so uncomplicated.'

'Ern, sometimes you've just gotta grab it and go with it, you know?'

Ern nodded and then replied, 'and sometimes you've got to know when to leave it well alone.'

Luke raised his eyebrows as he looked at Ern's face. 'You sound down, Ern. You want to come for a drink tonight? I said I'd pop in as Steph's doing a shift.'

Ern hadn't been into a pub since he'd stopped drinking. There'd been many times when he'd been around drink but not yet in any kind of bar. He hesitated before saying, 'That would be good. You want a coffee for now?'

'Hey, thanks that would be great. I'm going to try and earn some cash so I can get a round in tonight,' Luke said, standing up and playing through the notes on his clarinet to warm up.

'You're not going to earn much sitting around here,' Ern teased him. He stood up, slapped him lightly on the back and said, 'Give them some jazz. That always gets the feel good vote, which should bring the cash rolling in.'

Luke winked at him and began to play. Ern walked along the walkway and pushed open the door of Tony's. As he stepped into the

162

warmth, he saw Tony and the woman who had been working in there earlier, tentatively dancing through the tables, counting 1-2-3, 1-2-3. Ern leant up against the doorframe and watched them with a smile on his face. He thought about how he'd like to take Kate dancing one day. He could imagine her laughing as he spun her around, wincing as he treads on her toes. Ern chuckled quietly. As Tony whirled Liza round and swooped her into a dip, she exploded into giggles. Ern joined in her laughter which made Tony finally him notice standing there.

'Dammit, man!' Tony said with a laugh. 'That's the second time I've been caught dancing today!'

'You do it very well,' Ern said. 'This place would be full if everyone knew there was a rendition of Come Dancing going on.' Tony walked back behind the bar looking flustered and Liza dusted down her apron still unable to stop her giggles.

'What can I get for you, Ern?' Tony said.

'Two lattes, please Tony,' Ern replied, digging into his pocket for a handful of change. 'So it looks like it's all working out with you getting an assistant?'

Tony grinned back at him. 'Yep. I reckon it was a very good decision.'

Ern dropped the money on the counter, gave Tony a thumbs up sign and left the café with his coffees. He walked straight over the walkway to the Bank. He placed the cups by his feet before slotting his card into the cash dispenser. He had a momentary panic that he had forgotten his pin number, as it had been so long since he last used it, but he remembered it with the help of the pattern his fingers made as he punched it in. After delivering a coffee to the busker, he sat down by his patch, not bothering to put his hat down but making sure the 'Thank you' sign was clear for all to see. Whenever someone tried to give him some money, he waved them away and said 'It's fine. Thank you.' He sat there for a long time, enjoying the music and watching the dusk drawing in on the town. Then the office and shop workers started streaming out into the street; their heads down and tucked into their coat collars or scarves as they tried to adjust away from the artificial heat they had been blasted with all day. Ern thought about Kate many times. He reasoned that it was fine that he hadn't seen her today. After all, it was he who had written in that note that he would give her some time. His fate was in her hands. All he could do was wait.

As the busker packed his clarinet away, he shouted over to Ern, 'You still on for that drink?' Ern hated the excitement that was building in his head at the prospect of walking into the pub but was convinced he could control it. 'Yeah man. I'll just get a bite to eat and meet you over there, okay?' he replied.

'You're on,' Luke said.

Ern eased himself up and walked back towards his B&B. He ordered take-out at the Chinese takeaway he passed each morning as he made his way into town. He tucked the foil carton under his coat as he made his way up to his room, so as not to risk the landlady unleashing more rules and regulations on him. The noodles tasted good and Ern felt buoyant as he closed the heavy door of the B&B behind him and headed for the pub, with a fresh change of clothes on, just a half hour later. He looked up at the clear, starry night and wished that he had Kate's mobile phone number, just so that he could hear her voice. He really missed her voice.

Ern walked quickly to the pub and pushed the door open without giving himself time to change his mind. The familiar smell of beer and sweat hit him square between the eyes. He paused at the door and looked at the bar. The clientele were mostly office boys backslapping and raucously laughing. He could see Luke leaning against the bar, chatting to Steph. Fruit machines flirted and flashed from every corner; their jingles jarring with the juke box, which was playing some Eighties soft metal track.

Ern took a deep breath and walked to the bar. His intention was to get a drink, down it quickly and then go and join Luke, offering to get the first round in. His mouth felt dry with anticipation of that first sweet taste of whisky which he was well aware he had sworn he would never touch again. Tonight though, he wanted a drink. His mind seemed disengaged from reason. The noise around the pub was reverberating around the room and around his head. He didn't notice that he had broken out into a cold sweat.

The landlord saw him and began to walk over, eyeing him with suspicion.

'What can I get you?' the landlord asked.

Ern wanted to say 'whisky' but the word just wouldn't come. Phoebe's face flashed up in front of him. Disjointed scenes from that night all those years ago, scorched through his consciousness, forcing him to remember. Ern shook his head, trying to make it all go away. He saw Phoebe again and his eyes filled with tears. He saw the sea swelling, her teddy falling overboard, his daughter reaching, crying for her bear, him screaming at her to hold on but she wouldn't listen and then she was gone. Just gone. He tried to grab for her, losing his battle to stay upright and then there was this dull crack before blackness. All there was then was the cold of the water bringing him around and freezing all life out of him. He remembered looking around for her, screaming for her, taking in mouthfuls of salt water as he did so but Phoebe was nowhere. Just nowhere. Ern felt his stomach heave, snapping him back to the present.

'I'll say it again, shall I?' the landlord said impatiently. 'What can I get you?'

'Nothing,' Ern replied quietly. 'Absolutely nothing, thank you,' and he turned to walk away.

'Arsehole,' the landlord said, making no attempt to lower his voice.

'Yes,' thought Ern. 'I think maybe I am.'

As he walked into the blackness of the night, his hands tucked deep into his coat pockets, he went through the events of that night with a clarity that he had never allowed himself before. Ern knew now that he had intended, in his drunken idiocy, to kill both himself and Phoebe out at sea that morning. Tonight was the first night that he had accepted that was true. The realisation that his intention had been to murder Phoebe made him feel sick to the stomach. There was always stuff in the tabloids about broken hearted fathers taking the lives of their own children and he wondered whether he'd used that as some kind of justification that evening. His face pulled back into a snarl at the thought. His eyes felt as though they were burning. The anger he felt about his actions was becoming harder to control the more he remembered. He wanted to lash out at something inanimate so that the only thing to feel pain would be himself. Instead he walked hard and fast, marching along the seafront to try and place all the memories in the right order. He had been drunk but he had sobered quickly as Phoebe had been so happy. She made him play clapping games with her and sing nursery rhymes at the top of their voices. The spray of the water had cleared the fug from his brain and Phoebe had agreed that they should go and find some bacon and eggs somewhere, for their breakfast. They were heading back to shore to eat. Ern remembered now. They were laughing and Phoebe was looking over the edge of the boat saying 'Look Daddy, Look!' when the wave hit. He lunged to pick her out of the sea but the boat was turning and as he fell, something hit his head. Ern was grateful that finally he could remember. His greatest fear was that he had murdered Phoebe intentionally. Even though he was not blameless in all of this, he at least knew now that he did not kill her with his own hands. If he had been sober would he have been able to save her? The captain of the trawler that picked him up said that the surge had been intense and that I was lucky to be alive, let alone a small child. Ern would never know for sure whether he could have saved her and that was just something he would have to accept.

'I'm so sorry, Phoebe,' he whispered. 'I am so sorry.'

CHAPTER TWENTY-EIGHT

Kate had gone home and immediately changed into some pyjamas, cursing Jamie all the while. She understood that he would be concerned but she didn't think that she deserved that tirade. Even so, his words had stung badly and she had lost all confidence that she knew what she was doing. He had voiced all her worst fears and made her feel stupid for believing that it could be any different. She tucked up on the sofa with a blanket and watched mindless DIY programmes on the television, whilst sipping hot chocolate and eating half a packet of ginger nuts. Jamie had tried to call her on her mobile but each time she jabbed the divert button so that he went straight to answer phone. She didn't bother listening to his messages.

Kate fell asleep during Countdown and by the time she woke up it had got dark outside. Cat was meowing for her food and Kate's stomach was growling a macabre duet with her. She fed Cat and then opened the fridge, staring at the shelves as though a meal would magically appear but she decided there was really nothing she could cook with two strawberry yoghurts, half a cucumber and a mini bottle of champagne that someone had given to her on her birthday. She opened the freezer and it was just as bad – half a tub of ice-cream and some frozen peas.

Kate went back into the lounge and flopped on the sofa. Maybe if she went into town, she could get a takeaway? Maybe she could go into town and check out a few fast food places and suchlike until she found the right one? Maybe the right one would have Ern sitting at a table about to bite in to a hamburger? Maybe they could see each other and talk? Maybe he could prove Jamie wrong and everything would be alright?

Kate sat for a moment biting her lip like a guilty child. Then she quickly jumped up and bounded up the stairs two at a time to get changed. She picked up the first clothes she could find and slipped into them, ruffled her hair with her fingers and quickly dabbed some bronzer on her face with the hope it would help her lose the pale, sleepy look on her face. As she reached the front door, she quickly put on some of her emergency mascara, slipped on her trainers, grabbed her coat and ran out the door, slamming it shut behind her. As she waited for her bus, stamping her feet and hugging herself tightly to keep the cold at bay, she started to feel more and more guilty about not having seen Ern today. She felt awful that he might have thought she'd decided to have nothing more to do with him now that she knew the full story. Maybe he'd left town already? Kate stopped stamping and let that thought sink in. She decided that no matter what it took, she would find Ern tonight and tell him that she liked him. That she more than liked him. Or maybe she shouldn't? Perhaps she wouldn't tell him anything. Maybe she would just hold him and let him know that way how much she cared? But she had to find him. She had to.

By the time the bus arrived, Kate's face was strained with confusion and she was frantic with worry that Ern might have left town already. As she sat in the seat, with the driver throwing concerned looks her way, she willed the bus to hurry, hurry ('Get a bloody move on!') and get her into town quickly. Kate was the first to jump off the bus and she ran to the walkway, her coat flapping in the breeze. She went to his patch and looked down at his drawings. They were difficult to see as it was so dark but she knelt down and tried to see them with soft illumination that the orange streetlights cast onto each magical picture. She saw today's and smiled at the beautiful lily holding the lovers. She frowned as she looked down and saw the stem reaching out into anguished screams. She turned her head looked left and right trying to work out where Ern would go. She didn't know where he was staying and she had no idea where else to try.

At that moment, she saw the busker coming out of the pub, with his arm draped over the barmaid that Kate had chatted to from time to time when she went in there for a drink with Jamie or Beth. She ran over to them.

'I'm sorry, I'm REALLY sorry to bother you but have you seen Ern?' she asked quickly.

Luke looked at her and frowned. 'No, I'm kinda worried about him because he was due to meet us for a drink but never showed.'

Kate's eyes widened. 'He was going to meet you for a drink? In the pub?'

'Yep. I owe him a pint after all the coffees he buys me,' Luke replied.

'Do you know where he might be?' Kate asked anxiously. 'I really need to find him.'

Luke thought for a moment and then said, 'Well, I know where he's staying but…'

'Oh, tell me, please. Please tell me,' Kate said. The relief of finding some clue as to where he was had triggered tears of relief. She felt a fool sobbing in front of them but, more than that, she wanted to find Ern and as far as she was concerned that was all that mattered. 'I promise you I won't tell him you told me. I just really need to speak to him.'

Steph nudged Luke softly and said 'Go on, Luke. Ern's a big boy and she needs to speak to him. Give them a chance, yeah?'

Kate smiled at her. Luke straightened up and said, 'Okay, it's Highview B&B on the seafront. I've got a room there too. They don't allow visitors after 9pm so you'd better take my key to sneak in. The landlady is a stickler for rules.' He dug into his jeans pockets and produced a key fob that had one large and one small key with a huge plastic tag that read 'Highview, Room 8'.

'What room is Ern in?' Kate asked, taking the keys from him and wiping away the tears with her sleeve.

'He's in room 3,' Luke said. He put a hand on each of Kate's shoulders and looked her striaght in the eye. 'I know you've been seeing him a bit and I know I don't have the details but he's really a decent guy. I hope you get it sorted.'

'Me too,' Kate said, close to tears again. 'Are you going to be able to get back in tonight though if I have your keys?'

Luke looked at Steph and smiled. 'I've got a bed sorted for tonight, I think,' he said. Steph quickly chipped in with, 'Oh, go on then. But no making the toast in the morning this time, okay? You'll run the batteries out on my smoke alarm, keep burning it like you do.' Kate smiled at them, pleased at how comfortable they seemed with each other.

She walked a few steps away and then started running, shouting 'Thanks you two. See you around. Have a lovely evening. THANK YOU!'

When she reached the guest house, she was surprised at how awake it looked. She hadn't imagined that there were many tourists in the town at this time of year but all but one window seemed to be lit up. She counted the windows outside to see if she could figure out which was room number 3. Both of the windows on the second level were illuminated by the light inside but there was no movement as far as Kate could see. She walked up the five steps to the large Victorian front door and pushed the larger key into the bottom lock, turning it slowly until she heard it click.

Once Joyce was sure that all her visitors were in for the night, she had locked the front door and settled down in her small apartment on the Ground Floor. She had earlier winced at the messy, handwritten note the young busker had left, which had said that he would not be returning that evening. She had shaken her head at the unreliability of the young before writing a reply note to him which said 'As you are aware, you will still be charged for the room. I look forward to you settling your bill at the earliest opportunity,' which she slipped in the pigeon hole for his room. As she sat in front of the television, filing her nails, she watched the soap actress being interviewed on the chat show. She shook her head in disgust as she watched the actress soaking up all the compliments, giggling like a schoolgirl when Joyce was well aware she was not much younger than her. With a tut, she pressed the stand-by button on the remote control. She had hoped for silence but Bill was asleep in his armchair, mouth open, snoring softly. She pushed her foot out and nudged his legs. 'Bill! Go to bed,' she said curtly. Bill woke up and blinked heavily before closing his eyes and drifting off again.

When Joyce was satisfied that he wasn't snoring anymore, she went back to filing her nails. Tomorrow was her regular canasta morning with the other landladies in the town. Joyce knew that she was top dog amongst them all and with that came a responsibility for her to look her best. When she'd first been invited to their regular morning meetings, she had been shocked that their card game of choice was poker! She waited a few weeks before making her feelings quite clear – that poker was no game for ladies of their standing and that they should choose a more appropriate pastime. Of course none of them had known how to play canasta at first, so it had taken several weeks of tiresome tuition.

Joyce picked up the *Orange Flame* nail varnish that she had purchased earlier that day and began to brush long strokes onto her nails. Joyce knew that the colour was a perfect compliment to her white slacks and the turquoise jacket that she intended to wear. There was no excuse for sloppiness and she had to set an example. She had made an appointment at the hairdressers for nine o'clock in the morning, so Bill would have to do the breakfast sitting tomorrow. She looked over to Bill and shook her head. As much as it pained Joyce to leave Bill in charge of anything, sometimes needs must. She had been trying to get Bill to understand that she needed more than this. She wanted a small hotel in Spain, preferably somewhere upmarket like Alicante, where the clientele would dress for dinner. Maybe then they could host entertainment evenings with stars such as Leo Sayer or Jimmy Tarbuck. That was the sort of life she was meant to have. Not some kind of doss house for every ne'er-do-well who happened to be in need of a bed for the night. She spread her fingers over her knees and waited for them to dry.

She went over the other things she would get Bill to see to in the morning. There was the salesman in number 5. She was certain that he had been watching porn because she could hear all manner of strange noises as she went past his room earlier that evening. She had thought she had blocked all the porn channels on the small portables that were in each room but there were so many new cable channels it was difficult to keep up. Then there was the couple in number 7. All day, both today and yesterday, they had stayed in bed and kept the 'Do not disturb' sign on the door. It wasn't natural to Joyce's way of thinking. Also, from a logical point of view, it must mean that they had food in there, which was strictly against house rules. Bill would have to sort that out too. She was just remembering that he should also take a look at the toilet in number 6, when she heard the front door click. She jumped to her feet, blowing on her nails as she did so and headed for the door. No-one got past Joyce at this time of evening without her knowing about it.

Kate was only three steps up the flight of stairs when the ground floor door opened and Joyce flew out.
'Stop!' Joyce shouted. 'Who are you?'
Kate turned around and faced her, embarrassed to have been caught. 'I'm Kate. I'm… uhm… staying in room 8.' Kate couldn't think of anything else to say.
'You are not in room 8. That young busker chappie is staying in Room 8 and he told me he wasn't coming back this evening.' Joyce said, crossing her arms under her ample bosom.
'Yes,' said Kate, pointing her finger in the air in agreement. 'He's my brother.'
'You don't look like him,' the woman said, eyeing her with suspicion.
'No.' Kate tried to think quickly. 'Half-brother! He's my half-brother on my mother's side but we share the same aunties and nephews and stuff.' Kate tried not to let on that she'd just confused herself by that sudden invention of a family tree.
'Well, that's not acceptable. There are fire regulations and I need a full list of all patrons before I can allow you to stay. Also, there will be an extra charge,' Joyce said with a clipped voice.
'Why will there be an extra charge?' said Kate, looking confused.
'Administration,' The woman said bluntly. 'Now come and sign the guest book.'
Kate slowly stepped back down the stairs and looked at the big book that was lying open on the desk. She quickly tried to see if she could see the busker's name but there was only one name on the page and that seemed to be a woman. Kate picked up the pen and scrawled an indecipherable squiggle.
'What on earth does that say?' Joyce asked, tipping her glass up on her nose to take a closer look.
'It's my name,' said Kate with a cheesy grin, hoping that her sweetest smile might convince this amateur Miss Marple.
'Well then now I am sure you are brother and sister as you both have such abominable handwriting. Take this copy of the house rules and

we shall expect you for breakfast no later than half past eight tomorrow morning, is that understood?'

Kate had an urge to curtsey and say 'Yes ma'am' but instead she just nodded her head and started walking back up the stairs.

'Wait a minute!' Joyce shouted to her. Kate turned around slowly. 'Yes?'

'No checking the more dubious cable channels on your tv, do you understand? I will not have porn in my abode. Also, remember what I said about breakfast. We will not pander to latecomers and there's no discount for you skinny things who like to starve yourselves instead of eating good, wholesome food.'

Kate stifled a giggle. 'Oh yes, absolutely. And absolutely, positively no porn. I promise,' she said with an angelic smile. 'And 8 o'clock. No problem.'

'Very well,' Joyce said. 'Off you go.'

Kate found the door to number three on the second landing. She knocked but there was no reply. She tried again and finally she heard a key turn on the other side. Ern opened the door and saw Kate standing there. As she flung her arms around him, he buried his face in her hair and held her tight.

They didn't say a word to each other. They swayed into the room until the door could be closed behind them. Then they lay down on the bed and enjoyed being so close, kissing each time one of them released their hold a little.

Ern looked at Kate's face in the half-light, kissing her eyelids and her cheeks, ignoring her giggle as he kissed her nose and then finally her lips, which parted slightly as his lips met hers.

They made slow, quiet love with a sweet tenderness that there had not been the night before. As Kate lay in his arms listening to his breaths as he drifted into sleep, she didn't know whether to laugh or cry at the intensity of feeling she had just experienced. She opened her eyes and looked across at Ern's belongings that were neatly piled in his open suitcase on the chair. She could see that he had brought few clothes with him. At the foot of the chair was his tin of pastels and behind were several boxes of new chalks, stacked up and waiting to be used. She shifted her head slightly and looked at the photo that was propped up on the dressing table. She knew it must be Phoebe. The little girl had the same cupid's bow lips and twinkle in her eye that her dad had. She was grinning a cheeky smile and looking directly in to the camera. Kate smiled sadly back at her. Ern had plugged his mobile phone in to charge and Kate could see that a green light was blinking with unread messages. She wondered who might be calling him and whether they knew where he was.

Ern untangled his legs from hers and turned over towards Kate. She watched him open his eyes and look at her. They both smiled and Ern closed his eyes again.

'Are you not going to sleep?' he asked.

Kate spoke in a serious voice. 'I don't think I can. I'm racked with guilt because I promised the landlady no porn and I feel like I've betrayed her trust.' Ern chuckled and squeezed her tight.

'That wasn't porn,' he said. 'That was all perfectly natural and right.'

'It was, wasn't it,' she replied quietly. 'We're just right.'

'Yep,' Ern said, still with his eyes closed.

Kate forced herself to keep quiet. She wanted to know where they go from here. She wanted to know what his plans were and whether she was involved in any of them. She told herself that there was plenty of time for answers. Plenty of time.

CHAPTER TWENTY-NINE

The next morning, Kate woke up only to find Ern had left already. There was a note on the pillow, which simply read

Good morning, my darling.
You are amazing.
See you later ok? Xxx

Kate looked over to the bedside table and smiled when she saw that he'd made her a cup of tea before he left. She winced when she tasted it, the long-life milk having given it a stale, creamy taste. She slid her feet from under the sheets and sat up, hugging them to her. She picked up her clothes from the floor and dumped them on the bed beside her, glancing around the room as she did so. The photo of Phoebe had gone, as had Ern's mobile phone and his tin of pastels. Some of the new boxes stacked behind had been opened and their discarded wrappers lay on the floor. Kate let go of the sheet and padded over to the en-suite shower room, which was separated from the room with a sliding door.

On the sink there was only a tube of toothpaste, his toothbrush, a razor and some soap. Kate swished back the shower curtain and saw that there was another tiny bar of soap lying in the dish under the tap. She turned the taps and closed the curtain again, padding back into the bedroom to give the water a chance to warm up. She went over to his clothes, picked up one of his sweaters and hugged it to her, burying her face in the soft wool and breathing in the woody aroma it had captured from his roll-ups. She folded it back up neatly and went to the bathroom where the steam on the mirror told her that the water was now running hot. She stepped in, turned her back to the shower head and let the warm water soak her hair before she moved her body under the water so it would warm her skin. She took the tiny bar of soap and began to sing her favourite shower song at the top of her voice -Doris Day's classic 'Secret Love.'

Just as she 'told the golden daffodil' there was a sharp rap on the door. Kate closed her mouth tight and listened.

'Mr. Malley?' Kate recognised the voice of the landlady. 'Mr. Malley, would you please open the door now!'

Kate clamped both hands over her mouth to stop her giggles being heard. She thought about dropping her voice and pretending to be Ern with a cold or something but knew there was no way she would get away with it.

'Mr. Malley, or whoever you may be, we shall have words when you come down for breakfast.' Kate turned the water off when she was sure that the woman had gone away. She stepped out the shower and grabbed a towel from the handrail. She wrapped it around her body and went back into the bedroom. After she had got dressed, she made the bed and opened the door an inch or two, so that she could check if anyone was in the hallway. The coast was clear so she tiptoed out, clicked the door closed behind her and tiptoed down the stairs. As she passed the dining room, she heard the landlady loudly going through a 'to do' list with military precision. She quietly pushed down the handle of the front door but as she opened it, it made an almighty squeak. Kate heard the landlady say, 'And for goodness sake, make sure you oil the hinges on that door!' as Kate closed the door quickly and ran down the steps as fast as she could.

Ern looked out of Tony's spare bedroom window. The walkway looked different from up here. He could see the same people walking and the same people selling their wares but somehow their personalities were down on the ground and unable to reach him. He turned back to the board and the mocha brown paper he had carefully attached to it. He already knew exactly how he was going to portray Tony's coffee shop and it would be a tribute to Kate's picture on a smaller scale. He had realised yesterday that Kate's picture was missing one vital component that he would ensure was depicted clearly

176

in his. He had filled his tin with every shade of brown and beige imaginable. There were just a few other colours, one of which was the cobalt blue that Kate had bought him and one which was bright scarlet red.

He felt his mouth go dry at the anticipation of starting the new project. Ern had often thought that the flurry of doubt and expectation he felt when he went to start a new picture must be very similar to stage fright. He had one chance to make it work because any reworks had a tendency to make the image stale.

He sat down on the edge of the bed and looked at the blank sheet, imagining where everything would be placed and how deep he wanted the colour to penetrate into each section. As he pictured the image in his mind, it started to evolve and flow into other images; his thoughts and emotions were becoming part of the subject. Ern slowly stood up and looked out of the window again. He looked down to his patch and decided that all his work there was now complete. This picture would be the transition from what was out there to where he would start next. He nodded his head slowly, recognising what it was that he had to do. He pushed away his melancholy mood, picked up his chalk and began to draw.

Kate was pleased she'd gone home to change her clothes. Cat had been waiting at the door as she walked in. Kate had fed her and then had started to do some more on her painting. She hoped that this wonderful feeling inside of her would transport itself onto the canvas. She honestly couldn't remember the last time she felt this happy. After a few hours, she had stood back and looked at her progress. Kate felt tingles over her skin as she looked at it. It might have been the best thing she had ever created and she knew that much of that was due to Ern's influence. She made herself a coffee and sat cross-legged looking at the painting while she drank. Every now and then, she would pick up a brush and make a slight adjustment but mostly she just sat, looking at each little detail and checking that she had not missed anything or anyone out.

Kate decided that she would go and tidy her bedroom and then find something fabulous to wear. She put some Seventies disco on her stereo and danced around in her underwear, singing along at the top of her voice, picking up bits and pieces as she went and creating neat piles of clothes in the wardrobe and replacing all the books on the shelves. She changed her sheets and then lined up all the bottles and tubs on the dressing table so that it looked as presentable (and well stocked) as any counter in a department store. Kate dabbled with the thought that maybe she should try and change into Mrs Clean permanently but decided that then these moments of perfection wouldn't seem so perfect any more so it was best to stay just the way she was. Christmas every day would be no fun after a while.

Kate went to her wardrobe and chose her favourite jeans. She then decided that today was finally the day she would wear the red lambswool sweater that had been waiting, with its tags on, for a very special occasion. As she looked at her reflection in the mirror, she winked at herself and said 'Good job!', before running down the stairs, grabbing her keys and coat, blowing a kiss to Cat who was sitting on the stairs and slamming the door behind her.

As Kate stepped off the bus into the walkway, she was full of excitement and wanting to tell Ern about her picture. She walked briskly along, throwing a huge grin at the busker as he played. Kate sidled up to him and dropped the room key into his pocket with a whispered 'Thanks.' He winked at her without dropping a single note of the tune he was playing. Kate walked through a huddle of people to Ern's patch. She stopped abruptly when she realised he wasn't there. She ran over and looked down at Ern's pictures, realising that he hadn't drawn anything today.

Determined not to panic again, she walked over to Tony's and pushed open the door. The café was full and the customers' chatter reverberated around the room, overwhelming the music that Kate could only just hear playing in the background. She squeezed between several chairs to make her way to the bar. Tony wasn't in his usual place behind the bar, so Kate got her money out and tapped it impatiently on the wood, waiting for him to arrive. Liza walked out from the back room, drying her hands on a tea-towel.

'Hello. What can I get you?' Liza asked, smiling at Kate.

Up until this point, Kate had managed to repress all her anxiety about Ern not being there but seeing Liza instead of her good friend Tony was the straw that broke the camel's back. 'PLEASE could you just tell me where Tony is?' Kate said loudly. Her outburst was overheard by everyone in the café and they all turned to look at her.

Kate quickly apologised, 'I'm sorry,' she said to Liza and then turning around, 'I'm sorry' she said to everyone in the coffee shop before turning back to Liza and saying, 'I'm sorry. I'm sorry. I'm *really* sorry. I just wanted something to be the way it always is and Ern's not outside and then suddenly there's you and not Tony.'

Liza smiled at her and said, 'It's okay. Tony's out the back sorting out some more sanwiches. He's taken me on to help him out for a few hours a day, that's all. You want me to get him for you?'

Kate felt extremely embarrassed. She knew she was behaving like a spoilt child and the last thing she wanted was Tony giving her that friendly smile when she'd just made a complete idiot of herself. 'No, no. Don't bother him. Tell him Kate says hi, okay?' and with that Kate turned, made her way back through the crowded café and walked out into the street.

She pushed her hands into the pockets of her coat and walked down to the beach, with her head down, wondering why the hell everything had to be so damned confusing.

Ern was really pleased with how his picture had gone. It was Tony's coffee bar but it could easily have been the interior of a dark jazz bar with its muted tones and hazy atmosphere. Tony was dancing with Liza between the tables. Her back was arched away from him which allowed both of them to be shown smiling, enjoying their dance. The coffee cups and machine were at the back of the shop, with a mirror behind reflecting the scene in slightly lighter hues and softer lines. The bookcase was stacked with books of every size and colour. Sprites were reclining on top of some of the books, legs dangling, enjoying the spectacle of the two dancing in the centre. Faceless people were hinted at on the surrounding tables but with each pair or group, their hands were finely drawn so that you could see some were holding hands, others had clenched fists and a few held out their hands as though imploring for something. But over by the window was the main focus, as it was the only thing not to be drawn in shades of brown. A young woman was sitting with her back to the rest of the café, her curls cascading down her shoulders and over the back of the chair. She was dressed in a bright, cobalt blue sweater with faded blue jeans and red sneakers with polka dots on. The girl was gazing out of the window and over her shoulder a sketch pad rested on her lap. One of her hands was holding a pencil and the other was holding the top of the pad. In front of her, there was a steaming cup of cappuccino. Underneath her chair, a large tabby cat was curled up fast asleep. Ern took out a charcoal pencil from his tin and sharpened it with his pen knife, to an extremely sharp point in order to create the clearest lines. He went close to the drawing, being careful not to rest his hand against the chalk in case it smudged and carefully wrote some words onto the girl's sketchpad. He chuckled and said 'There you go!'

Once he was sure he had finished, he scrawled his name in the bottom right-hand corner, picked up his coat from the bed and found the fixative spray. He sprayed on the first light coat, being careful to use wide sweeping motions. The chemical smell immediately filled the room and even though he always found the pear-like aroma pleasing, he hurried over to open the window wide so the smell wouldn't invade the whole of Tony's flat. As he looked through the window and down to the street, he saw Kate walking away. Even though he had acknowledged earlier that people's emotions seemed to be unable to reach him up there, he could tell immediately that Kate was sad by the slow way she walked. All her usual bounce had gone and her shoulders were rounded forward. He watched to see which direction she would take and saw that she was heading for the beach.

Ern knew it wasn't going to be an easy conversation but she deserved to know exactly what he had planned. He sprayed another coat of fixative onto his picture, grabbed his coat and left the room, shutting the door firmly behind him.

CHAPTER THIRTY

Kate looked out to the horizon and saw dark grey clouds rolling in from the East. The beach was still bathed in sunshine but Kate knew it would be quickly fading as the sun started its slow journey over to the West. She knew it would soon be dusk and she would have the spectacular show of the starlings all coming in to roost on the pier. The first time she had seen them perform their amazing ballet in the air, she could hardly believe it was true. They would swoop and swirl above the wooden structure in unison before some instinct would make them turn and fold in on themselves creating a tea-leaf stirring in the sky. Again and again they would turn until finally, one by one, they would come to rest on the dome of the old theatre right at the end of the pier. Kate often wondered whether people had lost that instinct to flow together so naturally. Maybe their supposed intelligence had actually crippled their ability to consider the whole, rather than just themselves.

She pulled her coat tighter around her, tucking her hands away and digging her chin into the upturned collar.

Kate heard the pebbles crunch behind her and she rested her head on her knees so that her hair hid every part of her face. She didn't want anyone to be on her beach. She wanted to be alone. As the footsteps got closer, she felt her skin chill. She knew it was Ern without even having to look up.

'Hello Kate,' he said from behind her.

'Hello,' she said, still with her head buried. She heard him sit down next to her and then felt him nudge her knee.

'Here,' he said. 'I brought you a coffee.'

She lifted her head and took the cup from him without looking at his face. 'Thank you,' she whispered.

Kate lifted her head and looked out to sea. The sun was sinking rapidly and the sea was almost cut in half with the sparkling water meeting a dark, grey blanket reflection of the thunderous clouds that were rolling in rapidly from the West.

'I'm going home Kate,' Ern said. 'I'm sorry.' Kate felt like her heart had stopped beating for a moment. She breathed out slowly.

'Don't keep apologising,' Kate said quietly, flipping the lid off her cup and holding it close to her face so that the steam might warm her cheeks. 'I had a feeling that was what was coming, or had come already, when I couldn't find you. '

'It was always going to happen eventually,' said Ern. 'If I hadn't have met you, this life I've put myself in to might have gone on for months or years. I need to get a grip now and go and sort everything out. Get to a life I want to be living and that someone might want to share with me.'

Kate took a sip of her drink and thought carefully about her words. 'I was so excited about seeing you today. When I couldn't find you there was just this drum roll of disappointment in my head.' He put his arm around her and shuffled in closer to her. She rested her head on his shoulder. 'Why can't I choose anyone normal Ern?'

'Because *you* are special Kate.' Ern pushed one of his hands between her crossed arms and held her own hand in his. His cold fingers soon warmed with Kate's touch. 'I'm only doing this because of you. I can never be this person and make you happy. You deserve more.'

'What if I don't want more?' Kate asked, not really believing the question herself. She knew that Ern deserved better than her playing devil's advocate.

'I have had to make a decision. It would be easy for me to pretend that I can keep going on like this but that's not going to move me forward.' Ern put his forehead against Kate's arm so that they were both huddled together. 'It'll hold other people back to. I don't want to hold them back.'

'By that I suppose you mean me?' she asked quietly.

Ern nodded and replied, 'You and my sister, as well as the rest of my family. I know where to place all the memories now. I know that I have to accept what happened and try to make amends.'

'How?' Kate asked, without any hint of accusation.

'By moving on and getting things straight. I've got to start standing on my own two feet and prove myself, I suppose.' Ern thought about his own words for a while. He desperately wanted Kate to realise that this was the only thing that could happen. 'I need to make sure that I never even come close to going down that road again.'

'I understand. Of course I understand but….' Her words were left trailing in the air. She wanted to scream 'what about us?' but kept biting back the words. Ern kept talking and she listened carefully.
'If I stay here and try to sort things out, it will be like a get out of jail free card,' he said. 'The time I've spent with you, I can honestly, honestly say that it has been one of the most wonderful experiences of my life. But it seems unreal. I feel like I don't deserve it… or you. I need to go and make myself someone who deserves to be this happy.'

'What makes you think you don't deserve it?' Kate said, trying to keep her voice calm. 'What makes you think I don't deserve it? Why does male pride have to be so bloody obstructive?'

Ern didn't answer. They sat quietly and he whispered 'I'm sorry,' again. Kate turned her head and kissed him. They held each other for a long time, enjoying the closeness.

'I think I've got you into trouble with your landlady,' she said quietly.

'Oh, that's not very difficult,' Ern said 'What did you do?'

'I was singing Doris Day in the shower. I think she gathered that either you've had a surgical procedure or you had a woman in there,' Kate smiled and rolled her eyes up to the sky, desperately trying not to let herself be too miserable for him. She wanted him to remember her happy.

Ern chuckled and said, 'Whoops. I'll have to go in speaking in my best squeaky voice.'

Kate bumped against him whilst saying, 'Oy! I have not got a squeaky voice!'

'No, you have a beautiful voice,' Ern said, bumping her back.

Ern placed his finger under Kate's chin and turned her to face him. He looked at her for a moment and then kissed her softly.

'May I take you for dinner?' he asked.

Kate looked at him for a long time and made the decision that she was going to make the most of every last hour that they spent together. 'That would be lovely,' she replied.

Ern grinned and said, 'You look gorgeous but I would like to go home and get cleaned up. Would that be okay?'

Kate nodded and replied, 'Of course.'

Ern watched a seagull flying in from the shore, squawking to its mate. He followed its path with his eyes, as it flew over to an old couple sitting in deckchairs at the side of the promenade. The old woman was throwing bread to an ever increasing throng of gulls, their excited gabble sounding loud and aggressive considering their serene surrounds.

He looked at Kate and then back out to the sea. 'I'll be leaving in the morning,' he said quietly. 'I'm not very good at goodbyes.'

'Me neither,' said Kate sadly. She pointed her finger in the air and nodded her head once as she decided, 'We won't say it okay? We'll just know it and not bother saying it.'

Ern nodded in agreement and said, 'I'll see you later.' He kissed the top of her head as he stood up. 'Shall I meet you at Tony's and then we'll go on somewhere from there?'

Kate looked up at him and smiled. 'Perfect,' she said. As she heard him walk away from her, she buried her head again and allowed a few tears to finally run down her cheeks.

Edie buttoned up the top button on her coat and brushed off the stray breadcrumbs that were on her gloves. She'd only saved a few scraps for the gulls as she knew well that arriving on the seafront with a full bag of bread just led to the birds fighting and pooping all around her. The birds in the park had therefore eaten the lions share and it had also given her and Charley a chance to see if the bulbs that the council planted there each year were coming up yet. They had both been pleased to see that snowdrops were beginning to poke through. She looked over to Charley having a cat-nap; his flat cap had slipped over his forehead a little, making him look drunk. She threw the last of her stale bread to the seagulls and shook the bag so that all the crumbs fell out. Charley had been slightly miffed that she had chosen to give the bread to the gulls, as bread pudding was his favourite and he had argued vehemently that he should take precedence 'over some bloody birds' once he had seen her walk out the door with the bag in her hand. Edie had teased him that he had eaten quite enough bread pudding, which was why she had found it necessary to move the buttons over on all his trousers. Poor old Charley had taken it to heart though, so she'd put her arms around his middle and given him a little squeeze with the reassurance that there was just 'more of you to cuddle, my love.'

They often came down to the seafront in the afternoon. It was their way of keeping moving and feeling part of the world. She put her hand on his leg and shook him gently awake.

'It's getting chilly, Charley,' she said. 'We should be getting on home.'

'It is. Reckon we're going to get some rain before the week's out but it will do the potatoes some good. They've been suffering on the allotment, with all this dry weather.'

Edie nodded and made a mental note to pick up some King Edwards from the supermarket next time she went there. Charley tried hard with the allotment but he never noticed when she found it necessary to make the odd substitution now and again. She nudged him and said, 'See that young couple over there Charley?' Edie pointed over to Kate and Ern sitting on the pebbles. They remind me of us. You were always scruffy too.'

'Till you got your mitts on me,' Charley chuckled. 'It took me a while to get used to feeling like I was dressed in my Sunday best every bloomin' day.'

'Sunday best indeed,' Edie tutted and then patted his knee. 'Well someone had to take you on, love.'

Charles waggled his gloved hand towards Kate and Ern and said, 'We would never have done that in public,' and Edie turned her head to see the couple kissing, their arms wrapped around each other.

'Don't be such an old fuddy-duddy. Of course we did that in public. You're just all screwed up with your memory. Don't you remember that night under the pier... just before you left for National Service?'

Charles' face lit up into a grin, 'Ah, that was a good night, Edie,' Charley winked at her and she softly giggled. 'I remember all the starfish clinging to the supports of the pier. Thousands there were... thousands.'

You said it was the next best thing to making love under the stars, Edie said rolling her eyes skyward before she giggled again.

They sat in quiet contemplation for a few more minutes; Charley's mind filled with the memory of that night under the pier whilst Edie contemplated what to cook for their tea.

'Shall we go love?' she said, looking up at the clouds. 'I don't want it to start raining on us.'

'Okey dokey. Help me out of this damned deckchair. My bones have given up for the day.'

Doll took his hand and they stood together, Ern groaning loudly and Edie chuckling at his overacting. They walked along the prom hand in hand; popping four coins in the deckchair attendant's tin as they went by. The pier was on their route home and Charley wolf-whistled as they went past. Edie hastily poked him in the ribs.

'Oy, you… behave,' she scolded with a smile. 'Or you won't get that little bread pudding I made for you and hid at the back of the fridge.'

Charley smiled 'Ah, you do like to make me suffer, lady,' he said with a chuckle. 'C'mon then, my darling. I might get home in time for the football results.'

Kate pushed open the door of Tony's coffee shop and as soon as she saw Liza, she remembered her embarrassing outburst earlier. The café was empty now and Liza was clearing the tables. Kate went up to her and started to help loading up the trays. Liza flashed her a smile.

'I'm so sorry about earlier,' Kate said. 'I just got myself all worked up.'

'That's okay. We all have bad days,' Liza replied. She wiped her hand on her apron and offered it to Kate. 'My name's Liza. Pleased to meet you.'

Kate shook her hand and smiled. 'I'm Kate. I'm the local idiot who's addicted to Tony's coffee and has a tendency for embarrassing outbursts.'

Liza laughed and said, 'What can I get you?'

'A cappuccino would be lovely when you have time,' Kate said.

Liza picked up the tray and went behind the bar. Kate took a seat by the window and hugged her coat around her. Even though it was warm in the café, she still felt chilled to the bone. She didn't want to say goodbye to Ern but she knew that there was no point trying to stop him. She didn't want him feeling obliged and she also didn't want him ever to resent her. They both deserved to walk away from this with good memories. She got her small mirror out of her handbag and checked that her mascara hadn't run when she'd cried. She didn't want

186

Ern to know how upset she was. She made sure that she flashed herself a smile in the mirror before she closed it.

Kate saw some people stop and look at Ern's work out in the walkway. The woman knelt down and was touching the plastic. Kate felt a sudden panic that she should jump up to go and tell them to be careful, don't disturb the chalks but she told herself not to be so silly and decided she had to let it go. She'd already made enough of a fool of herself for one day.

'He-ey, Kate!' Tony's voice thundered towards her and she looked up at him with a smile.

'Hi, Tony,' she said. 'I thought you'd gone and retired to that villa you keep talking about.'

'Not yet, my friend,' Tony replied with a grin. He sat down in the seat opposite her and leant forward, resting his arms on his knees. 'Are you okay? You want to talk?'

'No, Tony. I don't want to talk,' she said. 'I wouldn't even know where to start.'

'Well, you could start by telling me you're okay,' he said. Kate looked at his concerned face and smiled.

'I'm okay. I really am. It's been an amazing week,' she said, turning her head to look out of the window again. The couple that had been looking at Ern's art had moved on and the walkway seemed to be completely deserted. Tony interrupted her thoughts.

'Ern's done me a picture. I had a sneaky look at it upstairs. It's fantastic!' he said. 'I'm looking forward to getting yours in here and then I can put them both up.'

'I shouldn't think mine's going to be a patch on Ern's,' Kate said. She had genuinely concerns that her efforts would look simplistic and naïve compared to Ern's amazing work which captured so much of his subject's feeling and emotions with apparent effortless ease.

'Well that's not what he said,' Tony replied quickly. 'Singin' your praises, he was. He thinks a lot of you, Kate.' Tony nodded as he said the last words as if to emphasis the truth in them.

'I think a lot of him too,' Kate said quietly. 'An awful lot.' She looked back to Tony and smiled. Liza came over and put the coffee down on the table in front of Kate. Kate thanked her and winked agreement at Tony as he said 'I'd best go and help clear up.'

Kate picked up the mug and closed her eyes as the warmth radiated from the china cup into her hands. She reminisced about the first time

187

she met Ern and every time since. She suddenly realised that she had barely given a second thought to her new job, but then told herself that she could do that once Ern had gone. For now, it was all about him and her.

The door opened behind her and she heard Tony do a loud wolf-whistle, followed by a 'Wow!'. She turned her head and saw Ern standing there in black chinos, a crisp white shirt and an extremely well cut black jacket. He looked slightly embarrassed as he walked up to Kate and kissed her on the cheek. Kate realised that her mouth was open with the shock of seeing Ern look so smart and she quickly clamped it shut again.

'Bloody hell,' she said.

'Is it alright? I mean it's not too much, is it?' Ern said, holding open his jacket and looking down at himself.

'No, no. Bloody hell no!' Kate said and stood up quickly, grabbing her bag. She looked at him and grinned. 'You scrub up rather well,' she said.

'Why thank you,' Ern replied with a chuckle. He held out the crook of his arm and said 'Shall we?' Kate slipped her arm through his and winked over to Tony. 'Yes, let's,' she said.

As they left the coffee bar, Tony shouted after them 'Have a good time you two. Oh and Kate you owe me for that coffee!'

Tony looked over to Liza who was loading the dishwasher. 'I don't know how I ever managed before you turned up, Liza,' he said.

'Oh, you would have got by,' she grinned. 'I thought you said this was only going to be a few hours a day though?'

'I kinda like having you around,' Tony said. He grinned at her and asked, 'If that's okay with you?'

Liza smiled back at him and said 'That sounds fine by me.'

As Liza wiped down the bar, Tony put on a cd before going back to clear the rest of the tables. Within a few minutes, he was humming along and swinging his hips to the music. Liza stood at the bar watching him and smiling. Tony saw her and held out his hand. 'May I have this dance madam?' he said.

Liza giggled and said, 'Go on then, but no more dips, okay? Is it a deal?'

'It's a deal,' Tony replied.

CHAPTER THIRTY-ONE

Ern shivered. 'It's cold without my coat,' he said. Kate hugged his arm tight and said 'You look gorgeous.'

'Why, thank you,' Ern said with a smile. 'Shall we eat here?' Kate looked up at the restaurant, which was lit up on the inside with candles on each table. There was just one other couple sitting at the back.

'Shall we sit in the window?' she asked.

'If that's what you would like,' Ern said and pushed the door. He held it open with his arm outstretched so that Kate could walk in first. The aroma of garlic and herbs immediately made her mouth water. They stood at the door to wait for a waiter to seat them.

A tall gangly man burst out of the swinging doors from the kitchen with such verocity that they hit the walls. The man was walking so fast that he managed to avoid them swinging back onto him as they closed again. He walked over to Kate and Ern, picked up a book from the high counter in front of the door and said, 'Names please?'

'Malley,' Ern said bluntly. The man perused his book and then said curtly, 'You do not have a reservation?' Ern shook his head and swiftly said 'No and if it's a problem we can always go somewhere else.' The waiter looked at Ern and sighed. 'No, no matter,' he said. 'Please follow me.' He started to walk off but Ern stood still.

'We would like to sit by the window, thank you,' Ern said. Kate glanced at him and noticed how much more confident he looked. The waiter turned slowly with a look of disdain on his face but as he went to speak, he saw Ern's confident expression and obviously changed his mind. He smiled a sickly smile and said, 'Of course, Sir,' swerving to the right and showing them to their table. He pulled a chair out for Kate to sit down, saying 'Madam?'. She removed her coat and passed it to him, trying to avoid giggling as she did so. Ern waited until she was seated before sitting down himself. 'Would Sir like to see the wine list?' the waiter asked. 'Yes please and we will also have a bottle of still mineral water with one glass, thank you very much.'

'Certainly Sir,' he said before scooting away. Kate looked at Ern uncertainly. She wasn't used to this new confident Ern. Ern looked at her and winked before chuckling. Kate finally allowed herself to giggle, pleased that most of her Ern was still there inside this new man sat in front of her. 'Well aren't you the assertive one!' she said, teasing him.

'I just want this night to be perfect, Kate,' Ern said, reaching out and taking her hand. Kate pushed her legs forward so that they touched Ern's legs under the table. 'It will be,' she said.

The waiter came back with the wine list and two menus tucked under his arm. He passed the wine list to Ern, who swiftly said, 'That will be for the beautiful lady opposite me.' The waiter seemed thrown for a moment but then passed it to Kate, before getting out a pad from his top pocket and unclipping a pen from his lapel. Kate didn't even bother opening it and passed it back to him saying, 'I'll just have a half bottle of your house red, please.' The waiter sighed again and put the pad back in his pocket, clipped his pen back on his lapel and then passed them each a menu. 'I shall be back to take your order,' he said, sounding so disappointed that Kate began to wonder whether she should have played along and studied the wine list before making her choice. They opened their menus and looked at the huge variety of dishes on offer.

'Do you think they do meatballs?' Ern said quietly. Kate looked at him and smiled. 'Oh, I think we can push the boat out tonight, don't you?' she said. 'Absolutely,' Ern replied.

Kate quickly looked down all the dishes and pointed out to Ern that they did do meatballs. 'Linguine con polpette,' she recited slowly. 'Gosh, that sounds so much more romantic than meatballs,' she giggled to which Ern nodded with a smile. As always, Kate checked out the dessert list before she could even consider what to have for the main course. If there was something that she simply had to have for afters, she would be frugal with her choice of meal but if there was nothing other than Tiramisu, which for no rhyme or reason she hated with a passion, then she would go for a great big steak. *Chocoholics Fix* stared back at her and she knew straight away that she had to have it. The waiter appeared at the table again, with a carafe of red wine and a glass for Kate. He poured her a small amount in the glass for her to taste it but she just said 'Oh, don't worry about that. Keep going. I'm not fussy about anything but a full glass.' He filled up her glass and with his pad at the ready, he asked, 'May I take your order?' He sighed as he said it, with what Kate sensed was a feeling of resignation. She reckoned he imagined they would order fish and chips or maybe jellied eels.

Ern said, 'I would like the Filetto Pepe Verde please… but hold the cognac sauce.' His accent and pronunciation of the Italian dish was perfect.

Kate cleared her throat, smiled brightly and said, 'I'll have the lemon chicken, please.'

'Pollo al Limone,' the waiter corrected her.

'If you prefer,' said Kate, managing to keep a straight face.

Once he'd gone, she took Ern's hand again and said, 'You know you never asked me the ten questions. I think you should ask them tonight. Not that there's much you don't know about me already.'

'Oh Kate, I think there are many wonderful things I still have to learn about you,' he said, squeezing her hand. 'Ten questions though. Hmm, that could be fun.'

'Careful now. Am I allowed to refuse to answer any?' she said.

'Absolutely not!' Ern replied with a grin. 'Tell me where you would go right now, if you could go anywhere in the world.'

Kate pretended to think seriously for a moment. 'I would go here because there's a wicked chocolatey dessert I'm looking forward to,' she said emphatically.

'Oh, that's not fair,' Ern chuckled. 'Tell me where you would go after you've eaten dessert then.'

Kate propped her chin up on her hand and gave it some thought. 'Barcelona. I went once about seven years ago and I absolutely loved it. Have you been?' Ern shook his head and replied, 'No, I haven't.'

Kate dropped her hand back down to the table and said, 'Oh for goodness sake, you would love it! The architecture is amazing and the atmosphere is amazing and the galleries are just incredible and at night there is this huge massive fountain that sings and dances and you can sit on the steps watching it drinking beer and…,' she picked up her glass and took a large sip of wine before adding, 'Ugh, it's just incredibly wonderful and amazing. All of it!'

Ern had been watching her face as she spoke. He loved the way she became so animated when she touched on a subject that excited her. 'Barcelona then. One day, I would very much like to see Barcelona with someone who could speak about it with such passion,' he said.

'I would love to take you, Ern.' Kate said, resisting the urge to ask him if that meant that she would be seeing him again. She decided it would be best to just imagine that it was just one of those things people say.

The waiter appeared with their meals. Kate thanked him and breathed in the citric aroma of her dish. She picked up her knife and fork and started to eat. Ern sat for a while still watching her and then, as he picked up his own cutlery, he asked, 'What's the thing you hate most in the world?'

Kate chewed and swallowed what was in her mouth before answering, 'Spiders.'

'Spiders? I can't imagine you being afraid of spiders. They're harmless,' he said.

'I'm not afraid of them,' Kate said with a mouthful of chicken. She swallowed and continued. 'I hate them. They're horrible and unnecessary.'

Ern smiled and said, 'But they keep all the flies at bay and make beautiful spider webs.'

'Fly paper does an adequate job of keeping flies at bay and spider webs, well, we could live without them,' Kate said, leaving no room for further argument.

'And where do spiders come on the list along with war and world poverty?,' Ern said with a chuckle.

'Oh, they're right up there,' Kate grinned back. She glanced out the window and saw Luke and Steph walking by. Luke's arm was draped over Steph's shoulders and she was hugging his waist. They looked so happy. Kate tapped Ern's leg with her foot and pointed in their direction with her fork. 'Happy endings,' she said with a smile. Ern looked at them as they went passed.

'I wish our ending could be different Kate,' he said quietly. 'You do understand though don't you?'

'Don't spoil it Ern,' Kate replied. 'I've said I understand. Let's just enjoy tonight, okay?'

'Yes,' he said and quickly stopped himself from apologising again. Kate popped some more chicken into her mouth and smiled at him.

They ate for a little while without saying any more. The waiter came back to check they were happy with their meal, to which they both nodded. He gave them a double-take as he walked away and Kate wondered whether he was secretly hoping that they were having a row. She put her knife and fork down on the plate. 'I think I'll save myself for dessert,' she said.

'I have plans, Kate.' Ern said suddenly, as though he had been storing up the words and they had just decided to gush out. 'I want to carry on with the architecture stuff for a while but also try and get together a collection of my own art to show at a gallery. Maybe I could even go back to college and get my teaching qualification and become an art teacher at some point. With that, I can go anywhere.' He looked up at her. 'They're not big ambitions, I know, but they are within my reach. If I can get my life pointed in the right direction then who knows where I can go from there.' He placed his hands in the middle of the table and Kate placed hers inside them. 'I would never ask you to wait for me and that is not what I want either…I wouldn't want that pressure on either of us.' Kate went to protest but stopped herself. She knew that promises at this stage were wrong and make everything more difficult. 'I just want you to know that I will never forget you.'

Kate swallowed hard and looked down to the table. 'Will we keep in touch Ern?'

'I tried to think about what would be best but, to be honest, I don't think I could take hearing from you and not actually being with you. I'm not sure that it wouldn't just stop both of us getting on with things.'

She took a moment to think and bit her bottom lip sharply to stop herself from crying. 'Yes, you're probably right,' she said.

'Are you ready for the dessert menu?' the waiter's voice cut through the moment. Kate closed her eyes, took a deep breath and lifted her head. 'That won't be necessary,' she said brightly. 'I would like the Chocoholics Fix please.' Ern looked at her before glancing up at the waiter. 'Make that two,' he said before looking back to Kate and smiling.

As they ate their dessert, they talked about people that Ern had met in the town and Kate filled him in on bits and bobs of local gossip. They talked about Tony and how Liza had transformed his smile into a huge Cheshire cat grin. Ern mentioned the poetry of the man who sat outside the coffee shop talking to himself. Kate agreed it was wonderful, dreamy words. They tried to imagine a past for him of travelling the world with a woman in every port until absinthe or some exotic drug had sent him into his own fantastical imagination. Ern told Kate about Annie, the flower seller, and how she lived alone. He told her how much Annie missed her children and grandchildren as they all lived so far away. Kate had nodded and said that she would maybe go and buy some more tulips, adding that maybe Annie would like to have one of Tony's coffees delivered by her now and again? Ern had smiled at Kate's good nature. 'I will always be able to picture you Kate, sitting somewhere along the walkway, chattering to someone.' Ern had stopped for a moment before adding, 'Or lying on your bed gazing adoringly at Johnny Depp.' Kate chuckled and said 'Ah, you're just jealous.'

Ern paid for the meal with a credit card, ignoring Kate's protestations about going dutch. Kate had sat back and looked at this new Ern that was just even more incredible and more wonderful than she could have believed.

They collected Kate's coat from the waiter and walked out into the icy air, which was made worse by a fierce wind that had blown up from the sea. Kate pulled Ern into a doorway with a giggle and they kissed. Ern squeezed her tight and said 'Oh Kate, I so don't want to go.'

Kate rested her head against his shoulder and slid her arms under his jacket. 'Then now is the perfect time for you to go,' she said.

Ern eased her back so that he could look in to her eyes. 'Why?' he said. Kate looked at how confused she'd made him and ran her fingers along his jaw. She put her hand behind his neck and pulled his face towards her for them to kiss. Then she moved her cheek against his and whispered in his ear. 'Because if you leave when you don't want to go, then there is always a chance that one day you will want to come back.'

Ern buried his face into her neck and kissed her lightly there. 'Wise woman, you are,' he whispered through her curls. He lifted his head and shuddered. 'Agh! It's freezing out here!'

Kate giggled and planted big warm kisses on his cheeks and a quick peck to his nose before saying, 'Then let's get a taxi.' She became more serious as she added, 'Come home with me tonight, Ern. Please?'

Ern smiled at her, took her hand and they both ran quickly to the main road, so that they could hail a taxi.

CHAPTER THIRTY-TWO

Kate heard the door click closed behind him. Right up until the last minute she had hoped that he'd stay. She sat up slowly and looked over to her cup of tea that he had just put on her bedside table along with another pink lined sheet of paper. She took the note and opened it. Tears filled her eyes as she read,

You are wonderful.
I have left something for you
at the walkway.
Goodbye my gorgeous Kate.
Xxx
p.s. I fed Cat, I can't resist her either.

Kate wiped the tears from her cheeks with the back of her hand and got out of bed quickly. She ran over to the window and opened the curtains to try and see him. She saw the tail-lights on a taxi blink as it turned the corner at the end of her road and disappeared from view.

She went back to bed and pulled her knees up to her chest, trying desperately to stop herself from calling a taxi and chasing after him. They hadn't talked much the night before. They'd got back to Kate's house and stumbled through the door giggling with Cat eyeing them with disapproval from her viewpoint on the stairs. Kate had made tea and they'd curled together on her sofa, listening to music and talking about childhood memories, most embarrassing moments and other such snippets of their lives that drew them closer into each other. When Ern had seen Kate's tidy bedroom he had teased her gently, telling her that her mother would be so proud and that Johnny must be pleased with his new neat surroundings. They had drifted in and out of sleep all night; kissing and holding each other, making love and enjoying the closeness that they might never share again.

Kate picked up the mug from the bedside table and took a sip of the warm tea. She looked over to the window and saw that the clouds were heavy and grey, moving across her window quickly as they were driven by the fierce wind. She looked down to her dressing table and saw that her mobile phone was blinking with a new message. The thought that Ern had maybe taken her number from the phone before he left, made her jump out of bed again quickly and grab the phone, jabbing the 'read message' button as she did so. It was a message from Jamie, which simply said 'I'm sorry X Call me X'

Kate pressed 'call sender' and listened to the ringing tone beep loudly in her ear. As soon as she heard Jamie's voice pick up and say 'Kate! How are you?' she burst into tears again. Jamie hushed her and gently coaxed her into telling him what was wrong. 'C'mon Kate, tell me what's happened and then I can help.'

'I love him Jamie but he's gone. I let him go. I know it was the right thing to do.' She put her hands against her forehead as if to force that point into her own mind. 'I *know* it was the right thing to do and I probably could have stopped him but I let him go,' Kate said, sobbing each word.

'I am not going to sit here and say 'I told you so' even though you might expect me to. I know I was pretty hard on you before, Kate,' Jamie said. 'I've given it a lot of thought since and I didn't give you enough credit. Let's meet up and you can tell me exactly what's gone on, okay?'

'There's no point, Jamie. I know he's gone and I know it's for the best. It's nothing to do with what you said, I promise,' Kate said. 'The worst part of it all is that so much of me resents that life isn't just easier. It's so unfair that I meet the man who could honestly, genuinely and completely make me happy…' She sat back on her bed and continued, 'but it was just at the wrong time.'

'There'll be a right time for you, Kate. I promise you,' Jamie said quietly.

'Thank you Jamie,' Kate said quietly. 'I'm glad you're not angry with me anymore. If you'd only met him, you would have understood.'

'Let's meet up. We can go to the greasy spoon or Tony's. Where do you fancy?' Jamie asked, trying to lighten the conversation.

'Come to my place at lunchtime Jamie. I'll make you cheese on toast, okay?' Kate said.

'That sounds like the best idea. It looks like it's going to pour down,' Jamie replied.

Kate looked out the window and saw the first drips of rain running in rivulets down her window. She held the phone away from her ear as she watched it, until suddenly she understood. 'No!' she shouted. 'No, no, no!' She could just hear Jamie saying 'Kate? What's the matter?' and she quickly shouted into the phone, 'I've got to go Jamie. I've got to go.' She pressed the button to end the call and grabbed her jeans from the floor, pulling them on quickly before pulling her sweater off the back of a chair and dragging it down over her head. She threw open the door of her bedroom and ran down the stairs, hopping over Cat by the front door and only just remembering to pick up her keys. She pushed her feet into her trainers and grabbed her yellow mac before running out into the rain.

There was a long queue waiting by the bus stop and Kate quickly decided that it would be quicker to run to the main road and get one of the many buses on that route. She did up the zip on her mac and started running as fast as she could, praying that the rain hadn't yet reached the side of town that the walkway was on. Once she got to the main road, she saw that the traffic was completely gridlocked with rush hour traffic and that two busses were caught up in the snarl way up on the brow of the hill. She let out an anguished, angry wail of frustration, turned heel and starting running along the pavement towards the town. Her hair was hanging in ringlets, weighed down with the rain as her hood flapped behind her.

As she ran, the rain became heavier, rushing through the gutters beside her and forcing the cars that crawled by to put the wipers on to their quickest setting. She shouted up at they sky 'Just wait. Just wait for me to see what he left for me, please!' not caring that people were glancing at her as if she were mad. She turned the corner and saw a bus indicating right to pull away from a bus stop. She ran after it screaming 'Stop!' raising her arms and waving them frantically. The bus stopped at the traffic lights and Kate ran across the road, swerving in front of it and banging on the door next to the driver. 'Please let me in,' she shouted. The driver opened the door and was protesting 'I can't let you on here, luv,' but she was already on and she dug around in her jeans pockets for some change. She burst into tears when she realised she didn't have any money on her and looked at the bus driver, tears running down her face. 'Please, I just need to get to the walkway in town. Please, it's so important,' she said. The traffic lights turned green and the driver said 'Alright then miss. Take a seat but if I lose my job over this…' Kate leaned against the plastic screen that separated him from boarding passengers and kissed it. 'Oh thank you, thank you,' she said, perching on the chair just behind him. She sat with water dripping off her and creating a puddle by her feet. She kept looking out the window, determined not to meet the eye of any other passengers. She didn't want to have to apologise for her behaviour. None of them knew how important this was to her. The traffic was clear past the lights and they arrived in town within a few minutes.

Kate jumped off the bus before the doors had finished opening shouting, 'Thank you, lovely man,' and running as fast as she could to turn the corner into the walkway.

When she reached the walkway, it was dark and the pavements were glistening with huge puddles forming. She stood still, suddenly not wanting to go any further. She watched the people hurrying up the street, hunched under umbrellas. She put her hands up to her face and wiped back the curls that were clinging to her cheeks and forehead before slowly walking up the street. As she neared Ern's patch, she saw the bright colours were already swirling in the water, cascading down into the drains like rainbows.

She walked closer and saw that Ern's art had all but gone. There were faint traces of the tulip's scarlet petals, the white lily with its bright green stem and the beautiful city sunset, but all the pictures were now washed together and the magic they contained was running away with each new gush of rain that pelted down on them. Kate knelt down and touched the slabs, watching the colours run past her fingers. She knew it was pointless trying to see any message Ern might have left but she carefully looked at every slab, trying to see a different colour or some shape she didn't recognise. She started to cry again. Warm tears ran down her face as the cold rain seeped in through the knees of her jeans and down the back of her neck.

A hand touched her shoulder.

'Kate?'

Kate turned her head and saw Tony standing there with an umbrella. He crouched down and held the umbrella over both of them.

'He's gone Tony,' Kate said quietly. 'Ern's gone.'

'I know, Kate,' Tony said, putting his arm around her. 'Come with me and we'll get you warmed up, okay?'

Kate sat looking at the slabs for a moment more before nodding her head. Tony helped her up and hugged her around the waist as they walked back over the walkway to his café.

The rush of warm air as they stepped into the café made Kate feel claustrophic. The radio was on and Kate was irritated at the cliché of it playing some sad blues song. She saw Liza over at the bar and tried to muster a smile. She raised her hand instead as a way of saying 'Hi.'

'Sit down there,' Tony said, guiding her over to the sofa by the bookshelves. Kate took off her mac and sat down, wiping her cheeks with the sleeve of her sweater. She kept her head down, her hair hanging over her face, not wanting anyone to see her this upset. She heard Tony talking to Liza and their hissed voices kept breaking through the sound of the coffee machine grinding fresh beans. Kate heard Liza say, 'She hasn't noticed. Tell her.' Kate pulled up her knees and hugged them, telling herself to stop crying. When Tony sat down on the chair opposite, he gently reached out and touched her knees, saying, 'Here's your coffee, Kate. Open your eyes. Look up.'

Kate looked at him and smiled weakly, taking the coffee from him, saying, 'Thank you.'

'Look up, Kate. Over there,' Tony said, pointing to the wall opposite.

Kate looked over and there was Ern's picture. It was a large, wonderful depiction of Tony's coffee shop. The dark brown colours were emphasised with touches of black and stark white as the light reflected from the chairs, tables and all the other things inside the place she cared so much for. Muted beiges and fawns were swirled to show customers huddled in corners, lovers kissing on the sofa and in the centre were Tony and Liza dancing. Kate stood up and moved closer. As she got nearer she saw herself in the picture, sitting by the window with a copy of Wordsworth's poetry by her side.

Tony came up behind her. 'I told him that was your favourite book, Kate,' he said quietly. Kate looked at herself, sitting there with a notepad on her knees, on which she could just see that small words were written on the page, surrounded by a love heart. She peered in and read them. 'You and Me.' Kate laughed despite her tears and said aloud 'Oh Ern! That is so cheesy!' She looked down and said 'Oh look Tony! He's even put Cat in it!'

Tony chuckled behind her and said, 'Cute, huh?'.

Kate wiped the tears from her cheeks with her sleeve, turned and smiled at him. 'Yes, very cute. Ern definitely knows how to schmooze.'

'Go and sit down, Kate,' Tony said. 'Drink your coffee and dry out a bit, okay? We're still here for you.'

Kate nodded and walked back to the sofa. She took a few sips of her coffee and looked again at the picture. Tony had hung it off centre and she could see that her painting would be perfect next to it. She liked that her and Ern would be next to each other in that way. It seemed right somehow. She looked over at Tony and Liza working behind the bar. She thought about what a good team they made. Maybe one day, things would be different for her.

She put down her mug and stood up, turning to face the bookcase. She let her eyes wander along the top shelf for her book and just before she got to it, she saw a slender book with a bright red spine, standing upright next to Wordsworth. She put her hand up and tipped it out of its place. As she brought it down, she immediately recognised what it was - 'Lady and the Tramp,' by Walt Disney. She took it back to the sofa and opened it up. Tears welled up in her eyes again as she read the dedication on the inside page,

'To Kate, A very special Lady, Love from Ern (her tramp), xxx'

Kate trailed her fingers over the page and whispered, 'You were no tramp to me, Ern. Please come back soon.'

Author's Note – For Len...

I sit here, outside, in this Sunday street,
with one coffee, one sandwich, one Marlboro Light.
My two buttoned coat is loose on my frame,
wasting away from the inside out
but my heart is strong, my love is true,
even though the wench beats me
till I'm black and blue!

His explosion of laughter blasts those that pass by,
Mind your own, don't look, as she tickles his chin,
whispers sweet nonsense, will-o-the-wisp,
to his bold serenade of some faraway folksong.

I sing to you, darlin', of the nights we shared,
warm wine mellowing our minds,
the curve shadows mirroring your hips wild roll,
before I read to you their imaginations,
conjured pearls of rhyme magicians,
smooth laudanum lies that end too soon,
chasing clouds across the waning moon.

Their hands loosely lace in a finger twine dance,
calloused tips drum on the hot metal top,
his tune recedes to a playful hum,
a beat that sways his frayed lace boot.

Look at them sitting, their grey faces strained,
flickering glances as they judge me, fear me,
their broadsheet pulp fiction spelling death and despair,
the devil may care...
the devil does care,
but they choose to pity me!
I pity them their bitter sweet irony.

His ice eyes dart, a glacier trap,
a mother curls her baby closer,
children mutter, hushed by shame,
as his cheeks glisten with her tears.

Will you stay, my love, just for today?
I try to hold them back, I try,
but one more, they say, one more pill to push you away...
for they will hurt you, you know,
and they will pull you apart, piece by piece,

204

tear your spirit from my soul
and your screams will drown in my heart.

Long, curled nails tear the bread, the ham, the cheese,
he mutters, tosses feathered pests a feast,
their frantic fluttering pleases him,
growls a chuckle, eases up, stoops low,

Will you help me home, lighten these limbs?
I know I shuffle as you skip so pretty,
but please, take my arm, rest your head on my shoulder,
let your curls fan my cheek in the breeze.
Maybe lie with me, kiss my eyes, my lips,
embrace me to ease this dark ache
and send me a promise, my sweetheart, that I will not wake.

Printed in the United Kingdom
by Lightning Source UK Ltd.
136398UK00001B/121-144/P